Praise for the

Red Dog Conspiracy

"Not only do you have a strong lead character, you also have others who complement her. This story takes us to a place divided into families and run by an iron fist. Finding a young boy is what it starts out as and ends up being so much more."

— LAURA FURUTA

"This is definitely noir, including the traditional breaking of the narrative timeline. People are doing nasty things for sometimes known, and sometimes not yet uncovered, reasons. It's what makes the world turn for the Families, who are in an uneasy alliance with shifting loyalties, cease fires, and outright aggression."

— MARGARET FISK, Tales To Tide You Over

"Patricia Loofbourrow has created a world of family intrigue combined with feuding households across the four quadrants of Bridges."

— JUNE LORRAINE ROBERTS, Murder In Common

"… a good read for anyone who likes mystery and suspense mixed with science fiction."

— IVORY MORTON, Beautyful Word

"… the political intrigue in this story is unrivaled …"

— TANGO WITH TEXT

"Beautifully written."

— GABRIEL CLASON

For more reviews, visit JacqOfSpades.com

FICTION BY PATRICIA LOOFBOURROW

RED DOG CONSPIRACY
Part 1: *The Jacq of Spades*
Part 2: *The Queen of Diamonds*
Part 3: *The Ace of Clubs*
Part 4: *The King of Hearts*
Part 5: *The Ten of Spades*

THE PREQUELS
Gutshot: The Catastrophe
The Alcatraz Coup
Vulnerable

THE COMPANIONS
Drawing Thin

The Ten
Of Spades

Part 5 of the Red Dog Conspiracy

Patricia Loofbourrow

Published by Red Dog Press, LLC

Printed in the USA

The Spadros Pot
East River
Bridge Stub Spadros 1B
Bridge Stub Spadros 3B
Spadros Promenade E
For more, visit JackOfSpades.com
To Spadros quadrant ->
Spadros Promenade E
To Spadros quadrant ->
Keevarde Spadros Station
To Market Center
Keycard Cafe
Snow Street
Stud Street
Bridge Stub adros 1W
Spadros Promenade W
The Old Plaza
Snow Street
The Cathedral
The Treasure
Main Road 3E
Scoop Street
The Rathole
uth ver
Snow Street
Shill Street
Spadros Promenade W
To Spadros quadrant ->
Bridge Stub Spadros 3W
To Market Center
Boot Street
Broadway Avenue
The Hedge
Copyright 2018 Patricia Loofbourrow

1900 years after the Catastrophe, the Merca Federal Union spreads across the North American continent in domed, steam-powered independent city-states, each with its own way of life.

The neo-Victorian domed city of Bridges is controlled by four crime families. A fifth faction fights to disrupt the fragile peace.

Private eye Jacqueline Spadros is caught at the center of it all. This is her story.

The Dilemma

The door slammed in my face.

A cold breeze flapped the corners of my overcoat, and I quickly reached up to keep my hat atop my head.

My lady's maid Amelia Dewey sighed. "I'm sorry, mum."

Carriages and horses, women and men passed by, never giving me a glance. The wooden banister snagged my glove as I descended the cracked steps. The midmorning light was weak, thin, pale.

Amelia glanced around. "Do we go on?"

Did I have any choice? "We go on."

But it was much the same on 24th Street as on all the rest. The response varied from fearful curtsies to angry curses. The answer still was no.

No, they didn't need an investigator.

No, they knew no one who might.

No, I couldn't come in.

"Fucking Pot rag" was the most blunt way it'd been expressed, but their eyes all said it.

The worst was on West 4th, when an old widow woman offered me charity. Even in the Pot I wasn't a beggar, nor — as some put it — a new way for the Spadros Family to gouge their quadrant.

I wasn't so far gone as to take their pity.

We returned home for luncheon. My butler, Blitz Spadros, opened the door for us. "Any luck?"

I sighed, shook my head, went past him into our home.

It was a good place, those few apartments. Now that I think of it, the place was built to be a boarding house. An entry, a small parlor through a door to the right. My two rooms lay to the left: the front one my bedroom, the next my office, each with their own bath and toilet. Another unoccupied room lay beyond that.

Straight ahead, stairs rose to a large room which had picture windows overlooking the street. Behind the parlor, a door led to our kitchen. The hall beside the stairs passed first the kitchen (accessible through a door to the right). Then the hall passed our empty room and turned behind the kitchen to the rooms Blitz and his wife Mary shared. A closet nestled under the stair.

The building was a duplex: our half faced onto 33 1/3 Street. It had a side door from the kitchen, which opened onto an alley barely wide enough to walk down.

This was all I owned in the world, and if something didn't happen soon, I'd lose it too.

I went through the parlor into the kitchen. My housekeeper Mary stirred a pot of soup. We often had soup these days.

Mary Spadros was a pretty woman of one and twenty, with pale skin and straight light brown hair. She smiled when she saw me. "Almost ready."

I slumped into a chair. "It smells wonderful."

Amelia came in. She now wore her maid's uniform, black with white hat and apron. "Mum, you need out of these clothes."

I let out a snort of amusement. "Always wanting to change me."

"You'll feel better once you're into something comfortable."

I did feel better, especially once my corset came off. I hated the thing. Even as a child, I hated anything which tried to constrain me.

We sat around the small kitchen table, Amelia bustling about to serve our soup and bread. A bit of graying black hair had fallen from its bundle under her hat to lie damp along her pale doughy cheek. While she placed my food precisely, she was more careless with Blitz and Mary's items. A bit of soup slopped over the side of Mary's bowl onto the white lace tablecloth.

Mary rolled her eyes, but not so Amelia might see.

I said, "Won't you have a cup, Amelia?"

"I may." She ladled the steaming liquid into a wide mug. "I'll sit on the back stair."

Amelia would seldom join us — sitting at the table with your "betters" was apparently forbidden to servants in Bridges. But this didn't bother me today. Amelia had made it quite clear that her first loyalty was to my husband, Anthony Spadros.

And Tony didn't need to know about this.

Once she'd closed the door, I asked, "What's our situation?"

Blitz put his elbows on the table. "We have this month's Family fees. We have enough to pay for your medication. And for food, if we're careful. The main problem is the property tax."

When Dame Anastasia Louis left me the deed to the building after her murder, it was about to be sold for back taxes. So his words disturbed me.

"Fortunately, it isn't due for a few months yet." He glanced aside. "Sawbuck should be here today with your allotment."

Tony sent money each month by way of his first cousin Ten Hogan (who everyone called Sawbuck), supposedly for "all I needed" — the minimum required by law for a woman "of my station." But it was much less than the Court had provided during my trial.

We'd had to replace the parlor windows several times after rocks and bricks were thrown in. A fine metal mesh placed outside the lower windows, held up two feet away by rods of iron thrust deep into the earth, stopped that. But we were still making payments for the work.

And I owed Mr. Doyle Pike — the lawyer who'd saved my life — a great deal. Aside from a few cases which were little more than messenger service, I'd earned nothing. I had no idea how to pay the thousands of dollars I still owed him. It was more money than I'd ever seen in my life.

After the trial, Mr. Pike immediately filed a lawsuit against the city for everything he could think of: false imprisonment, malicious prosecution, libel, failure to protect me whilst in custody. That last one almost got me killed.

We did everything the judge asked, yet one day Mr. Pike brought bad news. "The Four Families want no more scandal. The court has been instructed to delay until we give up." Mr. Pike had patted my hand, yet I could see his disappointment. "My dear, I can pursue this further if you wish. But it'll be less costly, both to your pocketbook and reputation, if we stop now."

I had no money to pay what I already owed him, much less continue on. But he'd shown no inclination to forgive the debt. Each time Mr. Pike had come calling since then, I'd told Blitz to inform him I was not at home. And I hadn't answered any of his letters. But I knew how this worked: eventually, he'd tire of being polite and hire enforcers.

Anyone Mr. Pike hired would hesitate to attack me, if only out of fear of the Spadros syndicate. But there were many ways to make my life miserable which didn't involve physical violence.

Blitz and Mary looked glum. They were living on the little they'd been able to save before they married and left Spadros Manor. I'd forbidden them to spend any of that on me, or if they did, to keep an accounting. But I knew they'd spent their money anyway — we still had meat in our soup, after all.

Blitz — also Tony's cousin — had been his night footman. Mary — the daughter of Tony's butler — had been Tony's maid. But since Blitz and Mary left Spadros Manor to become my staff, Tony seemed not to care if they starved.

As one of Spadros Manor's servants, Amelia had plenty. And I wondered if this was deliberate, a way for Tony to show what I could have — if I would only return to him.

Was he truly that petty?

Mary rested her hand upon mine. "You'll find someone who needs your help, mum. I know you will."

People were always telling me to "go back to the Pot." It was times like this that made me wonder if they weren't right to say that after all.

* * *

I couldn't spare a penny up and back several times a day for taxi-carriages, so my feet hurt most of the time. After our brief luncheon, I sat in my bedroom, put my feet up, and counted my business cards. One hundred twenty-seven left of the 500 I'd bought before the trial, with no way to purchase more.

4

I'd sent a card to my former dressmaker Madame Marie Biltcliffe (who used to arrange cases for me, until we'd fallen out) and received no answer. My best friend Jonathan Diamond had pinned my cards in places where families of the accused gathered and given one to every attorney in the city.

I wiggled my toes inside my boots. Twenty-three years old, and not much to show for it.

My birthday had come and gone, with my few retainers and the smallest Yule log for company. And every day, from the time I woke to the time I fell asleep, I wanted a drink. I wasn't sure that would ever leave me.

But I was free. I had a roof over my head, and my stomach was full. The steam pipes worked and the lighting too. I hadn't frozen over the winter.

All I needed was a job.

I lit a cigarette and read a day-old copy of the *Bridges Daily* Amelia had brought from Spadros Manor.

The new Mayor, Mr. Chase Freezout, seemed to be recovering from the terrible beating my father-in-law Roy Spadros gave him on the courthouse steps in early November.

At the Grand Ball on New Year's Eve, Mayor Freezout had given a brief speech from a rolling chair at the top of the balcony. But he hadn't been seen in public until now. According to the paper, he made a proclamation — "firmly grasping the lectern" — to denounce the "ruffians plaguing this city."

I imagined Mayor Freezout referred to someone other than the Four Families. The sight of the police standing idly by as he was beaten bloody by the Spadros Family Patriarch on the Courthouse steps couldn't have failed to make an impression.

Inventor Etienne Hart and his mother Judith had moved from their ancestral home at the racetrack to a mansion on 190th Street, Hart quadrant, right next door to Mayor Freezout's former home. The paper said the new Hart property was being heavily guarded.

I could only imagine. At the time, I felt certain Mrs. Hart was being questioned most thoroughly. She'd almost caused a war between the Spadros and Hart quadrants. But what would her husband Charles Hart do? As Patriarch of the Hart Family, he couldn't let a scandal of this magnitude go unpunished.

Inexplicably, Roy Spadros hadn't pursued the matter. Which was odd, because Roy hated Charles Hart more than anything else.

And why had Judith Hart turned against me in the first place?

From all my observations, she believed I was her husband's lover. The idea repulsed me — the man was old enough to be my grandfather! And while perhaps Mr. Hart had some feeling towards me, we had firmly resolved the matter. I regarded him as a rather dangerous but highly useful acquaintance.

But clearly Mrs. Hart was in league with the notorious Red Dog Gang, who'd tormented me and the Spadros Family for over a year now. District Attorney Freezout — now Mayor — indicated after the trial that Mrs. Judith Hart had been part of his framing me for the zeppelin bombing.

Could the motivation for all the crimes the Red Dog Gang had committed — kidnapping, blackmail, theft, murder — possibly be as simple as Mrs. Hart's jealousy?

I laughed aloud at the idea. You didn't bomb a zeppelin, killing hundreds of people, because your husband was in love with another woman. It was absurd.

So there had to be much more at stake. But what?

I sat up, squared my business cards, and put them in their case. If we were to survive, I had work to do.

I'd made it down 24th Street. With any luck, Amelia and I might visit the east half of 25th before darkness fell.

The bell rang.

I reached my door just as Blitz knocked. "Sawbuck's here."

I opened the door; Blitz stepped back, startled. Sawbuck loomed behind Blitz in the open doorway.

While the money was welcome, Sawbuck, not so much. I leaned on the door-frame. "Master Ten Hogan. What a pleasant surprise."

Sawbuck flicked out a dollar bill. "Here's your cash."

I almost laughed. A dollar. "Why doesn't he come himself?"

Sawbuck hadn't moved, the dollar still standing upright between his fingers. At my words, his face darkened. "Why do you think?"

He flicked the dollar into the air, and it fluttered down. "I've done my duty," he snapped, and stalked out.

Blitz picked up the dollar. "It seems Mr. Anthony has had a bad day."

That made sense. Sawbuck was utterly devoted to Tony, and had not forgiven me for leaving Tony the way I had.

The horror on Tony's face when he saw me and Joseph Kerr together that night in my study swam in front of my eyes. "I imagine so."

But I had to focus on today. "Amelia."

She emerged. "Yes, mum?"

My feet hurt terribly, but I could think of no other options. "Let's see how far we get on 25th."

The Scandal

As scandalous as it might sound, I, Jacqueline Kaplan Spadros — a woman still married to the Spadros Family Heir — worked as a private investigator. I'd left Tony over a year ago. My husband refused to divorce me; I refused to return home.

For the past six months, I'd been trying to get a case so I'd have money to pay my bills. But I cared about more than paying bills.

I had to find Joseph Kerr. I hadn't seen him since the night Tony caught us together in my study.

I didn't know whether Joe was alive or dead. He'd still been walking with a cane from his terrible accident a few months earlier. Tony had posted a monstrous reward for his capture, so the entire city searched for him, including the Four Families. How could he possibly have survived?

But my best friend Jonathan Diamond seemed to believe Joe was alive, and that thin hope was all that kept me going most days.

And I also had to find little David Bryce's kidnappers.

David's oldest brother Nicholas (who we children called Air) had been my best friend until my father killed him when I was twelve. One of the scoundrels who took David claimed he'd taken the boy simply to lure me into their trap. So I felt doubly responsible.

And though I rescued David Bryce, he was by no means well.

I visited David and his mother Eleanora during Yuletide. He'd gotten taller, thinner. Small dark hairs dotted his chin. Yet though he was now thirteen, he still rocked, curled into a ball, just as when I'd found him in that windowless basement over a year earlier.

That bright, happy little boy had been driven mad. And I would destroy those who took him.

Once my bills were paid, I could hire a taxi-carriage and pay my informants. I could find Joe. I could bring David's kidnappers to justice. I could start rebuilding my life.

So here I was, walking from house to house in hopes that someone would know someone who needed my help.

* * *

Amelia and I managed to cover the south side of East 25th Street before we had to return for tea. While waiting for Blitz to answer the bell, I wearily rested my hand on the sign attached to the wall below my door number:

Kaplan Private Investigations

Discreet Service For Ladies

Blitz opened the door. "No luck, huh?"

I shook my head. "Amelia, this time I'm glad to change out of these clothes."

Blitz said, "Master Diamond is here."

I peered past Blitz into the parlor. Tea had been set out, with small sandwiches upon a three-tiered sandwich stand Mary had found at a poorhouse sale.

Jonathan Diamond ventured over to greet us, his smile bright against his dark skin. Jon wore a forest green jacket and trousers, with a charcoal and green waistcoat patterned with the Holy Symbol his Family had taken for its own. His coiled black hair had been cut since I saw him the day earlier, and I wondered if his dastardly and frankly mad identical twin Jack had ever pretended to be Jon, even in play.

"Wait there," I said. "I'll be out shortly."

Jon stopped mid-stride and chuckled, giving me an extravagant bow. "Then, dearest lady, I breathlessly await your return."

He always did know how to make me laugh.

9

When Amelia took off my left boot, she gasped. Blood lay upon my sock. When she stripped the sock off, skin flapped there. "You've worn through a blister!" Her face turned angry. "Why did you not tell me it pained you?" She rushed to fill my wash bowl with water. "Soak your foot, mum."

The water was cold, but it felt good. I put both feet in.

A copy of the *Golden Bridges* had arrived, sent by one of my informants, apparently unaware I had no money to pay her for it. "Who paid the messenger?"

"The butler, mum."

Amelia would never refer to either Blitz or Mary Spadros by their proper titles, only "the housekeeper" or "the butler," and that after I rebuked her for her disrespect. From the way she treated them, she seemed to think they'd risen above their proper station.

Amelia insisted on combing the dust out of my thick curls and loosely plaiting my hair, so in the meantime, I read the paper.

The *Golden Bridges* ("Fuck the Fairy Tales, Get the Real Story") was a tabloid. Full of speculations and wild theories, rumor and gossip. But once in a while, it could be useful.

BRIDGES STRANGLER ATTACKS!

Another Man Dead: Police Blame City

Every five days like clockwork, the fiend some call the Bridges Strangler presents the police with a grisly parcel. Yet the Constabulary seems no closer to finding the scoundrel than when he first began attacking young men over a year ago.

Policemen have been fired and new ones hired, yet the deaths continue. The bodies are often discovered in lower east Spadros quadrant. Some blame the police in that sector for not apprehending the villain.

Commander Norman Pattsz, the official leading the Spadros First Precinct, was overheard at the nearby tavern: "All protocols have been followed to the letter! If the police were given resources to deal with crimes of this nature, perhaps lives might be saved."

The Spadros Family refuses comment, and their mouthpiece the *Bridges Daily* ignores the matter altogether. But our sources close to the Family have noted an unusual amount of activity in the Spadros syndicate. The *Golden Bridges* will investigate this more thoroughly to uncover the Real Story.

I felt pretty sure what the "activity" was about.

Spadros men had rebelled against Roy, rampaging since before my trial. They called themselves the "Ten of Spades" and agitated for Tony's death. They'd attacked Tony and Sawbuck inside Spadros Manor. One of them even tried to shoot me in the street outside the Courthouse during the trial. If it hadn't been for Jonathan Diamond, I wouldn't be here today.

The *Bridges Daily* had reported two days earlier about a shootout in Spadros quadrant not far from where I lived. A group of Family men were ambushed while delivering a set of chairs to the site of an engagement party which was to take place the next day. Three were killed and several others injured on both sides of the struggle.

This must be the work of these rogues. Who else would attack Family men helping civilians?

The big question was this: were the Spadros rogues in alliance with the Red Dog Gang? I suspected such, but had no proof as yet.

As I paged through the *Golden Bridges*, I found this:

DIAMOND FAMILY CONTROVERSY?

Five Diamonds In Heated Secret Meeting

According to our Inside Reporter, the five eldest Diamond Heirs met yesterday at the exclusive Baroness Hotel on Market Center. Sources at the hotel state that the meeting involved "loud and heated" discussion. One of the brothers had injuries to his face upon leaving. A bill for damages was presented today by the hotel to Diamond Manor.

Although the nature of their discussion is unknown, the rumors of unrest within the Diamond Family following the historic "Bloody Handshake" upon the courthouse steps last November between Patriarchs Roy Spadros and Julius Diamond may be confirmed.

There have been no reports of, or even further movement towards, peace between the Spadros and Diamond Families in any official manner. But the *Golden Bridges* stands ready to bring you the Real Story as these events unfold.

Hmph, I thought, as Amelia wrapped my foot. The *Golden Bridges* mainly stood ready to sell more copies.

The *Golden Bridges'* "Inside Reporter" had to be a great number of people, unless possessed with the skill of teleportation. I wondered who these men were. They were brave indeed to publish stories that the Four Families wished hidden.

* * *

Jonathan Diamond must have had a good appetite. By the time I returned to the parlor, half the sandwiches were gone and what little was left of the tea was cold. Mary brought in a fresh pot.

She'd made small sandwiches: mint found by the side of the road, rinsed and chopped into salted cheese she'd made from leftover milk, then spread onto day-old bread. They were delicious.

I turned to Jon. "I hope you're well?" My glance went to his water-glass, a bit of liquid still remaining from the tonics he took "for his health."

He smiled at me. "Well enough. And yourself?"

I ignored the pain in my foot. "Resuming business after being on trial is difficult, but I'll find someone willing to take my services."

"Have you contacted your former customers?"

This amused me. Every day, Jon arrived with a new idea. Yet today's idea was one he'd had less than a week after the trial. "Ages ago. They agree to be used as references, and would happily call upon me in the future, but have no need for my services today."

He rested one arm over the back of the sofa. "Alas, I have no mysteries in my life which need solving. I wish you'd allow me to help, just until you're on your feet."

At the time, just one foot. "I won''t allow it."

"Even as a loan?"

"I owe too much already." This thought discouraged me.

Jon leaned forward, elbows on his knees. "Jacqui, I'm not Tony, and I'm not Mr. Pike. I — I can't — I don't want to — I only want to help. If you'll let me." He gazed towards the floor. "You'll be honest with me, will you not? If you're in need."

I felt such fondness for him, and yet I was amused. "Today, I am truly not in need. Thank you for reminding me of that."

"But I don't want you to even feel anxious of need. I want you happy and well."

"Jon, I'm perfectly well." Other than my foot, which felt as if on fire. But mentioning it would only worry him.

He clasped his hands together, dropped his voice so only I might hear. "But are you happy? Is this," he glanced around, "what you truly want?"

Am I happy? The question had arisen many times in my life up to then, and only a few of those times had the answer been yes. I leaned back, surveying the room. Then I chuckled. "How could I possibly be unhappy with you here?"

Jonathan blushed, smiling to himself. "You insist on flattery when I ask a simple question. Being happy when no one else is around, now **that** is a worthy goal. Just happy with yourself."

His words struck me, and my eyes stung.

"I'm sorry, Jacqui. But I don't think you're happy at all."

But this is what I wanted! "I couldn't breathe there. I couldn't think. The place was killing me." Being with Tony was killing me, with his neediness and his constant fear for me and his lies. Night after night, having to pretend I desired him, all the while screaming inside ... "I felt caged."

"I don't want you to go back if you don't want to. But you have to consider what you do want. What you need to be happy. Really, truly happy." His dark eyes peered into mine. "Because you don't know how long you have before the Dealer collects your cards."

"Have you heard anything about Joseph Kerr? Anything at all?"

Jonathan leaned back, glancing away, an edge to his tone. "The search continues. I've not heard of any sightings, not of him, or his sister, or his grandfather. Even their maid has disappeared."

"I know you dislike him, Jon, but —"

"Dislike is the wrong word. I've seen what he's done — is still doing — to you. What he's done to other women. What he's been accused of, is being accused of to this day."

"Could he not be innocent, though? Is it possible all this talk is only talk? Slander? How can you cast him aside on rumor? He's been your friend, Jon. And he's only shown me the very best."

He faced me. "On this matter, we can never agree. Yes, he's been cordial. But I don't trust him. And I've seen the anguish of the women he seduced then abandoned. The little girls with his eyes clinging to their mothers as they were dragged to a life of whoredom in the Pot." He pointed towards my bedroom. "I carried you from that very place, where you lay near dead because of him. Don't ask me to consider his nature, Jacqui. Because it disgusts me."

I stared at him, appalled. "How can you say this?"

"Because I'm being honest with you, something you can't seem to be, even to yourself."

I recoiled, thrown into thought. Was I being dishonest with myself? Surely not.

It didn't matter how I felt about Joseph Kerr not being with me during all that had happened. It didn't matter how hard it was for me to understand what people claimed he'd done. I couldn't pass judgment on him without hearing his side of the story. It would be unfair. "I love him, Jon. I love him with my whole heart. Nothing you say will ever make me stop loving him."

We sat in silence. Yet I felt a turmoil inside. I did love Joseph Kerr, despite the rumors and accusations. I feared for his safety. I wanted Jonathan to understand.

"If what I said could make you stop loving him it wouldn't be love," Jon finally said. "I don't want you to stop loving him, Jacqui. I just want you to see Joseph Kerr for what he is. So you can know who it is you love. That's all."

Mary came in to collect the dishes, and I considered Jonathan's words. Could it be possible that Joe hid things from me? That I didn't know him? Could any of these accusations be true?

I remembered that afternoon when I nearly drank myself to death at the thought they might be true, and I shuddered. "I don't want to return there."

Jonathan glanced over his shoulder in the direction I stared, at my bedroom. Then he sat beside me and took my hand. "You don't have to drink to face the reality of life. There are other ways."

I felt lost. I didn't know what those other ways were.

Jonathan rose, still holding my hand. "Call your maid, get dressed. I wish to take you on promenade."

"I've been walking all day!"

"Then we'll go for a drive. Mrs. Dewey!"

I gaped at him. Why was he addressing my servant?

She hurried in and curtsied almost to the floor. "Yes, sir?"

"Make Mrs. Spadros ready. We're going on a drive."

She stopped, mouth open, and glanced back and forth. Then she recovered, curtsying low. "Yes, sir, at once, sir."

There was no blood on my foot wrappings, which pleased Amelia. She re-wrapped my foot in a thinner bandage and cautioned me not to walk further.

When I emerged, Jon said to Amelia, "Pray tell the housekeeper Mrs. Spadros will return after dinner."

I stared at him, astonished. "Jon —"

"You have been without gaiety long enough. I wish to take your thoughts from trouble and put them on more joyous matters."

"Well —" I wasn't sure this was a good idea, with my foot the way it was.

"Then it's settled. You have your handbag? We're off."

Amelia stepped in his way and curtsied low. "Sir, may I speak with Mrs. Spadros one moment?"

He stepped back. "Of course."

Amelia drew me aside and whispered, "You don't intend to leave me here?"

"Why should you come? You weren't invited."

She seemed confused. "You mustn't go to public dinner without your maid. It would cause scandal!"

"Amelia," I said. "After all your protestations about sitting with your betters, you wish to impose upon Master Diamond? I'm surprised at you."

Amelia gaped at me, eyes wide. "But, mum, you don't understand. Your husband —"

Tony's reaction to Madame Biltcliffe's former shop maid Tenni sitting at the table with us flashed through my mind. "Would be furious at the very idea!" I gestured towards the kitchen, where Mary prepared dinner. "Will you go? Or must I inform her myself?"

Jon stood watching, too far off to hear our conversation. Amelia went crimson. "No, mum." She vanished into the other room.

Jon said, "Will she not attend you?"

"It's not necessary." We had plenty to eat here. Or she could eat at Spadros Manor as she usually did. "All will be well."

Jon's eyes widened, but he opened the door for me. "Well ... if you're certain."

"Absolutely." My foot did hurt a bit, but surely the carriage wasn't far.

Jonathan Diamond's white and silver carriage sat parked on the corner twenty yards to the right. "They asked us not to park on your street," Jon said, "as it's too narrow for others to pass."

I'd wondered where it had been.

Jon's footman was a serious-looking man a bit darker-skinned than myself wearing the white livery of the Diamond Family trimmed in silver. The footman never glanced at me, but said to Jon, "Do we await any others, sir?"

Jon hesitated. "No."

"As you wish, sir."

We got in, sitting side by side. The horses' hooves rang on the gray cobblestones as we set off.

"Your carriage is so warm," I said. "How is it done?"

Jonathan grinned. "My grandfather's invention. It runs on a dry-cell battery."

I didn't understand, and I supposed it showed, because Jon said, "It needs no wires, nor even a generator. The mechanism holds electricity inside itself for later use."

"Oh." I felt impressed. "How ingenious!"

The sun shone pale between the rooftops and alleyways as we passed. We turned onto 24th, then onto the main road toward Market Center.

Streetlights were being lit. Shops began lighting their lamps inside. Workmen and shop maids trudged along. As we approached the Pot, the Hedge loomed in the distance, coming closer, then flanking the road on either side.

I thought of my people, still caged behind wrought iron. Still living in squalor. "This part of the city reminds me of what we've lost, Jon. All of us."

"I know." Jon squeezed my hand, then winced, rubbing a spot on his chest. "So tell me true: what would you enjoy? Shall we visit the river? I believe we have warmer days ahead. Perhaps we could take my boat out."

Our carriage drove onto the wide stone bridge towards Market Center. "That sounds wonderful! How have I never seen your boat?"

"I'm not much of a sailor." Jon shrugged. "I've never given it much thought. My mother gave it to me when I came of age." At that, he glanced away.

That would have been a year or so before Mrs. Rachel Diamond's terrible accident.

Jonathan said, "But with all my duties, I rarely have chance to take it out. I let my men use it from time to time." Then he winked, flashing a wry smile. "For the Business."

I grinned at him, making my face all innocence. "How would I possibly know what you mean, sir?"

Jon laughed full out then, until he winced.

"Is something wrong?"

He shrugged, not meeting my eye. Then he let out a cough, wincing as he did so. "Perhaps a twinge of pleurisy. I've had it before: it's most annoying." He took a heating pad from a pouch in the carriage-wall and pressed it to his chest. "The heat helps."

"My poor dear. But you feel otherwise well?"

"Of course! Don't let this worry you."

The carriage stopped in front of the restaurant we'd often had luncheon at during the trial, a favorite for the police. Jon returned the heating pad to its pouch in the door. "Wait here. Keep the curtains closed."

He closed the door; I put my injured foot up on the black velvet bench seat across from me.

For weeks after the trial, reporters flocked to my home, asking for interviews, wanting my photo. Blitz made it sound as if there were a waiting list, offering to "get them to the front of the line" — for the right price. That did help with Yuletide, and with the year's order for my morning tea.

At the time, I had no lover. Yet I wished for no children. Twice, men had tried to violate me, and the cost for the tea my mother had given me was worth the peace of mind.

Amelia was scandalized when she heard of the bribery, but her opinion didn't bother Blitz in the slightest. "If these men are silly enough to offer a bribe," he'd said, "I'm silly enough to accept it."

But eventually even that stopped, and Tony's dollar a month didn't go as far as I liked. Looking back, I don't think Tony had any notion whatsoever of how much things cost.

Jon tapped the window, which startled me. The door opened. "It's safe."

People walked past, but I saw no sign of Spadros men, rogue or otherwise. So I followed Jon into the restaurant.

The place was much the same as before: wood-paneled walls, large windows before an outdoor patio. We were taken to a small curtained back room much like what they had at the Ladies' Club. As we passed those dining, we were the subject of not a few stares and whispers. Some of the stares weren't friendly.

The room could be seen through the diaphanous white curtains, lit by an electric chandelier over the table. Market Center seemed to have the most reliable Magma Steam Generator in the city: the island had not once lost power.

We sat at the large round table facing the curtains, a seat between us. The waiter took our drink order — tea for us both. Although the sheer curtains were drawn, I could see — and feel — the stares in our direction. "How the tongues will wag tonight."

Jon seemed startled. "You think so?"

He invited me, so I assumed all was proper. Had he not thought this through? "Let me see ... my husband and I have not been seen together in public since the trial, not even at the Yuletide Spectacle. I don't appear at the Grand Ball —"

Tony had asked me, Jonathan had asked me, even Mr. Charles Hart had asked me. Which was within his rights, as that year's host for the Ball. But I had refused them all.

"— or the Celebration of the Coup. And I'm seen in society for the first night since the trial ... with you." I gave him a thin smile.

Jon put his hand to his forehead. "I'm sorry, Jacqui. I didn't consider how this might look. Should we go?"

I chuckled. "Of course not!" I raised my voice, staring at those staring back until they turned away. "Let the tongues wag — I have nothing left to hide."

That was true enough. The trial had laid every scandal bare — my business, my homeland, the details of my marriage. The only thing which hadn't been exposed was my dalliance with Joseph Kerr. Which, if what Doyle Pike's grandson Thrace said were true, could be revealed at any moment or used to Doyle Pike's advantage. And of course, Roland, Tony's illegitimate son by Jon's sister Gardena.

The boy's true identity was a secret I hoped would never come to light, for everyone's sake.

Jonathan opened his menu, and so did I, but I'd been here so many times I already knew what I wanted. "Don't fret yourself, Jon. All will be well. I'm grateful you thought to give me a night out."

Jon took a sip of tea. I so loved the sight of his dark, dark skin against the white china. He glanced up as the waiter entered. "I think we're ready to order."

After the waiter left, I mentioned the *Golden Bridges* article about his brothers. "What happened?"

"Your news report told it in as much detail as I know. Other than which brother received the blow." He gave a grimace.

"Surely it wasn't you?"

Jonathan let out a short laugh. "No, I wasn't even there. Betony insists on trying to make peace, while Cesare desires nothing more than to show his contempt for everyone. Betony stepped in between my other brothers, and was hurt for it." Then he shrugged. "At least, that's what he told me."

"Oh, Jon ... was he hurt badly?"

"Nothing chipped ice won't solve. But I fear for them all."

He seemed to struggle with what to say, and I remained silent.

"My parents care about us. But my mother's true love was her tinkering. Nurses and maids raised us, yet we were shown little affection. I think they were instructed to keep their distance. My brothers never formed a bond with my parents." He shrugged. "I feel as if rambling."

"No, I understand perfectly." I thought of my mother, and all the women who raised me instead of her.

"My brothers lack something," he tapped his chest, "inside. Especially when it comes to our father. We were sent to school in the countryside as boys barely old enough for instruction. My father claims it was for our safety, but they see it as abandonment. Dismissal. Betrayal. While they're well-taught in the ways of governance and survival, they have little love for or understanding of my father. Or his plans for this Family."

Julius Diamond had made many powerful enemies. And ones not so powerful, but who might become so. For example, Tony.

I didn't think Tony would hurt his son's grandfather. But Julius Diamond was the one who kept Tony from seeing Roland any more than he did.

"Many in Diamond quadrant are disturbed, Jacqui. They fear even the rumor of an alliance with Roy Spadros. They fear he'll turn on them. Many remember friends lost to his torture room during the Diamond Purge. I don't know if you remember those days. After Jack's manservant Daniel was murdered —"

I stared at him in horror. *By my father. With Roy Spadros watching.*

"— we went to war. Daniel was a Diamond sworn, if not a Diamond born, and we had to avenge him. But then a year later, my father brokered a cease-fire. I understand his reasons now, but Jack and Cesare never forgave him."

Jack Diamond and his oldest brother Cesare in agreement on anything was a chilling thought.

"Jack has been obsessed with learning why Daniel was there that night, even to this day. But Cesare felt shamed by what he saw as our father's weakness." Jonathan let out a weary sigh. "All Cesare can see is the Spadros Family's crimes. 'Better to die than ally,' he says; many in our Family agree. On the other hand, Betony cares only for peace, and if promised it, will follow anywhere. He loves and admires Cesare, and hopes that with his influence, he might temper his path." Jon shook his head. "But of those five, Betony is the youngest." Jon glanced away. "I fear for us all, Jacqui. My father extending his hand to Roy Spadros may do what nothing has in a hundred years — shatter the Diamond quadrant."

"Your father's in danger."

Jonathan smiled at that. "We're Diamonds, Jacqui. We're always in danger. Yet I fear you may be right where my father is concerned." He let out a breath, shoulders drooping. "There's no reasoning with him. His way is right, no matter what anyone says."

Julius Diamond had treated Tony abominably, and snubbed me the one time I visited his home. But he tried to speak kindly to me in the storm room during the trial, and a part of me hoped he might survive this.

Waiters set our food before us. It smelled delicious.

Once they left, Jon said, "Mr. Charles Hart has inquired as to your well-being."

Jonathan Diamond and Charles Hart seemed to have an unusually close relationship for a Patriarch of one Family and the youngest son of another. "I hope he's well?"

Jon shrugged. "He sorely misses his grand-daughter —"

"Oh? Where has she gone?"

"When Inventor Etienne left the racetrack, he took Ferti with him." Jonathan shook his head. "On the face of it, the matter seems obvious: a man bringing his daughter to their new home. But in reality, the situation is unpleasant."

Miss Ferti Hart had a serious impediment: while she was the same age as Mary, her mind was that of a small child. "How so?"

"Mr. Hart claims the others care nothing for the girl; Mrs. Judith only brought her with them to spite him." Jon began to cut his lamb roast. "Are you sure you won't see him?"

"Why does Charles Hart wish to call on me? With everything that's happening, it seems like the last thing he'd want to do."

Jon shrugged, focused on his plate. "He wants to offer his support. I think he misses the time when he saw you every day during the trial."

I took a bite of mashed potatoes. Mr. Hart seemed entirely besotted with me. I couldn't understand it. "Tell him ... I'm concerned only for his welfare. He must calm his quadrant and resolve matters with his wife. Then I shall be happy to see him."

"He worries for you, Jacqui. He only wants the best for you."

"Tell him I'm perfectly well." Then I smiled at him fondly. "Look at you. Forever asked to play the messenger."

Jonathan chuckled. "I suppose such is my lot. Yet here I am, enjoying an evening with fine food and my dearest friend. So it's no bother at all."

* * *

On our return, Jon had his driver pull up to the door "for my safety," and stood with me at the door until Blitz opened it. Amelia had gone home, as she usually did before dinner.

I went into my room to change into my house clothes — with Mary's help — and I let Mary comb out my hair before she went to bed. I could change into my nightgown without her.

I sat at my tea-table with a cigarette, my foot up on the chair across from me.

Dinner with Jonathan had been lovely. Yet my troubles still remained. How was I going to pay my property tax?

The problem seemed insurmountable: I couldn't force anyone to hire me. I wished the Red Dog Gang had never made me their target. I had no shortage of clients before they interfered in my life.

What had I done to offend them, other than to have the misfortune of being sold to the Spadros Family? It seemed so unfair.

The clock struck midnight. I yawned and stubbed out my cigarette, well-ready for bed.

A large fist hammered the front door.

From far down the hall, Blitz said, "What the hell?"

The hammering resumed.

"Coming, you bastard." I heard Blitz stalk to the door, open it. "What the fuck do you think you're doing?"

"Get out of my way," Sawbuck growled.

Although my first impulse was to rush to my door, I decided the best course of action might be to sit still.

A moment later, Sawbuck burst in without knocking.

"It's a good thing I'm still up," I said, "or you'd have some explaining to do."

"Half the city's speculating about you and Jonathan Diamond. How could you **do** this?"

"How was I to —?"

But then, I reconsidered. Jon **did** say we were going to dinner. Then it dawned on me what Amelia had been referring to. What Jon's footman referred to. Why Blitz and Mary had been so quiet since I returned. "Come in, Ten. Sit down."

He shook his head and leaned on the door-post.

"He was only trying to cheer me. It was an innocent mistake."

"Jonathan Diamond **knows** better! When I left him, his father stood ripping him to shreds." A laugh burst forth. "Doing a finer job than I ever might."

"How is he?"

Sawbuck snorted. "Master Diamond? He's —"

"No. Tony."

Sawbuck came in, closed the door, and leaned on it, eyes shut. "Mortified. Devastated. Furious at you both." He spoke bitterly. "But he can never stay angry at Master Diamond for long." He opened his eyes. "You either, I'm afraid."

"Afraid?"

"If you're determined to be here, the best thing is for him to let you go and get on with his life."

Empty blackness lay outside my window. "All I ever wanted was for my husband to be with his son." Why was Tony so fixated on me? "Can you not persuade him?"

"No. And before you ask, that handshake on the courthouse steps did nothing to hinder the alliance between Diamond and

Clubb. Nor is Miss Gardena — or her father — more willing to consider a reconciliation with Mr. Anthony." He shrugged. "So far as I know, anyway. I'm not privy to such matters."

Our eyes met. "I'm sorry, Ten. I truly am."

He glanced away.

"Please tell him that. Nothing I have ever done was meant to hurt him."

Sawbuck stood there for a while, eyes unfocused. Then he glanced my way. "What the hell happened to your foot?"

The Lead

Brilliant white flashed in the gutters as I moved. The grimy gray cobbles crunched, and my breath steamed.

No one stood in the intersection. No one peered through the broken windows or hid behind the bombed-out steam automobiles. But I felt someone there. I turned, turned again.

Someone watched me.

Frightened, I ran past a horse's crumbling skeleton and hid inside the shattered ruin of a carriage.

A man-shaped shadow moved from the darkness, icy fingers seizing my wrist. "I have you now."

I screamed, jerking awake, heart pounding, bathed in sweat. My room was dark, but moonlight painted the street outside bluish-white. I couldn't feel my right hand.

Blitz ran to my door, knocked. "Mrs. Spadros? Are you well?"

"I'm all right," I panted. "Another dream." I felt disoriented. My hand tingled. "Sorry to wake you."

I heard Blitz chuckle. "Wasn't asleep." He usually slept in the early morning, once Mary woke. "Do you need anything?"

I flopped down onto my pillows, weary. "No. Thank you."

"I'll be off then. Rest well."

I'd left Spadros Manor but the nightmares didn't stop. I'd gotten free of the Family, yet they didn't stop.

Misery swept over me as I curled on my side. Tears slid to my pillow. When would this ever end?

* * *

The next morning, a letter came:

The invitation to enter your quadrant has been withdrawn.
But I am always here for you.

I hope this morning finds you well. — JD

I smiled fondly, folding it away. The letter lay upon plain paper, but I had no doubt it was from Jon. No matter what anyone said, Jonathan Diamond was a prudent man.

Then I took it out again. Jon had sent a full sheet, whilst writing upon less than a quarter of it.

Clever man. I retrieved the writing box Tony had given me for our anniversary. With a few strokes of my pen-knife, I had paper to write Jonathan back. Between my writing to Pip Dewey and the other messages I'd sent, my paper supply was nearly gone.

Amelia's son Pip seemed well, although he wrote less often than he had. He was eleven now, and wrote of learning to bake pastries, helping the meat man skin a hog.

Pip never spoke of his mother, nor she of him, but they seemed to have less animosity towards the other, and for that I felt grateful.

Pots clanked in the kitchen. Mary was reheating their dinner's few leftovers into a soup for our luncheon.

Mary Spadros had become a strong and faithful ally, working night and day to make my reduced situation work. How did I deserve such devotion?

She loves Blitz. And Blitz had allied himself with me. Although now with how little we had, I hoped he wasn't reconsidering.

Blitz had spoken with our mutual friend Vig and his cook Natalia, who as one of the Romani had connections I could only dream of. But while Vig and Natalia sent a nice basket for Yuletide, they knew no one who needed my help.

I didn't want to go to the Clubb Family for aid, nor to Mr. Hart. While they'd helped me greatly, I didn't trust them. In either case, I feared what they might ask in return.

I was one of the Dealers' Daughters, a descendant of those who had survived the sack of the Cathedral during the Coup a hundred years earlier. Mrs. Regina Clubb thought she could use me to force the Cathedral to give up their secrets — whatever those were. I wanted nothing to do with that.

The Clubbs also wanted an alliance with Diamond quadrant. In exchange for help during the trial, Mrs. Clubb asked me not to impede Gardena Diamond's courtship with her son Lance.

Mr. Hart's motivations were less clear. He'd been at my side through the entire trial. He'd offered an alliance with Diamond quadrant in exchange for Cesare Diamond's testimony on my behalf, not knowing Cesare had grudgingly decided to testify.

Yet despite his wife's obvious distress, Mr. Hart had come to call on me twice since the trial. He'd sent a whole roast ham at Yuletide, and red roses every week since like clockwork.

This seemed excessive to the point of being disturbing. I felt glad I didn't know Jonathan Diamond wished to go to dinner before I'd gotten dressed. I might have worn the much-too expensive necklace Mr. Hart gave me during the trial and caused even more scandal.

Powerful men didn't give free favors. Eventually, Mr. Hart would ask for something in return.

Those who wish men to rule the Cathedral are the real enemy.

Delicious smells wafted into the room. From the kitchen Mary called out, "Breakfast is ready." I heard Blitz open the door from the hall to the kitchen; his footsteps moved around the room.

The Cathedral only closed twice a year. At full nightfall on Yuletide Center and Midsummer Night, the Eldest sat in front of the great flat raised area which we children were never allowed to touch. And every time she spoke, she began with those words.

She was the oldest woman I'd ever seen, before or since: skin lined, hair long and white, eyes of bright blue.

Even then, she'd been helped to her seat, walking with a cane. Could she possibly still be alive?

The last time I was permitted to view her audience was on my twelfth birthday, Yuletide Center, just a few days before Air's death. Once I'd been sold to the Spadros Family, though, I'd been cut off from even this small sharing.

I remember sitting curled up at the door of the room I shared with Ma. I would listen to the Eldest's voice rise and fall, never quite able to hear her words, but taking a bitter comfort in the sound just the same.

It must have been much the same as what she'd said before:

You are the Dealers' Daughters.

May you be worthy of their sacrifice.

I sighed, feeling melancholy. *May we be worthy of their sacrifice.*

There had to be someone who needed my help.

I sat back, amused. They certainly wouldn't come to me.

My foot still hurt quite a lot when I trod upon it, and old blood marred the white bandage.

I dressed, put on my house shoes, made my bed as Amelia had taught me. I retrieved my business cards and my map of the city, then put them on my bed, ready to go.

I brought my tea-tray to the kitchen. As I expected, a pot bubbled on the stove as Mary chopped carrots.

Mary set the knife down. "What are you doing in here?"

I laughed. "Nothing's broken. Besides, I heard you say breakfast was ready."

"You best sit down. If Amelia catches you up on your feet, she'll tan me."

I quickly sat, putting my foot on the chair beside me. Then I realized Mary was joking.

"I had an idea," Mary said. "What if we put a garden on the roof, like the man across the way has?

"I didn't know there was a way up there."

"Blitz found one. The area isn't big, and the roof isn't reinforced, so we can't put a great weight upon it. But we might grow something light, like greens, that don't require much soil. And we can use the bits of dirt beside the front steps for potatoes."

"Excellent!" This could help ease our problems. "May I ask you something personal?"

She set a plate of scrambled eggs and a glass of milk before me. "Of course, mum."

"Why are you helping me?"

Mary laughed as if this were the funniest thing in the world. "Oh, mum. You're helping **us**! Don't you see? No matter what happens, we've been raised to serve as butler and housekeeper by the Lady of Spadros. No matter where we go, we can say that.

"I was a house maid, the youngest of many; my husband, a night footman. While we lived in Spadros Manor, there was little chance of bettering ourselves. But you've given us more than we could've ever imagined. Our families boast of our achievements —"

I never considered this.

"— and our friends envy our good fortune." She smiled to herself. "We have as much stake in your success as anyone."

"That's good to know, as I so want to succeed. My fondest wish is to travel, make my way independent of Family schemes."

Mary gaped at me. "What would you do?"

I shrugged. "Many things. But I like the idea of being truly independent, free from the entanglements of want and custom. To travel, own land, and have a business which helped others." At the time, the form of such a thing was only vague to my mind, but speaking the words inspired me. "One thing I might do is rebuild the Spadros Pot, make it good again. The Cathedral shouldn't lie in ruins. One day I hope to be its benefactress."

Blitz came into the kitchen from the back hallway. "They should never have forced such a woman as you to marry. A pity only widowed women may own land in Bridges."

Mary laughed. "And rich ones at that."

I smiled at them, thinking only ever about being rich. *One day.* "Did you rest well?"

Blitz chuckled. "I did." Then he frowned. "Why are you in here?"

Mary said at the same time, "What will you do today?"

Blitz said sternly, "She'll do nothing which involves walking." He turned to me. "Amelia told me your foot was skinned beneath!"

"The ball of it, yes. But it's much better."

Blitz snorted, shaking his head. "You're not used to such exertion." He pulled out the chair across from me and sat. "This needs a better plan. Perhaps put an ad in the paper. Looking for someone in need of an investigator does you no good if you can't do the job once you find them."

I felt abashed.

"And we need the doctor to look at your foot." Blitz got up wearily, and his movements made his thoughts plain: *one more thing we must pay for.*

"No, Blitz, I won't have it. You've done enough for me already."

He gave me a pinched smile. "In this we'll have to disagree."

"You can't have saved this much. Where are you getting the money?" I knew they didn't want to take money from the Spadros Family, but surely the temptation was there.

"If you must know," Blitz said, "we've used our money from the auction. So you see? Everything's fine. But you must restrain yourself! Nothing good will happen if you keep on like this."

The bell rang.

Blitz gave an exasperated sigh. "Now who can **that** be?"

He returned with old Dr. Salmon, who laughed when he saw me. "My dear, what have you done to yourself now?"

He and Blitz helped me to my bedroom, Mary trailing behind. Once the others were gone, Dr. Salmon closed the door, examined my foot, then applied a salve. "I don't believe there's any injury to the bones. But this blister is quite deep." His face changed, as if he had come to some decision. "You must stay off your foot for a week. No promenade. No outings." He took a small jar from his bag, placing it on my tea-table. "Have your maid change the dressing daily and use this salve. I'll send a walking-stick over for moving around the room. But no pressure on your foot whatsoever. It needs time to recover."

A week? I'd give it a day and see how it felt. But I knew how to answer instruction. "Yes, sir."

Then something occurred to me. "How did you know to visit?"

He laughed. "Why, I got a telephonic call in the midst of night from your husband."

I snorted. "Ten Hogan. Why am I not surprised?"

"I don't understand."

"Master Hogan was here last night. He told my husband of it."

Amusement flashed past his ancient gray eyes, but he quickly recovered. "I see." He rose. "I'll visit again in a few days. But if the pain increases, contact me at once."

"I will." Then a thought pushed all my plans aside. "How much do I owe you?"

He smiled. "I was merely on my way to an appointment, and came to call on a dear friend." He patted my hand. "No need to fret."

After Dr. Salmon left, I sat with my injured foot up, my shawl beside me, feeling weary. I'd tried so hard to make this work! If I truly couldn't go out, how might I find clients?

Posting an ad for my private investigator business in the paper was out of the question. The public revelation that the Lady of Spadros had run a business right under Tony's nose had shamed him terribly. Going door to door in our quadrant was bad enough, but an ad would broadcast it to the entire city.

There had to be some way to find work. There had to be.

I'd never return to Spadros Manor, especially now that Tony had re-allied himself with Roy Spadros.

People had died to get me out of there!

I could put an ad for a tenant, though. We had an extra room.

Why hadn't I thought of that before? "Blitz!"

He sauntered to the open doorway with a wry smile. "You rang?"

I laughed. There wasn't a bell system in this building. "We should put an ad for that room sitting empty."

His eyebrows raised. "Now why didn't I think of that?"

"Because we'd decided last year not to even try with the trial going on. But the trial's well over, and surely someone needs a furnished room with board."

"I'll have Mary look round to see the going price for this street. Whoever's taken over for Mr. Monarch —"

"It's Mr. Howell. The new guy doesn't want to go round, so he's making him do it." I'd run across Mr. Eight Howell a few days earlier. After Mr. Monarch's murder, it'd taken a while for Sawbuck to sort out who was reliable enough to be given charge of our street. Mr. Howell had been doing it for many months already, and I suspected — from his sour expression — that he'd been taking a bit extra for himself in the meantime.

Blitz laughed. "Fair enough. I'll see him, then. I don't want Mary in a saloon, not with those rogues about."

"Might you bring the papers in my right desk drawer, please? And a pencil."

He returned with them a few minutes later.

I came across Joe's letter.

> I hope you're well. Please visit tomorrow after luncheon.
> Look forward to our meeting. — Joe

How pathetic the note! How childish the writing! How little his letter said, and how much value I put upon it!

Was Jonathan Diamond right? Did Joseph Kerr really abandon me to run after other women?

In the Pot, one might have other relationships without it being offensive. Which made this even more difficult to understand. Why would he not tell me of them? Why say I was his only one, when he had children with these women?

To leave me alone was bad enough, but for him first to take all my money ...

Joseph Kerr couldn't have known that Tony — or his men — wouldn't kill me when Tony caught us together. He couldn't have known Roy Spadros would pardon me, or the Clubb Family would help me, or that Mr. Hart would stand by me, or that the jury would acquit me. Or that the man who shot at me would miss.

If it hadn't been for Jonathan Diamond, and for the plot the Patriarchs had concocted, I'd be dead now.

I had to talk to Joseph Kerr, to look him in the eye. I had to know why he left me sitting at the zeppelin station. Why he never came back for me.

And as I gazed upon the page, my heart sank. What Tony must have felt when he saw the imprint of my lips upon the letter!

Dismayed, I crumpled the page, threw it away.

Sooner or later, either Joseph Kerr's body would be found, Tony's men would capture him, or he'd come to me. But pining over him wouldn't pay my property tax.

I surveyed my notes about the only case I had — finding David Bryce's kidnappers. It wouldn't pay the bills either, but at least I was doing something.

The information I found might even be useful. The information I'd found about Jack Diamond had saved my life.

Jack Diamond was Jonathan's identical twin. But the man couldn't be more different if he tried. Jack was a madman, accused of the most heinous crimes possible: torture, kidnapping, murder.

As far as I could tell, Jack still blamed me for my father shooting his manservant the night I was sold to the Spadros Family. He'd publicly threatened my life more than once, in front of witnesses. His status as a Diamond heir and position as Keeper of the Prison were all that kept from being either prosecuted — or eliminated.

But as Mr. Pike once said, even scoundrels deserved justice.

So I'd told his oldest brother Cesare — who hated me for his own reasons — about my belief that Jack had been framed for David's kidnapping and the extortion of merchants in Spadros quadrant.

In exchange, of course, for Cesare testifying to my innocence at the trial. I don't give free favors, either.

I couldn't have cared less who framed Jack Diamond. My concern was David Bryce's abduction. While the scoundrel Frank Pagliacci claimed he took David, he was clearly being directed by someone more competent.

I paged through the sheets I'd written over the past year. Then I turned one over and began to create a time-line of the known facts. If I could understand the logic of the Red Dog Gang's leader — whoever he was — perhaps I might reason out his next step.

Before Yuletide, 1898:

Young black-haired woman gets into Madame Biltcliffe's office under false pretenses. The office later broken into & (only) Invoices stolen.

Kitchen maids stealing my letters.

At first, I thought these maids simply wished to give the Red Dog Gang information about me. But as it turned out, they only had to use my handwriting to forge Tony's signature on invoice paper, and they had "proof" that I'd shipped the materials used to bomb the zeppelin.

I gazed upon Jonathan Diamond's letter resting on my desk. So why steal so many? One long letter would have been more than sufficient to copy my handwriting. There had to be some other reason for their theft that I couldn't yet deduce.

Man in White (NOT Jack: "Forty at least," shorter & heavier than Jack Diamond) visits Eleanora Bryce's shop.

Morton (aka Master Blaze Rainbow) meets with his "business partner" aka Federal Agent Zia Cashout (very strong accent, red hair). With her: Frank Pagliacci, claiming to be with the DA's office; Birdie, a young female secretary with black hair; and a police detective. They offer Morton information he needs if he will lure me to a meeting with their informant.

Morton never met this lead, the informant Frank spoke of. Was the man even real? And who was this police detective? Morton had never described the man to me. Was he a real detective, or was this another impostor?

I hoped the latter was true, because I felt certain Frank Pagliacci was the Bridges Strangler. If the police were being paid by him ...

I rubbed my arms and put on my shawl.

Dec. 22, 1898: David taken.

Later: Mrs. Bryce goes to the police station. A couple waiting there (one is very good-looking, the other has red hair and a very strong accent) tell her to contact Madame Biltcliffe.

This sounded like Frank and Zia. Mrs. Bryce also told me the woman was from some area in Dickens called "Little Island."

New Year's Eve 1898:

I receive Forged Letter to Eleanora's shop

Red Dog stamp on alley Wall

David's disappearance had been amongst the first of many, most ending in strangulation. The stamp of the same red dog had appeared at many of these scenes: the mark of the Red Dogs children's street gang.

But these children denied anything to do with it. And as it turned out, a group of men were using the Red Dogs' stamp —

often a stamped business card left on the bodies — to frame these children for kidnapping and murder.

These men called themselves the Red Dog Gang. Yet they'd murdered at least one of the Red Dogs boys, a fifteen-year-old named Stephen Rivers who'd tried to help me find David.

Were any of the children in the Red Dogs still alive?

Somewhere in this, Morton was hired to oversee one of the Red Dogs "treys" — a group of three boys — to learn who framed the gang. Stephen Rivers had been one of those boys; a young man named Clover led them.

But by all accounts, Morton already had a case. A case important enough to visit a man he believed to be from the DA's office. So important that Morton was willing to participate in a wild scheme involving disguise and deception, just to gain access to a lead.

So why take a second case at the same time?

This always brought me back to Morton's employer. Morton constantly evaded the subject.

The fact that Morton's employer would care about a boys' street gang seemed odd in the first place. To set up an organization of boys spanning the city then ask grown men to direct these boys to throw rocks at windows stretched belief. It seemed unnatural, staged, and I understood neither the meaning nor reason for it.

Then it came to me.

Someone planned to incite chaos in Bridges, perhaps to step in later with themselves as the logical solution. A man who planned to run for Mayor, perhaps?

It seemed a reasonable plan.

Then a more cunning man deduced the play and suborned it. Perhaps he made friends with these boys then discarded them. The first man, alarmed at boys disappearing and his Red Dogs being blamed, hired Morton to investigate.

Master Blaze Rainbow had worked with Miss Zia Cashout for years, not knowing she was a Fed. He'd trusted her. He'd spoken of the case with her. She told him she'd found someone — this informant — who could lead him to the people behind this plot.

This was not two cases, but one.

I shook my head with a sigh. Morton could never have known Zia would betray him to the very people he searched for. They used Morton to help lure me to them. If Morton hadn't turned on them, aided me instead, I'd be dead today.

I pulled out the forged letter I'd received on New Year's Eve 1898, calling me to Eleanora Bryce's shop. On Madame Biltcliffe's stationery, still faintly scented with her perfume.

Madame's perfect black hair, her lovely face and form. The bruises the false Spadros men had given her. The hurt in her eyes, her angry words to me when we last spoke, the way she wouldn't look at me as she testified during the trial.

I couldn't think of that, not now. Pushing it from my mind, I found the note of apology and comfort she'd sent the day of the verdict and compared the two.

The handwriting in the first letter appeared to be hers, but written as if in great haste. Yet the letter "t" on this first letter had the same curl-up the handwriting expert had pointed out at the trial in the rest of the forged documents.

For an instant, I thought: if I'd refused to answer Madame's call, perhaps I would have been spared all this.

But David Bryce had already been taken. Yes, he was ruined, perhaps forever. But if not for me, he might be dead. Strangled, like the rest. First Eleanora Bryce had lost her oldest son, Air, then her next son, Herbert, both to murder. What would she have done if she'd lost David as well?

I flipped the page over to read it, then back. So much had happened! I was still on New Years Eve, over a year prior.

Man in Brown watching me outside Eleanora's shop.

Red Dog Stamp Card in my coat pocket at the Ball.

"Very good looking Man" with "dark tuxedo" calling himself Frank Pagliacci hires Tony's men Duck and Crab for $100 each at the Grand Ball.

Where did Frank get this kind of money? In a city where a taxi-ride could be purchased for a penny, $100 was a fortune.

New Year's Day, 1899: Man in Brown outside Joseph Kerr's
house. Party Time shipment hijacked (to lure Tony??).
Tony attacked with pipes (not guns!). Duck and Crab taken
by FP's men. He forces them to spy on us using blackmail.

So maybe Frank didn't have this kind of money. If he'd given the
men their money, he'd have no need to blackmail them into
working for him later.

Wait, I thought. After Frank captured them, Crab and Duck were
told to follow me and Tony while wearing brown. Yet I'd seen
someone following me the day earlier. Another of Frank's men?

I never got a good look at the Man in Brown. But I could very
well have been followed at various times by more than one man.

January 1899:

Roy Spadros receives letter from "young black-haired
woman" telling him of the attack on Tony. She knows
things few others know.

Herbert Bryce looks for David: found strangled.

Stephen Rivers looks for David: complains to police of Man
in Brown following him, found strangled.

Mrs. Bryce and I meet Morton in the Diamond Pot. He
directs us to a warehouse: Man in Brown and Man in
White are carrying a boy to a Carriage. Eleanora identifies
this Man in White as the man who visited her shop before
David went missing.

I still wasn't clear on what Morton was doing there. He claimed
he believed the kidnapping was a pretense, a way to lure me to the
meeting with their informant. Morton claimed he didn't know the
boy was even real until he met with Eleanora.

I wasn't sure I believed him. He'd helped me greatly over the
past year, even at risk to himself. But I felt certain Master Blaze
Rainbow hid something vital.

On Morton's yacht, Zia pretends to be Deaf. Morton claims
her as his maid, then sister.

I trace carriage to the Stables on Market Center. Stable-Master says the Man in Brown gave the name Frank Pagliacci & the carriage was stolen, then returned.

Hand-carved wooden button (only enough ever made for two jackets) and David's hair found in carriage AND Party Time + shoe polish.

Tony's men bought one of the jackets for Morton after his yacht was destroyed and his clothes ruined. The other jacket was purchased by a red-haired woman who signed her name Maria Athena Spade. Which apparently was pronounced "Spa-DAY:" it was Italian for the Holy Symbol the Spadros Family had taken for their own.

Yet this woman wasn't Zia: she lacked Zia's very strong accent.

Jan. 28, 1899: David found in basement of Jack Diamond's Shoe Polish (& Party Time) Factory. Ten men attack. Frank Pagliacci shoots at us from shadows, claims plan to destroy the Spadros Family. I shoot FP. Man in White appears.

Zia goes missing.

Frank's men and Feds chase Morton?

Again, it was difficult to tease out the truth here with Morton and Zia. And the Feds. I had trouble telling when Morton spoke true and when he lied.

Why were Frank Pagliacci and his men in Jack Diamond's factory in the first place? How did they got access?

Someone in Jack Diamond's factory betrayed him.

I felt certain his brother Cesare would inform him of our discussion, if he hadn't already. Perhaps the fact I offered aid might dissuade Jack from pursuing and tormenting me further.

Before Queen's Day, 1899: A Man in White tries to blackmail Mr. Roman (jeweler) when he won't pay for false gems bought from Dame Anastasia Louis.

Jonathan knew nothing of this man, nor of Jack ever going to Spadros quadrant. I suspected this was the same one who'd come to Eleanora's home before David was taken. The man went so far as to take on Jack's crazed affectations of dressing all in white and shaving his head!

> Feb. 15, 1899: Dame Anastasia hires me to collect from jewelers who did not pay. Tells me Frank Pagliacci is alive & she knows him. He beat her horse badly & she fears him. She wants to leave Bridges & escape him.

Thinking of Dame Anastasia, all that happened, the way she died — it seemed so unfair. Did she know what Frank Pagliacci planned?

She couldn't have known. The way she spoke, her concern for my welfare — she truly cared about me. At the end, she feared Frank more than anyone.

Then a horrifying thought: she knew Frank would kill her.

Dame Anastasia planned to leave in secret. Who betrayed her? Was it one of the many "young men" she surrounded herself with? Or did her ridiculous great-nephew tell Frank they were leaving? The man knew the date and time they were to leave at least a week prior. And he seemed overly forthcoming to anyone who paid him attention. Why would she trust him?

I pushed my anger aside. Dame Anastasia Louis — and everyone around her — was dead. If I had any chance of bringing Frank and his crew of scoundrels to justice, I had to focus on today.

> Late February, 1899:

> Man in White visits Eleanora "to cause mischief." Neighbor men chase him with bricks.

> I see Zia on Market Center. In love with FP. She claims Morton tried to kill her.

> Morton's boat exploded as he slept in it — he thinks by Feds. Same accent as Zia when sleepy: claims Zia is a family friend who betrayed him.

Clover, a young man in Morton's Red Dogs trey, had saved Morton's life after this explosion. And for that I felt grateful.

But no matter what Morton believed, I very much doubted the Feds would blow up a gentleman's yacht. Or chase him around the city, either. This seemed like Frank Pagliacci — reckless, not too smart, and overly extravagant.

Frank Pagliacci had already posed as part of the District Attorney's office. Were Frank's men now posing as Federal Agents? That could be hazardous to their health if any of the Families caught up to them.

Next, I wrote:

Stable-Master murdered.

I receive a letter from Marja: your Ma is next.

Marja wasn't one of the Dealers' Daughters, so she didn't live in the Cathedral. She was my mother's friend, one of the women who helped raise me, Joseph Kerr, and his twin sister Josephine. Marja had been the Kerr family's housekeeper for a while after Joe and Josie's grandfather took them to Hart quadrant.

Gardena is blackmailed: asks me to help. In return, I ask her to smuggle Ma out of the city.

Feb. 28, 1899:

Marja murdered.

Grief hit me so fiercely that I couldn't continue to write. Marja loved us so very much. As I held Marja's hand in the twilight, blood pooling around her, her last concern was for Josie.

While there had been rumors of Joseph Kerr around the city, no one had ever mentioned his sister. Were Josie and her grandfather still alive?

Though I'd vowed to Marja as she died that I'd protect Josie, I'd never been as worried for Josie as I was for Joe. Josephine Kerr was the leader of the street gang I ran with as a child, the High-Low Split. She was also the smartest, most capable person I knew. If anyone could keep away from the Four Families, she could.

And Josie was completely devoted to her brother. If Joe made it to her that night, she'd be taking care of him.

Heartened, I went back to my list:

Regina Clubb claims she has a witness: a "young black-haired woman" killed Marja. Names: Birdie, The Little Bird, Black Maria, the Death Card. This woman leads the High-Low Split now & has murdered those opposing her.

Morton claims the young black-haired female secretary he saw with Frank Pagliacci shot at him. Same woman??

Besides the conspirators, Morton was the one still-living person who'd seen the woman we thought might be Black Maria. I needed to contact him. But how?

Clover knew how to contact Morton once — perhaps he might do so again. Trying to obey the doctor, I hopped over to my writing box and brought it back to my seat. I wrote to my friend Vig: he might be able to locate Clover for me.

Several people had seen "Black Maria," all giving the same description: young, around my age, with black hair, a fine figure, porcelain skin, and long delicate fingers.

Black Maria was another name for the Queen of Spades, the title which rightly belonged to my mother-in-law Molly Spadros. The only reason for another woman to use the name would be to claim ownership of the Spadros quadrant.

Regina Clubb also said that Black Maria consorted with a "notorious rake" named — not surprisingly — Frank Pagliacci.

How could the High-Low Split have been subverted by these people? Could Joe and Josie being taken to Hart quadrant by their grandfather have led to this?

Surely Josie would have prepared others to take over should anything happen to her. Where were the people she'd chosen? Some of them were sure to be people I knew. Were they murdered by this woman? Or were they now working for the Red Dog Gang?

Mar. 1, 1899: Gardena's "blackmail meeting" is a diversion for the zeppelin bombing. Ma and Dame Anastasia planned to take this zeppelin. I am caught at the station.

How cruel these men were! To murder Dame Anastasia, try to murder my mother — then frame **me** for it?

And why blackmail Gardena Diamond in the first place ...?

Suddenly, I knew what Gardena was **really** being blackmailed about: her son Roland. Which meant someone else knew about him. But who?

Gardena's father would have been more than discreet whilst trying to arrange a marriage for her over the years. But Lance Clubb knew, which meant his parents knew, and possibly his older sisters and their husbands as well.

Other than my poor Nina and her older sister Kitty (now a cloistered Dealers' Apprentice), I knew little about the Clubb sisters, and even less about their husbands. Who might they have told?

I shook my head, dismayed. There was no way to know how many people had already learned of Roland's existence.

If, as Frank Pagliacci said, David Bryce's kidnapping and all this turmoil was intended to destroy the Spadros Family, an attack on Gardena was a fine way to attack Tony. She'd treated Tony horribly, her father had treated him worse, yet he defended her still. He loved Gardena and their son, perhaps more than he loved me.

Not that I cared about that part, not really. My concern for Tony was that of a sister for her younger brother. I wished no harm on Tony, but I never consented to be his wife. It seemed best for all concerned for me to go, so I did. I wanted them to be a family more than almost anything.

Too bad Sawbuck didn't see it that way. He could make a powerful ally.

The far kitchen door's bell jingled. A few minutes later, Mary knocked. "Your cane's here, mum."

"Just set it here by me. And would you bring a glass of water?"

"Of course, mum."

I took a long drink of water, wishing it were wine, then returned to writing my list:

April to November 1899:

Young black-haired woman buys large amount of gray cloth from Eleanora Bryce.

Driver from the night Marja shot (did he see Black Maria??) is murdered using a trap: a hole in the street covered with gray cloth.

District Attorney Chase Freezout and Mrs. Judith Hart frame me for the zeppelin bombing.

Spadros men attack Tony and Sawbuck, call themselves the "Ten of Spades."

Jack Diamond caught outside Eleanora's house — she insists Jack was NOT the Man in White.

Rogue Spadros man kills several guards, tries to shoot me outside courtroom.

During trial: Evidence of woman forger.

Were Black Maria, this woman forger, and Maria Athena Spade three people? Or were they the same woman?

The only way to know was to find Maria Athena Spade so I could learn what she knew. Was she part of the Red Dog Gang? Or — as Sawbuck suspected — was her name simply being used by them? We'd never know until we spoke with her.

But she'd disappeared. And the man who sold her the jacket was now dead. Not by the Bridges Strangler, but the same way Joseph Kerr's uncle died: shot in his office.

Perhaps there were two killers loose in the city.

For now, Maria Athena Spade was my only real lead. I had to find her and persuade her to talk to me. But I had no idea who she was or where she might be, and no one else seemed to know either.

I'd run out of money to do any further investigation on the matter. Until I got a paying job, I was relegated to walking the streets of Spadros quadrant to find one, a target on my back.

I peered at my bandaged foot. I didn't know how much longer I could keep on like this.

The Woman

The front bell rang, and Blitz answered it. I put my list away.

Mr. Doyle Pike said, "Is Mrs. Spadros home today?"

"I'm afraid —"

"It's all right, Blitz," I called out, "you can let him in."

Silence, then, "Come in, sir."

I was positive Blitz was annoyed with me even before he knocked; his face only confirmed it. "And where would you like to receive your guest, Mrs. Spadros?"

"Here, unless you wish to help me move to the parlor." I heard the back door open and Amelia hurry through the hall.

Blitz hesitated. "That might be best." He glanced back. "Let me call Mary."

"I'm here," Amelia panted. "Mum, let me get you presentable."

Blitz retreated.

Amelia set her coat and hat on my bed, adjusted the maid's cap she wore underneath, then began fixing my hair. "What did the doctor say?"

I blinked. "However did you know?"

"Your foot, mum. That's not a bandage we have here."

"I'm to stay off it." If I said a week, she'd take that as set in stone. "He'll be back in a day or two."

"Very good, mum." She slid my house shoe on, offered her hand for me to rise, and let me lean on her as I hobbled into the parlor with my cane. Walking on one foot using only a cane wasn't as easy as it looked.

Mr. Doyle Pike, my attorney, rose with a surprised look on his face. "My dear, if you're indisposed —"

"I'm perfectly well." It was stupid to have avoided him all this time, when he could possibly be of help. I sat, putting my foot on the table. It was indelicate, yes, but it hurt more when dangling upon the ground.

Amelia rushed to drape my skirt so my ankle was hidden, face crimson. "I'm so sorry, sir, she's been —"

Mr. Pike waved her off. "My dear, I have granddaughters older than this. I've seen an ankle before." Then he said to me, "I won't keep you long."

"I know — you want your money."

Amelia made a hasty retreat, perhaps sensing my mood.

"Well, yes, but —"

"I don't have it."

"Well, that's unfortunate." He reached for his briefcase. "May I —?"

"But there is a way you might help."

He leaned forward. "I'm listening."

"You use Mr. Jake Bower as an investigator. I want you to refer clients to me as well. Surely you see widows, or need access to where only a woman might go."

He leaned back, returning the paper to his case. "Are you sure this is wise, Mrs. Spadros?"

"That's not for you to decide. I've been an investigator seven years. I have references a-plenty. But I need work if I'm to pay you, and —" So far, Doyle Pike had freed me from both Prison and gallows. Yet I felt sure this man intended to cheat me at some point. I suspected he'd done so already. "— I'd like a copy of every page I've signed so far."

His face made an impressed "oh" for a moment, then he rummaged around in his briefcase, handing me three sheets of paper. After this, he leaned back with an amused smile and surveyed me for several seconds. "I may just have a case for you."

"Is that so?"

"A widow came to me asking for help. Her family is being harassed, and her daughter is missing. I can help with the first one, although it puts me in a precarious position. But perhaps you might be best suited for the second."

"I specialize in missing persons. Or does she believe her daughter's been taken?"

"No, the girl — well, shall we say, the spinster: she's twenty — left a note for her mother. But it's been several months without word, and her mother's frightened." He smiled at me as one might smile at a child. "Perhaps when you have children you'll understand."

I had no intention of having children, but I nodded just the same.

"Very well, then, Mrs. Spadros; I'll send her over."

* * *

Once Mr. Pike left, I looked over the papers I'd signed. But I didn't understand some — well, most — of the words.

So I sent for Mr. Trevisane. Mr. Trevisane was Tony's lawyer. But he'd also helped me during my trial, mostly with explanations of what was going on, and what things were called. Surely he could help me read these papers.

Then I returned to my room — with Amelia's help — and studied my list again. And I began to create a diagram of this Red Dog Gang's structure.

Everything I'd learned of this Red Dog Gang pointed to two men: a Man in Brown named Frank Pagliacci, and a Man in White impersonating Master Jack Diamond.

Frank Pagliacci and the Man in White began with at least ten men at their beck and call. Morton and I killed most of them at the Diamond Factory when we rescued David Bryce over a year earlier.

Four women worked with these men. First, the rogue Federal Agent Zia Cashout, who had red hair and a very strong accent. The handwriting expert said a woman forged the letters and invoices presented at the trial. A red-haired woman without an accent signed the jacket invoice using the name Maria Athena Spade. And then whoever Black Maria really was.

The kitchen door bell rung far off. A few moments later, Mary knocked. She carried a vase. "Your flowers, mum."

The red roses from Mr. Hart made me recall the forged invoices he'd presented at the trial.

The Red Dog Gang bought wigs!

Up to then, I couldn't deduce why they'd bought these. But now I understood: to disguise the women.

Or perhaps just to disguise one woman.

Zia had too strong of an accent: in Bridges, she'd be recognized the minute she opened her mouth. But if Black Maria wore a red wig, she might have signed for the jacket.

No wonder the coat seller ended up dead: he could identify her.

The handwriting expert said the wig invoices were forged. Did the handwriting on the jacket invoice match them?

I hesitated to write to Tony. I'd caused him so much hurt already. From Sawbuck's demeanor, I could see that Tony was still in a great deal of turmoil and distress. But perhaps Sawbuck might be able to get the invoice for me without disturbing him. "Blitz?"

A moment later, Blitz appeared. "What can I get you?"

"See if Sawbuck has the invoice for the jacket. He'll know which one I mean."

Blitz glanced at my pile of papers. "You found something."

"I might have. It won't provide money, but at least I'm keeping myself busy."

Blitz chuckled. "If it keeps you off your foot, that's good enough."

I ignored him, focusing on my list. Who was the woman forger the handwriting expert described during the trial?

The handwriting expert had been one of the Feds, and so was Zia. Could Zia be the woman forger?

I had no idea what Feds were taught. As a child, I was taught that Feds were vile betrayers who abandoned us in the Pot to misery and squalor after the Coup. I'd never seen one until I met Zia, but all us children knew to kill them on sight. If only I'd known she was a Fed when I had her in front of me!

But Mr. Pike had gotten a Fed to testify for me. The handwriting expert's information was helpful, yet to use it left me feeling vaguely unclean.

So we had Zia Cashout and Black Maria for sure. These two women could have done everything I'd seen so far.

But if there were only two women working with this Gang, then Black Maria was quite the talent. Able to hold sway over the High-Low Split children's gang as an adult? That in itself would be quite the feat. Over a thousand children and several hundred former gang members stood in her way, none who'd take kindly to some outsider pushing in. And she could shoot as well.

Marja's body lying under the street lamp outside Vig's bar appeared before my eyes.

But somehow I doubted that this false Queen of Spades would write her real name on an invoice. The real Maria Athena Spade was likely innocent, and probably terrified, especially if Spadros men searched for her by name.

I looked over my list. Mrs. Clubb said Black Maria consorted with Frank Pagliacci. Did Zia know?

There was already a great deal of evidence that Frank Pagliacci was a cad. Not only did Zia seem firmly attached to him, but before she died, Dame Anastasia told me he was her lover. Yet none of them seemed to know about the others!

Zia's outraged face when I told her Frank was a murderer came to mind. I couldn't see Zia taking kindly to Frank having a second lover. It wouldn't have surprised me one bit if Zia had murdered Dame Anastasia. If Zia knew about Black Maria, she'd surely try to kill her.

So perhaps Frank went between the groups to keep the two apart. This might be how their leader communicated with them. Frank had been repeatedly described as a well-liked and attractive man, perfect for such work.

Someone was strangling young men. Someone was shooting people at relatively close range. If the false Red Dog Gang and the High-Low Split operated separately, that explained the two different sets of deaths.

But why? Were all these strangled young men related to the Red Dog Gang in some way? Or had Frank Pagliacci begun killing for his own amusement? Only the police — and Frank himself — might know the answer to that question.

And who led these people? I felt sure we'd not seen the Red Dog Gang's leader yet. What terrible hate he had for us. But why? What had the Spadros Family done to him? What had **I** done to him?

His attacks were so personal. He'd directed David Bryce to be taken specifically because he looked like Air. This man had two women I loved as mothers killed. He almost killed my real mother, framed me for murder, and had a man shoot at me — for what?

This clearly was meant to torment me. But I couldn't think of anyone I might have insulted so.

From everything I'd learned so far, this Director had to be much older than the others. And crafty. Devious. Perhaps more so than I.

He'd gleaned decades worth of information about the Spadros Family few others knew. Information which had gotten lesser men maimed and killed in the most horrible ways. So he had to have planned these attacks for some time.

Yet he had to also be highly persuasive to make such different groups as this false Red Dog Gang, the High-Low Split children's street gang, and the rebellious Spadros men follow him. He'd likely been able to gather the information he had precisely because of this persuasive nature.

And he had to have a great deal of both money and influence to be physically able to do what he'd done so far.

At one point, I thought this leader was now-Mayor Freezout. But the terrible beating Mr. Freezout took at the hands of Roy Spadros bitterly proved that wrong.

But beating Mayor Freezout was a good play on Roy's part. Roy showed the Four Families' dominance to everyone in the city, and it was unlikely Mayor Freezout would trust Mrs. Hart again.

* * *

Although I'd called for Tony's lawyer earlier that day, I expected to receive some clerk. Or perhaps a messenger with a date to visit his office in the future. To my surprise, Mr. Trevisane himself arrived just after tea. "How may I help, Mrs. Spadros?"

"Would it offend to have you look at some documents —"

"Why, no —"

"— **without** informing my husband?"

49

Mr. Trevisane hesitated. "As your husband's attorney, I must inform him of anything which affects his legal position. This includes any agreements you might have made with others."

"Wait. My husband's responsible for my debts?"

"For as long as you're legally married."

I felt stunned. "That's unjust!" No wonder Tony had been so opposed to my taking on Mr. Pike as an attorney.

"Perhaps so." He spoke as if discussing a small child. "But it protects honest merchants from the frivolities of women —"

I gaped at him, appalled.

"— you see, no matter what a wayward little wife may purchase, merchants have assurance under the law that they'll be paid."

I swallowed, speechless. After a moment, I said, "Thank you for your counsel, sir. I'll have no need of your help today."

"If you're sure —"

I struggled to my foot, using the cane. "I am. Quite sure. Thank you." I called out, "Blitz? Pray see Mr. Trevisane out."

Once the man had left, I collapsed into the chair, appalled.

Blitz came in. "Are you well?"

I stared up at him. Was this how all quadrant-men saw women? "I'm not certain of much anymore."

Blitz knelt beside my chair. "Tell me what happened."

I shook my head. "Are we even human to you?"

"I don't understand what you mean."

I leaned my face on my hands, the cane clattering to the floor. "It seems I don't understand anything here."

"What did he say?" Blitz hesitated. "Did he hurt you?"

I began to laugh. "No, well, not like that. I don't think it's anything a quadrant-man would even understand."

Blitz picked up the cane, leaning it on the arm rest. "If you say so. But something's upset you. How can I help?"

I needed help. I had to learn what Mr. Doyle Pike had done — without Tony learning of it. "See if Mr. Thrace Pike is available to speak with me."

Thrace Pike was Doyle Pike's grandson, one of his many law clerks. But he seemed to have some attraction to me. Perhaps I might use this to my advantage.

"I'll send a message right away." He stood. "Anything else?"

Get me a drink? The thought appeared seemingly from nowhere. No, that wouldn't do to say, not after everything that'd happened. "Help me to my room?"

Blitz gave me a kindly smile. "Of course."

I let him help me to my room. But nothing was well at all.

I despised gambling. But I would have wagered every cent I had that Mr. Trevisane was on his way to Spadros Manor to tell Tony that I hid something of a legal nature.

Why did I call Mr. Trevisane, of all people? This would only disturb, upset, and distract Tony, at a time when he most needed to focus on the Family's survival.

* * *

Mr. Thrace Pike sat in my parlor the next day. A man of one and twenty with sandy hair and very dark eyes, he'd arrived precisely at noon. The instant I entered, he sprang up, his eyes widening at my cane. "What can I help you with, Mrs. Spadros?"

"Please, sit, sir. I won't take much of your time."

Thrace Pike hesitated. "Very well. But I can't stay long: my grandfather doesn't know I'm here."

So he'd deduced this wasn't a social call. I presented the papers to him. "What do these say?"

His face sobered, growing paler with each page he read. Finally, he glanced up, yet didn't meet my eye. "You owe my grandfather 1% of the price of the gems Dame Anastasia sold — erm, lent — the jewelers. From the peak of their market value."

Worse than I thought. Speculation had driven gem prices to horrendous levels before they crashed. "I understand."

"And he's charged monthly interest. Starting from when you signed." He gulped. "Over a year ago."

"What does monthly interest mean?"

Mr. Pike blinked. "Um, uh, it's a ... a percentage fee. For paying late. It's added to the bill every month. And the next bill's fee is derived from the entirety."

From the entirety? How was this possible? "And the terms of repayment?"

"10% of your current income, each month. Starting from when you signed. Including the stipend given you by the Court during the trial." The page trembled. "You're already in serious arrears. And there's a late penalty prescribed. Starting from your first month's default."

And all in writing, so there would be no doubt.

Doyle Pike planned this from the day he decided to help me by dunning the merchants for Dame Anastasia. And the form was printed, with blanks to fill in. So he'd done this to many others. And he knew that Tony — no matter what he might say, think, or feel — would be obligated by law to pay. "Why would he do this?"

Thrace Pike's face was as disbelieving as mine must have been. "I understand nothing about my grandfather. I marvel that I came from his line."

There must be a way to counter this. "Are these fees — no, how excessive are these interest fees?"

A bitter laugh burst from him, swiftly subdued. "Forgive me. No. Not such that you could challenge him. The entire contract is legal."

So much the worse. "What do you suggest I do?"

"Do?" He raised his face with such a stricken expression that for an instant I felt sorry for him instead of myself. "I don't know."

I smiled at him. "I'll think of something."

We moved towards the front hall door; I'd been experimenting with using the side of my foot to walk on. Out of curiosity, I asked, "How does your work fare?"

He stopped before the parlor door, which remained shut. "I'm the laughing-stock of the firm. I'd hoped to become a prosecutor. Yet the District Attorney's office won't see me. I suppose it's that I was on the defense team for your case. Against Mr. Freezout."

Mr. Freezout had been the District Attorney at the time. Losing my case must have been a blow to the entire department. But I felt certain that the real issue was what his wife had done during the trial. "I'm sorry."

He shrugged. "It's not your fault."

"I don't blame your wife, sir. She did what she thought best." What she'd done was throw the city into riot when her expose of

Doyle Pike's plan was printed in the *Golden Bridges*. The noise from the turmoil allowed an assassin to murder a squad of Court guards from behind during his plot to kill me.

"You're very kind." He opened the door. "The City doesn't see it that way. We're to be fined, in lieu of prosecution. She's to get leniency. Because she was with child."

Gertie Pike had given birth to a son a few days after the trial. "I see. I hope she and your children are well?"

He nodded, but never met my eye. "Very well. Thank you. Good day, madam."

Thrace Pike opened the door. Blitz stood in the hall; Thrace took his hat from him and left.

Blitz closed the front door and said, "So how bad is it?"

I still stood in the parlor doorway, leaning on my cane. "It's pretty bad."

* * *

I never learned who told who what, but just after dinner, Sawbuck appeared at our door.

Amelia had gone home. The dishes were cleared, and we'd been sitting around the kitchen table. I didn't feel like getting up, so I had Blitz bring Sawbuck in.

I never noticed before how big the man was. He didn't have to duck to get in the room, but he about filled the doorway. He scowled when he saw me. "What the hell is going on?"

"It's nice to see you, too," I said. "Why don't you sit down? Would you care for some coffee?"

Sawbuck just growled in disgust.

Mary and Blitz made a hasty retreat into the hall.

Sawbuck pulled out a chair and sat across from me.

Since he didn't say anything, I said, "Is there something I can do for you?"

He said quietly, "What the fuck have you gotten Mr. Anthony involved with?"

"He has nothing to fear. He mustn't become anxious over the matter. It's entirely under control."

"Like hell it is," Sawbuck said. "You have no income, or had you forgotten?" He leaned back. "Just how much do you owe?"

I hadn't exactly calculated it. "A good amount. But I promised to repay it, and I shall."

"With what? Your 'cases'?" He leaned forward. "Why don't you stop playing detective and return home where you belong?"

Playing detective? "I have been a professional investigator since long before my marriage. I'm sorry you don't trust me. But surely you haven't forgotten?" Sawbuck grew up in the Pot just as I did — why were we even having this discussion? "Women of the Pot pay their own debts."

He grimaced, appearing chagrined.

I had an instant of grief, which I pushed away. "I never expected my husband to become involved. Or even to learn of this." I wished I would have trusted Tony. I should have told him about the trouble I'd been in when I signed Mr. Pike's first paper. "I want him upset as little as possible."

"Then we're in agreement. So how shall we proceed? We can't kill Pike —"

A startled laugh burst from me. "What?"

"If I recall, he keeps files on each client. It's how he really makes his money. That investigator of his finds secrets his clients would rather not reveal, in case they don't pay. Sometimes even if they do. So we can't just kill him. I'm sure he has some mechanism to release his secrets should he die under suspicious circumstance." Sawbuck shrugged. "It's what I would do."

These quadrant-folk were insane. But Thrace Pike had tried to warn me about his grandfather. And I didn't listen. Had I told the man anything harmful? "I already have a plan. Doyle Pike has a case for me. And he's agreed to send me cases to investigate in the future." I shrugged. "It's a start."

Sawbuck's gaze turned inward, as if he were considering something. "Very well." He stood, gesturing for me to stay seated. "Keep me informed."

"I will. Thank you." Then I remembered. "Did Blitz tell you about the invoice?"

"He did. Unfortunately, it's nowhere to be found."

"What?"

"We believe the man who shot at you took it with him when he left to join the rogues."

Unbelievable. "So they planned for everything."

"Yeah," Sawbuck said. "Looks like they did."

* * *

That night, I couldn't sleep, so sat up with a cigarette, my list laid on the table, my mind filled with anxiety.

How could I even begin to pay Mr. Pike?

I imagined this "case" he had for me. A widow, he said.

She'd likely pay a few pennies a day, enough to hire a carriage, perhaps even enough to buy more writing-paper. But not nearly enough to pay the thousands I now owed him.

I remembered the Grand Ball, why, to this day I don't know. How opulent the room was! What delicious food! How lovely the clothing! We sat with friends, we toasted with champagne.

At the time, I'd thought it bitter. How I wished I had some.

And I recalled Major Blackwood, sitting near the other end of our table, with his bawdy anecdotes and custom-made uniforms. At the time, he seemed a silly, fat old man, ever revisiting the past.

Yet he'd never said a word about finding me dressed in a blood-spattered maid's uniform after I rescued David. And he showed real depth and kindness at my Queen's Night dinner.

Was he still making the party circuit, feasting at all the high-born tables in Bridges? He'd found a way to live free of the Four Families.

Was Jonathan right? Worse, was Sawbuck right? Had I made a terrible mistake by leaving Spadros Manor?

The mere thought of returning made me feel ill.

I'd made my choice. I had to stop this fretting and focus on what I could do.

But try as I might, I could think of nothing to add, and finally, exhausted, I went to bed.

* * *

Two days later, someone knocked on the door. When Blitz answered, a woman said, "I look for the Kaplan Investigator."

55

With my room right next to the front door, I heard the woman plainly. A thick accent, a heavy, faltering tread. I listened as Blitz brought her to my study, then knocked on my bedroom door.

"Come in."

"A woman to see you. She wouldn't give her name. Do you need help getting around?"

"No, I can manage." I could walk without the cane — on the side or heel of my foot — well enough to be presentable. So once Blitz disappeared down the hall, I went to my study.

The woman was at least fifty and stout, with wavy black hair graying at the temples. She dressed in widow's brown, yet of fine make, with expensive jewelry and a big, fluffy fur coat. Her complexion, olive, her eyes, dark brown. She rose to take my hand (and kiss both my cheeks). "You are woman investigator?"

"I am."

"Thank you to see me, Signora."

I sat behind my desk. "How may I help?"

"My daughter, she gone a year. My sons, the police, they look but don't a find." She clasped her hands together. "This my baby, please, you must a help. I pay whatever you want, my husband left us good money."

She could pay. I doubled my usual fee for uppers. "One dollar a day, plus expenses."

She didn't flinch. "Expenses? I not a know that."

"If I need to hire a taxi-carriage, or find special documents."

The woman nodded. "Whatever you need."

I struggled to keep my excitement in check. She hadn't paid me yet. "You pay the first week in advance. You only pay for the days I work. I keep records, if you ever want to see." I rested my elbows on the desk, and gazed into her eyes. "I always find who I look for. Always. I have a list of people you can speak with."

She opened her handbag. "I pay now." She handed over a five and two ones.

She carried a huge amount of money for a widow. What street did this woman live on?

I wanted to make sure there was no mistake here. "I find everyone I look for. But sometimes I find them dead."

She gazed down, eyes reddening. "I know. You can no bring a life. But I want a my girl home." She turned her eyes to mine. "Please? Dead or not a dead. Bring a my girl home."

I took a deep breath, straightening. Her plea seemed too much like Eleanora Bryce's for comfort. "Do you have a portrait of her?"

"Si, Signora," the woman said. She handed me a full portrait behind glass in a golden frame.

Just approaching womanhood, seated, knees turned sideways, hands in her lap, she faced the camera. I instantly recalled what Madame Biltcliffe said about the girl in her shop before the break-in. *Very pretty, very young. A lovely figure and straight black hair. Porcelain skin, blue eyes. Ah, a gorgeous girl.*

Alarmed, I turned towards her. "What's your daughter's name?"

"Maria Athena Spade, Signora. She's my youngest. My baby girl. I must a find her."

The Case

The one woman I most needed to find. And when I most needed money, her mother willing to pay anything to get her back. "Who told you to visit Mr. Pike?"

She seemed surprised. "My neighbor across a street." She spoke as if wishing to ease my mind. "I live on the Market a Center. My husband Giovanni was — how you say? — he bought a cattle from Nitivali and sold at stockyards. We move from Milano when Maria Athena small. Giovanni, he die last year from his a heart. I have nine sons and Maria Athena." Her eyes fell. "And a now she gone." She peered at me. "Can you help? Or no?"

I took a deep breath, heart pounding. This felt like a trap.

Every time the Red Dog Gang made a play, they used a distraction to divert me from what they were really doing.

What were they really doing?

This had to be a trap, like when they took David Bryce.

Yet it wasn't just a trap for me. If I were seized, would Tony, Jonathan Diamond, and Charles Hart stand idly by? And the Clubb Family was obligated to assist if called upon because of their alliance with the Spadros Family.

So if the Red Dog Gang played their cards right, this could become a trap for the Four Families as well.

But since I knew it was a trap, perhaps I might trap them instead. "I can help."

"Oh, thank you, Signora," she said, relieved. "Thank you."

* * *

Mrs. Spade and two of her sons lived on the north end of Market Center with their families.

"We had money for a bigger, but we no like a the quadrants," Mrs. Spade explained. "No mafiosi, my Giovanni say. So we buy room both a sides and put in the doors."

"Tell me what happened when Maria left."

For an instant, she seemed confused. "Oh, Maria Athena. We say Maria Athena. She go out and a no come back. On bed was a note."

"Do you have the note with you?"

She handed over a short note, but I couldn't read it. I'd never seen this handwriting before. "What does it say?"

She glanced away. "Spadros men search for her, and she no more a put us in the danger. But not a worry, she safe."

"And you're sure this is from her."

"Si, Signora."

"So why come to me? Why go to my lawyer?"

Her face filled with compassion. "Husband not a with you at a the trial. And his men attack!" She shook her head, face disbelieving. "Lawyer get a you free." Her gaze turned inward for a instant. "I no blame a you stay here." Her face turned commanding. "You not a go home to that." She straightened, gave a satisfied nod. "You good a mind. You find a my girl."

An outsider widow speaking little of our language, her only daughter missing. Yet she could look past the ways I might be unsuitable, even though for all she knew I was allied with the men who'd driven her daughter away in terror. "So you knew about my lawyer, and your neighbor told you to go to him?"

"Yes, Signora. But I not think to go until a she say." She gave me an "I don't know why I didn't think of it" smile.

"What have the Spadros men done?"

"Day and night a they come. Police no help. My sons bought a the guns."

This seemed worse than I imagined. "Are you sure these are Spadros men?"

"They wear a the — how you say it?" She reached across my desk, pinched my sleeve.

"Uniform —?" I recalled what Tony said in Spadros Manor's dining room last year. *Jacqui, our men only wear livery on specific occasions. Someone's impersonating us.*

Her face turned concerned. "Signora, what a happen?"

I turned to her. "These aren't Spadros men. Bad men tried to harm the Spadros Family. They stole uniforms —" this seemed quicker than to explain the matter "— and pretended to be Spadros men to ruin our name."

She stared at me, mouth open.

"Spadros men asked about her because her name was used to buy something which could help us find these men."

"What thing?"

"A brown men's jacket."

Mrs. Spade scoffed. "My sons, they no wear a brown!"

Plus the jacket was in a low-card shop well below the means of this family. "I never believed this was her. But we can't know the truth until we find her."

"What a you mean?"

"They've frightened her into leaving home. But why? Did she see or hear something she shouldn't have? The only way we can know is to find her."

Mrs. Spade cried out, "Oh, my girl! What evil chance entangled you?" She clasped my hands. "Rescue her from a the villains!"

"Where might she go? Friends, family?"

The woman shook her head. "We only family. My boys, her friends a no find."

"Please tell them if they think of anything which may help, they can send a message here." I handed her ten of my cards. "The more I know, the faster I can find her."

She rose with a determined air. "They will a write today." She held out her hand. "Thank you, Signora."

Once she left, Blitz peered in. I jumped up, squealed in glee. "We're saved!" I handed him the seven dollars. "She's rich, and I can help her."

"What are you doing up without your cane?" Then his face turned skeptical. "What exactly does she want you to do?"

* * *

Blitz sent for Sawbuck at once. "He needs to know there are more Spadros impersonators out there."

I really didn't want to deal with Sawbuck right then. I wanted to find this woman.

Maria Athena Spade felt she was safe. So where was she?

I inspected the letter. Other than the word "Spadros," I could read none of it.

It had none of the signs of copying the handwriting expert mentioned during my trial. But I couldn't assume it was genuine.

I returned to my room, slid off my house shoes and put my foot up. Something made me think Mrs. Spade didn't tell me everything.

A knock at the front door. Blitz answered it. "Good day, mum. Come in."

Then Blitz knocked on my door. "Mrs. Eleanora Bryce of Bryce Fabrics to see you. I have her in the parlor."

"Have her come in here." I didn't want to get up again if I didn't need to. "Would you ask Mary to bring us some tea?"

"Right away."

A few minutes later, in came Eleanora Bryce. Although like Mrs. Spade, Eleanora dressed in widow's brown, Mrs. Bryce's clothes were old, much mended. Her graying straight brown hair was parted in the center and braided around her head under a lace cap.

She drew back when she saw my foot up and the cane on the wall beside my tea-table. "Are you hurt?"

I smiled warmly at her. "Almost well." I took my foot off of the chair. "Please, sit. Are you and David well?"

She dusted off the seat, then sat. "Well enough. What happened?"

Normally such a question would be indiscreet, or even nosy. But I'd known Eleanora Bryce since I was born, and we'd gone through a great deal together. "Too much walking. It was silly of me."

Eleanora gave me a fond smile. "You always were a headstrong girl." She patted my hand. "I'm glad you're almost well."

Mary came in, poured tea for us, then left.

"You didn't come all this way just to see me. What's wrong?"

She stared at her teacup, hands in her lap. "Do you recall the gentleman who helped me and my sons? Before we came here."

"I do! Is all well?"

She shook her head. "He arrived just after the New Year. But they won't let him into the city."

I blinked. "He's been held since January? Why-ever for?"

"They won't say. When David was first taken, the police placed a notice to stop him coming into Bridges." She drew back a bit. "He was a suspect! But he'd never harm anyone." Her voice dropped to a whisper. "He believes the Clubb Family seeks a bribe."

This was ridiculous. "Blitz!"

A moment later, he opened the door. "What can I help with?"

I hesitated. "Call a Memory Boy, if you please."

"The one I sent should be returning soon. I'll let you know when he arrives."

I turned to Eleanora. "You were right to come to me." My stack of papers sat beside me; I turned one over and handed her a pencil. "Write his name and anything you think might help his case."

She moved her teacup aside and began writing.

I'd never seen Eleanora write before, and from the effort she made, writing seemed something she seldom did.

But she sat up with a relieved smile. "There!"

She pushed the page to me, clearly proud of her work:

Constable Trey Highcard of Dickens Police

Helpd me & Sons

A goode man Indeed

Wishs to Marry & Settle

"Oh," I said, taken aback. "He's asked you to marry him?"

She beamed, blushing. "He has. Through the post. I've accepted."

"Oh, Eleanora." I rose and hugged her. Of all the people who deserved something good to happen, she'd be at the top of my list. "I'm so very happy for you." After a moment, I returned to my chair. "I believe I can help."

"If you could, I'd be most grateful. We'd both be in your debt."

"This reminds me," I said. "I have something I've wanted to give you for some time."

I went to where I'd hidden the change I meant to give her before I fled Spadros Manor. I pressed the envelope into her hands: twenty-six cents, most of it pennies.

But when she peered inside, she put her head on her arms and began to weep. "Thank you so very much."

I rested my hand on her shoulder. Bryce Fabrics was on 2nd Street. While her Family fees were just two cents a month, with her rent, her fabric shop barely made enough for her and her son David to survive. And I recalled Jonathan's words to me. "I want you and David to be happy and well. I want you not to be anxious of need."

She raised red eyes to mine. "I'll never forget your kindness."

And in her eyes, I saw David — no, truly I saw his older brother Air, who he looked so much like.

If only my father hadn't shot him. If only I'd trusted that Eleanora would care for him, get him the medicine he needed. If only I'd obeyed my Ma and stayed in that night. Listened to her warnings about my father and his treachery. I owed this woman much. "I'll get your Constable freed, never fear."

* * *

After she left, I considered who to contact. Regina Clubb had not once responded to my messages, and I wondered if something were amiss. Sending a message to Mr. Clubb, or even his son Lance, was out of the question if his wife refused to respond.

About an hour after Eleanora left, the bell rang; Blitz answered it.

Werner Lead's piping voice came in from outside. "Master Hogan says to come to him. It's not for me to hear your message."

I chuckled and put my house shoes on. Werner was one of the Memory Boys, sent to carry messages too secret to be written. Problem was that these children remembered everything, both written and said, and who knew who **they** reported to?

"Very well," Blitz said. "Thank you."

I went past Blitz and outside.

My narrow street was busy, with messengers, delivery-men, and the occasional carriage trundling past. The woman across the street and two doors down was sweeping her steps until she saw me. She gave me an unfriendly glare and went inside.

Werner Lead was perhaps ten, with white-blond hair and blue eyes. He stood at the bottom of the steps, gazing up at me. "Good day, Mrs. Spadros." Two older boys with sandy hair stood beside him, watching everything but us.

Werner wouldn't enter a private home, so I went down the steps and sat before him. "I need your help."

He beamed, doubtless sensing an extra fee. "I'd be happy to."

"Mrs. Regina Clubb doesn't answer. Does she get my messages?"

He hesitated. "I tell them to her."

"Do you really? The Queen of Clubbs comes out to see you each time you call? I find that hard to believe."

The boy bit his lower lip. "Sometimes her butler takes them."

As I suspected. And who might **he** tell them to? "Do you know who holds outsiders who come into the city?"

"Oh, yes, Mrs. Spadros. I know that! Mr. Mikhail Bettelmann."

"I've never heard of him. How is he related to the Clubbs?"

"He's married to Mrs. Karla. She's the third grand-daughter."

"I see. So he's not too old."

Werner shrugged. "He's pretty old. At least thirty!"

"If I give you a message to Mrs. Karla Bettelmann, could you give it to her personally?"

The boy's face brightened. "For certain. She always comes out! Sometimes she gives us milk and cookies."

I felt sure these boys had been warned not to accept food from their customers. But that wasn't my affair. "Well, then, tell Mrs. Karla this: 'I wish to meet regarding Trey Highcard. Please inform me of the date and place.' That's the message. The entire message, you hear? Add nothing to it. You must tell it to her ear alone. And I must have an answer from her personally." I glanced back: Blitz still stood there. "Give him his fee."

Blitz handed the boy his fee. Then he returned up the steps, and the door squeaked a bit.

I said to Werner, "You'll get that same fee when you return with her personal answer. From her lips. You understand?"

I grinned to myself as he and his brothers hurried away. The Clubb syndicate made their real business selling secrets. Yet who would dare divert Regina Clubb's messages? The butler, for certain. And whoever paid him to do it.

If I cared — and I didn't already have a case to run — I'd sniff out that mystery. But if I could get former-Constable Trey Highcard out of a Clubb holding cell, I'd have done my duty.

Blitz had my cane in hand, and brought it to me. "I'm sure you heard what the boy told me when he arrived."

"I did."

"Fancy a trip? Best Sawbuck hear your news firsthand."

I grabbed hold of the iron banister to pull myself to my feet. "Get Amelia; I'm sure she'll want to change me again."

A plain carriage arrived a half-hour later. Dark brown, without Family symbols upon it. All the Families used them. If you happened to miss the black horses with silver tack, you might mistake it for a taxi-carriage.

My former day footman Skip Honor beamed for an instant when he saw me, quickly moving to his carefully neutral demeanor. I got in; Amelia and Blitz followed.

But I hadn't thought the matter through. Sawbuck's house was on 190th street, and the closer we got the more anxious I felt. It was too close to Spadros Manor, too easy to just bundle me over there, never to be seen again. Locked in day and night, with men watching my every move. My hands shook. The carriage felt stifling. "Stop," I said. "Stop!"

Blitz grabbed the speaking tube. "Stop the carriage!"

I got out just in time.

"Oh, mum," Amelia said, fanning me. "This was a mistake. You've had much too much excitement today."

I sat on the step panting, my heart pounding, bathed in sweat. "I can't go back there," I sobbed. "I won't. I'll die."

Blitz said, "When have you ever been to Sawbuck's house?"

Amelia glared at him. To me, she said, "Let's get you back inside." Once I was in, she closed the door, pulled the curtains, and sat beside me. "Now what's this all about?"

"I'm not going back to Spadros Manor ... I won't. I'll take my life before I go there again."

"Shh," Amelia said. "We're not taking you there."

I felt like a small child. "You're not? I'm not to be locked in?"

"No, mum." Amelia pulled me to her chest. "My poor girl ..."

I began weeping again.

"If you'll bite like a dog, Pot rag, you'll be treated like one."

Footsteps, grating on gravel, going away, leaving me alone. Bars, a locked gate. The space was small, smelled of animals. The lock was too high to grab properly. I rattled the gate in the dim humid air, feeling trapped, frantic. "Let me out!"

It was getting dark. Did they mean to leave me here forever? I screamed. "Let me out!"

With a shock, I realized where I sat.

Amelia peered at me, face concerned.

I got my handkerchief. "I'm sorry."

"I wish I might burn Mr. Roy's cards a thousand times," Amelia murmured, "for what he's done to you."

Roy Spadros had done so much worse to her than he'd ever done to me. But even so, I felt better.

Amelia said, "Do you want to go to Master Hogan's house? Or just go home?"

"If it's really just Sawbuck's house — I'll go."

* * *

Sawbuck had a smallish house on 190th in the middle of the block, three blocks from Spadros Manor. The house had a small courtyard inside a high wrought-iron fence, just as the rest did. But three men stood guard on the sidewalk, armed, tipping their hats as I emerged from the carriage. The middle one opened the gate for us.

Sawbuck's butler escorted us into a parlor not much larger than my own. Four chairs sat around a round wooden table. A long sofa lay along one wall. Several small portraits — one of my mother-in-law Molly — sat upon a mantel above the fireplace. Other than that, the room was bare.

It seemed Master Ten Hogan didn't do much entertaining.

"Took you long —" Sawbuck said, then stopped, staring. "What's happened? Why did you bring her here?"

Blitz and Amelia stared back, cheeks pale. I slumped into a chair, my cane clattering to the floor, and put my face in my hands.

"Maria Athena Spade's mother was just at my house. Men wearing Spadros livery threatened them."

Sawbuck sat across from me. "Mrs. Spadros, you look sick."

Amelia spoke in Sawbuck's ear. He stood, held out his hand to me. "I'm taking you back to your apartments."

I rose, taking his arm. We got into the carriage and were silent the entire trip.

Mary answered the door, glancing back and forth between us all. "What happened?"

Once we were inside, I don't know why, but I began to cry.

Amelia opened the parlor door. "Come sit, mum."

I sat on the sofa. "I — I'm s-sorryyy." I felt ashamed that Sawbuck saw me like this. "I don't know what's wrong with me."

Sawbuck snapped, "All of you, out."

He sat across from me. Once they left, he said, "There's nothing wrong with you." He gazed off to one side. "For a while after the first time I killed a man, whenever I saw a gun I would set to shaking. I'd get sick as well."

I wiped under my eyes, my handkerchief stained with makeup, and recalled the men I'd killed. The men who had me, Morton, and little David trapped in Jack Diamond's Party Time factory. The man who tried to violate me the night I left Tony. I wasn't sure they'd affected me at all.

"But I had to keep going," Sawbuck said, "for Mr. Anthony's sake. He doesn't know the half of what I've done for him. I was the only one I knew could protect him — from his father, most of all."

So Sawbuck didn't know that Roy wasn't Tony's real father. What might he do if he learned the truth?

"One day you may have to walk in there again. I don't know why. You certainly don't have to go there now. But whether you return or not, you have to keep going. Do what you have to do to survive. I don't know for who or what, but —" he leaned forward, rested his elbows on his knees "— you have to find your reason. There's something only you can do." He looked down. "That's all."

This was the longest speech I'd ever heard from him.

I didn't know why I kept going. It certainly wasn't for Tony, not then. Was it for David Bryce?

Looking back, I think not. I think it was really for the hope of finding Joseph Kerr. Learning what happened to him. Hoping that he might be alive. At that point, I would have forgiven anything, if I might only see Joe again. I nodded.

Sawbuck smiled to himself. "You may come through this yet."

"May I ask something?"

"Of course."

I'd made Tony's life miserable. "Why are you helping me?"

Sawbuck blinked. "You're one of us."

I glanced away. I wasn't one of them. I never wanted to be one of them. The Spadros Family had about destroyed me.

But if it gained Sawbuck's help, I'd let him think whatever he wanted to.

The bell rang; Blitz rushed to answer it. "I'm sorry, Inventor Call, Mrs. Spadros isn't —"

I said, "It's all right, Blitz, you can let him in."

Blitz came into view. While he looked nothing like Tony, at this moment he had his face in a mask remarkably like his cousin's. "Inventor Maxim Call, mum."

Blitz **never** called me "mum."

I went to him, angled so the Inventor might not see me. "I'm sorry, Blitz," I whispered, "but he came to me. I should see him."

His face turned resigned. And for an instant, I glimpsed how difficult the life of a butler must be, especially to a man as spirited as he. I patted his arm as I passed, hoping that might help. "Inventor Call!" I curtsied low. "To what do I owe this tremendous honor?"

Indeed, I was astonished to see him here He'd refused to even write, let alone grant me audience, the last time I'd offered him help. At the time, I presumed that he must need my help so much that he came here himself to beg my forgiveness.

Which in itself was inconceivable. What had changed?

Inventor Maxim Call was an ancient, wiry man with brown skin and the piercing blue eyes of his distant cousin, Roy Spadros. Completely ignoring my cane, he came past without a word.

I gestured into the room; Sawbuck had risen, moved around to the sofa, bowed low. "I'm sure you know Master Ten Hogan."

Inventor Call eyed Sawbuck, but didn't offer his hand. "I do."

Sawbuck didn't seem put out by this at all.

"Please sit, sirs." I turned to Blitz. "Tea, if you will."

Inventor Call sat on the sofa at least two feet from Sawbuck. I sat across from Inventor Call, intrigued as to what he might have to say. Yet he seemed hesitant to speak.

Etiquette dictated that Sawbuck stay at least ten minutes after the arrival of another guest so as not to give the impression of dislike or hurry. As hostess, I must make the time a comfort rather than a duty. "I hope you and your men are well, sir."

"We're well busy. Just added a new Apprentice."

"Congratulations," I said.

This seemed to surprise the Inventor. "Why, thank you."

I gestured to Sawbuck. "Master Hogan has my husband's full confidence, so you may speak without fear."

Inventor Call gave a soft snort, glancing over at Sawbuck, then back to me. "I seldom fear to speak, young lady, even to one so impertinent as yourself."

Well. "I meant no offense, sir. I simply wanted no waste of your time. Since you're so busy."

Sawbuck gave a slight bemused smile.

Mary came in with a tea tray, set it down, and began to pour.

Inventor Call glanced up at her. "I've seen you before." In her clothes fit for the street, I'm sure he wondered why she was pouring tea, instead of some maid.

I said, "This is my housekeeper, Mrs. Mary Spadros."

She set the teapot down and curtsied low.

"She's been promoted from the Manor," I continued. "You likely saw her there. We have no house maid as yet, so she's been kind enough to assist me."

Mary smiled, cheeks pink, as she passed a full cup to Inventor Call. It was rather impertinent of him to even speak of my servants in their presence — much less to them.

Sawbuck took his cup from Mary, blew upon it, then sipped it. "How goes your work, sir?"

"We're making progress," Inventor Call said. This line of questioning seemed to relax him. And I wondered if he felt ill at ease speaking to me, my position in the social hierarchy unclear as it was. "We've found several more Magma Steam Generators here in Spadros quadrant. Yet it takes time and men to search each one. But the power outages —"

There'd been one here in Spadros quadrant just the week before.

" — have become a distraction most unwelcome."

"I imagine." I took my cup from Mary, who curtsied and left. "Are these caused by the Generators, the pipes, or wires, or what?"

"Some of all." Inventor Call seemed surprised at **me** asking the question. "Each case differs. It takes hours, sometimes days, to find the problem." He let out a sigh. "These lines are ancient, built five hundred years past. Maps of their routes through the city were often lost in the Coup. Burnt, or rendered unreadable." He sipped his tea. "We're having to redraw the city one disaster at a time."

The Coup caused this. I felt a smug sense of pride. *You thought to destroy my people, but you've only caused your own downfall.*

Sawbuck leaned forward. "What are your plans?" He set his teacup and saucer upon the table. "The Heir will wish to know."

"Yes, of course." Inventor Call glanced quickly at me, then back at Sawbuck. "We wish to hire two more Apprentices at least —"

This surprised me: I'd never heard of there being more than eight, due to the time needed to train and oversee them all.

" — and put out word for more tradesman's and tinkerer's apprentices. Those working with metal are the most in need, but glass-men, carpenters, and miners are needed as well."

"Miners?" Sawbuck seemed surprised. "You wish to expand your work outside the dome?"

"We need more material if we're to repair these mechanisms. Some use rare ancient metals seldom found here. We could purchase them from Azimoff, but the cost —"

Sawbuck rose. "Make a list of what you need and send it to me." He reached into a breast pocket and produced a card. "I'll present the necessary details to our Heir."

Inventor Call looked up at Sawbuck with new respect. He took the card. "Thank you."

My injured foot twinged as I rose. "Will you be off, then?"

"I'll return tomorrow so we may finish our work."

Not sure what Sawbuck referred to, I sat and picked up my teacup, which had gone cool.

The second reason for my astonishment at Inventor Maxim Call's visit was the way he declined to see me the first time. It was, shall we say, most rude. "How may I assist you?"

"Mrs. Spadros, we need your help."

Do you now? "In what way?"

At least he had the grace to blush. "You have connections in the Cathedral, do you not?"

What should I say? Very few people knew my mother was still alive. "It's been many years since I lived there. And my mother is no longer —" I stopped then. Ma owned the Cathedral. If she was thought dead, in whose name was it owned now?

"I don't wish to remind you of a painful time. Yet if you had some connections there, some way to —"

I frowned. "Some way to what?"

He glanced away. "There's something important about the Cathedral. It's on the map you gave me —"

Yeah, then you kicked me in the teeth when I asked to help you again.

"— but we're not allowed in." He glanced away, color high in his cheeks. "Even our agents were detected and thrown out."

I felt outraged. "You dared to spy upon the Cathedral of the Blessed Dealer?" For a moment, I couldn't speak. "I trusted you. I gave up my map." I felt ashamed now that I'd done so. "And now you want me to spy upon them, too?"

The Inventor said nothing, chin held high.

I couldn't believe what I was hearing. "I gave you my map freely, out of good will. And whilst I fought for my life, I offered my help freely once more. Yet you dismissed the Lady of Spadros like some bastard servant girl!" Worse, he did so in the presence of a Memory Boy. I felt dismayed: by now, half of Clubb quadrant knew of his insult. "And now you ask for even **more**?" I stood. "I have had great respect for you, sir, but my help ends here. You may go."

He rose. "Mrs. Spadros, I —"

"The time for apology was when you came in that door." I pointed. "Go. Or I'll have you escorted out."

Inventor Call drew himself up. "Very well. But you have not heard the last of me."

Try to frighten me, will you? I gestured to the door. "You have one minute, sir. Or the manner of your removal will not be pleasant." I'd kick the scrawny old man down the steps myself.

He left.

Blitz came in. "Do you think it wise to refuse an Inventor?"

"To be perfectly honest, I don't care!" What could he possibly do about it? "He forgets that until now, I was the only one who helped him. But apparently that wasn't good enough." I felt bitter. "Let him report to Spadros Manor, then. Let him get his help from there."

* * *

That night after dinner, a knock came at the kitchen door to the alley, far off. Its bell rang as the door opened and shut.

This case to find Maria Athena Spade was a trap. I felt sure of it.

But what kind?

The fact that Mrs. Spade was directed to me of all people spoke of planning. The neighbor who just happened to mention Mr. Pike. Who just happened to visit when I was sure to be home. Who just happened to think of this woman. Who just happened to trust me.

It spoke of spies.

It spoke of someone who knew me quite well, or at least thought they did.

But I couldn't imagine who might set such a trap.

A soft knock. "Mum," Mary said. "May I enter?"

"Of course. Come in."

Mary had grown since she married, both in height and in demeanor. Gone was the shy playful newlywed. In her place stood a woman proud and fierce as a lioness, her light brown hair done up in an elegant bun swirling round rosy cheeks.

"I'm quite proud of your work," I said.

Her cheeks grew rosier. "Mum, we must speak."

I gestured to the chair. "Please sit, if you will."

She did so. "My husband and I are concerned for you. The Inventors are powerful allies, yet just as powerful enemies."

I smiled to myself. "Who called?"

72

"A Memory Boy." She hastened to add, "Not Werner Lead, mum, another. Your husband commands you to attend him." She hesitated. "I sent reply that you would not."

"Oh?"

"I hope I didn't speak wrongly, mum, but the way you reacted to even going near —"

I smiled at her fondly. "You did exactly right. But I feel surprised that you dared do so."

Her eyes and nose reddened. "Mum, I'm your housekeeper. **Your** housekeeper, not his. I'm sworn to protect you with my life." Her head drooped. "I never thought it would come to this."

"I'm sorry to put you in such a position."

She shrugged. "I've known Mr. Anthony since I was born. I was never allowed to play with him, of course — none of us were. But I looked up to him. I admired him, as I did my older brothers." She sighed. "I hoped better for him. I hoped better **of** him. That he would command you go there, after —"

I swallowed a lump in my throat. "His men are in open revolt; perhaps he believes I am as well. He's terribly afraid, Mary, and men who are afraid do things outside their natures." I forced myself to smile. "Don't judge him too harshly."

Tony had to play Anthony Spadros, the Heir, or we would all die. And I knew he hated it with every bit of his soul.

But I couldn't take care of Tony any longer. I couldn't comfort him, hold him, pretend to desire him, tell him what to do, let him have my body whilst screaming inside. I'd had enough. I'd done enough. He had to find a way through this on his own. "I'm not going back, not even on his command." I reached over to pat her hand. "You did exactly right."

She took out a handkerchief, wiped her nose. "Thank you, mum."

"And tell your husband I'm sorry about what happened with the Inventor." I don't know why I hadn't spoken to him earlier — with my anger at Inventor Call, it never crossed my mind.

Mary smiled. "He understands, mum. He spoke without consulting you." She tucked a loose strand of hair behind her ear. "He only wants the best for you."

"I know that." I leaned back. "When I first came to Spadros Manor, I never expected to be here, with the two of you." I giggled at that. "Of all people."

Her eyes widened. "I remember! I was just turned ten. You looked a sight." Then her face fell. "No one was ever kind to you. My mother whipped me with her belt when I said so. She told me it wasn't my place to go against Mr. Roy's wishes. It was the only time she ever did." She took a deep breath, let it out. "Now, of course, I understand how afraid she was for me. A few months later, what happened to Mrs. Dewey —"

Amelia. Roy Spadros had violated her, forced her to give birth to Pip, and terrorized her and her husband ever since. "You must have all felt horribly afraid."

She gave several quick nods, face pale. "No one knew what Mrs. Dewey did to provoke him. We feared the same, or worse, should we defy his commands."

Indeed. Roy Spadros was well-known for torturing his victims to death. "That's why I had to get away. Why I can't go back. Just one reason of many."

She leaned her elbows on the table, hands clasped under her chin. "I know we can make this work, mum. Especially now that you've secured a case. How can we help?"

I sent Mary off with a list of things to do in the morning. Purchase more writing-paper. Break Mrs. Spade's large bills into money we might use, especially pennies for the taxi. Of course, we must set aside ten percent for our Family fees.

Ironic, that Mrs. Spade's money should go to the Spadros Family. But aside from moving out of the quadrant entirely, there was nothing else we could do. The ability of these men to sniff out extra cash was uncanny, and I dared not defy them.

Then I wrote to my contacts. Who was Mrs. Spade's neighbor? What were her connections? Did she have any family or friends in the group of rogue Spadros men? I needed to know everything I could about her.

I also wrote to Mrs. Clubb. Had she any further information about Maria Athena Spade? To the point, when I might meet with her informant? This informant was the only one who might put it to rest whether this young spinster was Black Maria or not.

Then I hesitated. This shouldn't be sent to the Clubbs in writing, I thought. Putting the page aside, I made a notation to contact a Memory Boy in the morning.

* * *

The next morning, I got a copy of the *Golden Bridges* and a letter:

Mrs. Spadros —

I was given your name by my mother in regards to Miss Maria Athena Spade.

During the past eight months, we have searched the entire island, going door to door. Fliers have been posted over the Plaza, with a reward offered for information. All of her friends were interviewed, both by us and the police. So far, we have learned nothing. To the best of my knowledge, my sister is not on Market Center.

In deepest gratitude,

Mr. Giovanni Spade, Jr.

This had to be Maria Athena's oldest brother.

I heard Mary move about the kitchen, the familiar clank of pans, and I shuddered, suddenly grateful she was safe.

Nothing good could come from a young woman gone missing. How afraid Maria Athena's family must be!

Blitz said something far off, and while I couldn't hear his words, I got a feeling of dread. I put on my robe and went to the kitchen. Blitz and Mary stood in the middle of the kitchen, turning towards me in surprise, faces pale.

I said, "What's happened? What's wrong?"

Blitz held an opened letter, the Holy Symbol of Spadros Manor upon it. "Major Blackwood has been murdered."

The Lesson

For an instant, I felt confused. An old Army man who spent his evenings telling bawdy stories at parties. "Who would want to murder him?"

"I don't know," Blitz said, "but a card stamped with a red dog was with his body."

The Red Dog Gang.

Why would they kill Major Blackwood? He seemed harmless. He wasn't in a Family. He had nothing to do with any of us. It made no sense. "Was that why my husband wanted to see me?"

Blitz glanced at the letter, then shrugged. "It must have been."

"But why is he so concerned? Other than that it involves the Red Dog Gang."

Mary said, "Didn't he attend Queen's Night dinner last year?"

"He did," Blitz said, face thoughtful, "And that would make two out of the eight guests at that dinner party who are now dead."

I hadn't considered that aspect of the matter.

"Send condolences to his family," I said, feeling downcast. "I'm truly sorry he's gone. How did he die?"

Blitz let out a breath, glancing away. "He lives alone. He was strangled in his bed." He peered at the page, then at me. "Isn't that what happened to the Bridges Stable-Master?"

I went back to my room, bathed. My foot looked almost well. I used the salve, re-wrapped my foot, and got dressed. Put on my makeup, fixed my hair.

But the whole matter puzzled me.

Was this the work of the Bridges Strangler? After over a year of luring young men off the street, why would the scoundrel kill an old man in his bed?

Or was this the same man who murdered the Stable-Master?

Perhaps, instead of two killers on the loose, we had three.

* * *

Around midmorning, the Memory Boy Werner Lead came by. "Mrs. Karla Bettelmann will meet you Friday, June 19th, for luncheon at the Clubb Women's Center."

"What does Mrs. Karla look like?"

"She has brown hair and brown eyes. She likes to wear brown, or sometimes green."

"Very good! I have another message for you."

His eyes widened. "Wonderful!"

"But it must be given to Mrs. Regina Clubb. It's important."

Werner looked uncertain. "I'll try my best."

I felt a sudden compassion for this child, alone in a huge city with just his two older brothers for protection. And his coat, of course. Attacking a Memory Boy held the death penalty, and the attacker's entire neighborhood was denied messenger service for a year. The latter meant everyone watched out for the Boys whenever their bright red jackets appeared.

"Here's the message: 'I await the meeting with your witness. Third time's the charm.'"

Werner's cheeks turned pink. "I'll bring it right away."

I told Blitz to pay the boy double his fee, then went to my room.

But before I could sit down, the kitchen door jingled as it opened and shut. It sounded like Amelia. Crying!

Alarmed, I rushed in. "What's happened?"

Amelia shook her head, sobbing.

I rested my hands on her shoulders. "Did Mr. Roy hurt you?"

"Oh, mum," she said. "They made him shoot them."

I peered at her, perplexed. "They made who shoot who?"

She wiped her face. "I'm sorry, mum. Mr. Anthony."

Fear spiked through me. "My husband's been shot?"

"No, mum, I'm sorry. I'm not telling it right." She took a deep breath, let it out.

"Sit down, Amelia. Tell me what's happened."

The rogues who'd ambushed the Spadros men earlier had been caught. These men were tied, hooded, taken to the Gap in the north Spadros Hedge (quadrant-folk called it the Rathole) and shot.

But that wasn't what upset Amelia. What upset her is that Roy forced Tony to shoot them.

"One of his men fancies one of our kitchen maids, mum. He told her Mr. Anthony did it. He grabbed their hair through the sack over their heads, put the gun to their heads and fired." She began to shake. "He killed all four of them. He got sick after. And now he sits, just staring!" This sent her into another bout of weeping.

Oh, Tony ... "Don't berate him. So far as I know, he's never shot a man before."

Amelia became angry. "**Berate** him? That sweet boy, forced to do this, by that — that monster!" She rushed into the hall, her footsteps pounding up the stairs.

I went into the parlor to peer out of the front window.

And I recalled a day back when I was fifteen. I was in the Pot. It was afternoon, and the leaves were just turning golden. Joseph Kerr, his sister Josie, and I sat on a pile of rubble. It was well past what the quadrant-folk called the Old Plaza, on the way to the tunnel under the Main Road.

I held Joe's hand. Josie sat a bit off with this other kid, who was maybe fourteen, just talking. And while they were talking, I realized Josie was teaching this kid how to cut someone's throat.

"You have to do this where someone sees," Josie said. "Someone too far away to stop you. Do it boldly, and show no fear. When I hear the tale of it, we'll speak again."

The boy paled, but nodded, backing away to scamper off.

Josie turned to me with her beautiful sweet smile, the sun making her golden curls glow. "If he wants to be one of the High Cards, it's the only way. He must prove himself, and make them all fear him. Or the other kids won't follow."

In the silence of my apartments, I leaned my forehead on the cool glass. "Life burns the weakness from us all."

Amelia sat facing the picture windows upstairs. I sat next to her. "That sweet boy, as you call him, is Heir to the Spadros Family. Would you rather see him dead?"

"No, mum."

It was a hard lesson for Tony, but one I didn't see a way around. "Mr. Roy made the right play."

"How can you say that?"

"Amelia, the men must see Mr. Anthony do this, not once, but many times. They must believe him to be strong so they can respect him. They have to trust that he would get vengeance for them should they be attacked. Or imagine themselves under that hood, if they're inclined to believe otherwise. Do you understand? No matter what he is inside, they have to believe he can become just as heartless as Roy Spadros. They have to believe he can hold the quadrant, or else he never will."

* * *

I returned to my desk. Some of my informants had written back. Nothing seemed out of the ordinary about the Spade family, or the neighbor who'd referred her to Mr. Pike.

I took out Mr. Spade's letter. It was good to know Maria Athena wasn't on Market Center, but that was the smallest area of the city. The woman could be in any number of places, in any of the four quadrants, under a dome over six hundred miles across.

And all my investigations so far seemed to be going nowhere.

Generally, when my investigations seemed to be going nowhere, I needed to do something else. So I took out the music Blitz had me working on and went to the piano to play.

Jonathan had given me the piano the year earlier, when I was under house arrest. My playing had improved over the past year, and the credit went entirely to Blitz. I told him once that if he tired of being a butler, he could open a shop teaching piano.

Blitz came over to lean on the piano. "Nice work." He pointed at a part of the page. "A bit slower here." He'd entirely taught himself to play, years ago. But I taught him how to read the pages in return.

"Have you heard when the Major's funeral will be?"

Blitz shrugged. "Once the police investigation is done."

"Please let me know: I'd like to attend."

It was after tea when Sawbuck arrived, and for a moment, I'd forgotten he'd promised to do so. He seemed concerned. "Are you feeling better, Mrs. Spadros?"

"Entirely. My foot is almost well."

"That's not what I meant."

I felt confused for a moment. "I haven't gotten sick again, if that's what you mean."

He leaned back, relaxing. "You mentioned Maria Athena Spade's mother came to call. What did she want?"

I didn't actually want to talk about this, for several reasons.

"So it's true," Sawbuck said. "The mother hired you to find her."

I gaped at him. "However did you know?"

He smirked, just a bit. "Any luck?"

"No," I said. "All I know is that she's not on Market Center."

"I could have told you that. The family's been posting fliers around the Plaza with a hefty reward for months now."

I felt deflated. "Don't go over there, Ten. Her sons bought guns for the next Spadros man at their door-step."

Sawbuck raised his eyebrows. "Sheep with claws!" Then he chuckled. "Why would we have need to visit them?"

"So ... how do you think I might find Maria Athena?"

"If I knew that, Mrs. Spadros, I'd pick her up myself. But the Family has more important things to worry about."

The rogue Spadros men. "How many are still at large?"

"Perhaps twenty."

"You don't know for certain?"

He hesitated. "Twenty are unaccounted for. But there's been rumor of unrest within their ranks — it may be that some are dead."

These were not just Family in the general sense. You couldn't become a Button Man without being related to Roy and Tony in some way. And most of our Associates were related to them as well. "I'm sorry, Ten."

He nodded, not meeting my eye. "They made their choice, Mrs. Spadros. I would much rather them back safe, alive and well." At that, our eyes met. "But you know this doesn't end that way."

The Tabloid

Despite Sawbuck's words, I felt encouraged. If there was unrest within the rogues, that could lead them to make a mistake which Tony and Sawbuck could exploit.

That evening, the doctor came by. "Have you been walking?"

I shrugged.

"Does your foot still pain you?"

I shrugged again.

"You must take care, my dear. It's healing. But if you overdo, another blister may form. You might even do damage to the underlying muscles or bones." His face turned stern. "If you can't be trusted in this, Mrs. Spadros, I'll be forced to put a cast on it."

"I'll be fine," I said. "I have nowhere I wish to walk to."

Grudgingly, he left, saying he'd return in a few days.

After dinner, I opened the *Golden Bridges*.

THE FOUR FAMILIES ARE COWARDS!

Vile Midnight Attack

The attack on our Establishment by the Four Families shall be avenged! By the time you read this, we will have moved our presses to evade the villains. Slaughtering men as retaliation for printing the truth shows the true nature of the vile fiends who keep their boots upon the neck of this city.

No longer will we keep silent! We promise not only
the Real Story, but the Entire Story.

Good grief, I thought. With all that's going on, now the *Golden
Bridges* attacks us?

I turned the page, and to my horror, saw that it wasn't just the
Four Families they chose to attack.

WHOREDOM IN SPADROS QUADRANT?

Mrs. Jacqueline Spadros receives men both high and
low into her home at all hours. Unsavory rumors
swirl about the Real Story behind her absence from
Spadros Manor. Little construction has occurred in
the year since then, so despite her statements before
the Court, it seems she is not at her apartments to
renovate them. While she has a lady's maid, that
woman departs before dinner, possibly to maintain
her reputation.

Why has her husband cast her out? Why does this
admitted Pot rag not return to where she belongs?
Why do these men from several different quadrants
write, call on her, and send flowers?

Has a brothel formed in the midst of Spadros
quadrant? We vow to bring the Entire Story.

After reading this, my hands shook, my heart pounded.

What happened to the *Golden Bridges*? This didn't even sound
like the same people writing. It was as if some power struggle had
occurred, and the men with any sense or decency lost the battle.

How did they know these things? Why would they attack me so
publicly, in such a personal way? Had I not suffered enough?

I went to the window, peered out through the mesh in front of it.
They must think me vulnerable. No wonder Sawbuck came to see if I
were safe.

Frightened, I flung the paper into the fire. Then I locked the
windows, drew the curtains, and hid under my covers.

I felt sick. How could I go in public again? How could I allow anyone to come to my home? How would tenants ever dare to take rooms here? I felt as if there were now a taint upon me.

Curled under the covers, my weeping slowed. I still felt shaky, vulnerable, afraid. But if I were to ever be safe, I knew I had to consider this logically.

The death of the *Golden Bridges'* man had disrupted some balance. More unstable men had taken control of the paper.

Yet why attack me? Could they possibly blame me for their man's murder? I didn't understand what I'd done to deserve this.

I peered out from under the covers. A small piece of the Golden Bridges lay unburnt on my hearth.

How had the *Golden Bridges* managed to survive so long? How had it been able to speak truth and sense in a city where looking at a Family member wrong might earn you death?

The *Golden Bridges* had been rude and at times vulgar, but it had also been entertaining. Funny, even.

And now, it seemed, everything had changed.

Then it occurred to me: how exactly did Gertie Pike meet with the *Golden Bridges* to tell them about Doyle Pike's plan?

I wouldn't have the slightest idea how to contact them, even if I wanted to tell them something. Which meant that Mrs. Pike had information I didn't. More to the point, she might know what was happening with the *Golden Bridges* now.

Normally I wouldn't care. But since they'd decided to attack me, I needed to find out. Perhaps I could find a way to protect myself.

So early the next morning, I made ready to go to Market Center.

What hadn't Mrs. Spade told me about Maria Athena's note? If I were allowed to see Maria Athena's room, it could hold some clue as to where she went. And I might be able to speak with this neighbor of hers.

Then I'd visit Gertie Pike and get that mystery sorted — if the woman would talk to me.

* * *

Blitz didn't want me to go to Market Center by taxi-carriage.

On this I would be undeterred. "I can't go to see Mrs. Spade in a Spadros carriage, Blitz, I just can't."

So my cane and I were off to the taxi-stand. After driving to the Main Road, we went over the bridge to Market Center. Then we passed the Palace grounds, which the quadrant-folk called their Plaza. The Palace was gone long since, razed after the Coup.

The taxi-carriage slowed. "Road's closed." The driver's voice came from the brass speaking-tube, sounding tinny. "There's police up ahead."

Police did indeed swarm around the building. I went to a young Constable guarding a barricade. "What's happened?"

"A woman was found dead."

This seemed alarming. Yet I couldn't tell the man who I was. "I was just to visit my sister. Please, sir, tell me. Was it Mrs. Spade?"

The Constable's face softened into compassion. I wore one of my charcoal walking dresses with a black veil: it must have appeared as if I were in mourning. "Let me check for you."

The officer returned a few minutes later. "Your sister is entirely well. It was her neighbor across the way."

The woman who'd advised Mrs. Spade to go to me for help.

"Do you want me to tell your sister you're here?"

I couldn't risk being involved in a murder in any way, not after just being tried for murder myself. "I'll come back later," I gestured at the commotion, "once all this is sorted. Thank you, Constable."

I took a taxi to the other side of the north end of Market Center, near where Mrs. Gertie Pike lived. Servants, law clerks, and other workers on the island lived in this area.

Gertie was married to Mr. Thrace Pike. I wouldn't call us friends, but I did know something of her: she'd almost gotten me killed.

I raised my veil and knocked on her door.

Gertie Pike was one and twenty. Lank blonde hair, pale skin, uneven teeth, eyes too close together. An out-of-fashion house-dress. When she opened the door, she tried at once to slam it shut. Anticipating this, I stuck my cane in the door. "I'm not here to hurt you, Mrs. Pike. I just want to talk."

"What do you want?"

"I have a question it seems only you might answer."

"Does this involve one of my husband's law cases?"

"Not at all."

At that, she let me pass. Her voice was tinged with regret. "I'm not allowed to know of his law cases anymore." Her little girl toddled barefoot across the wooden floor, while a babe of six months slept in a small cradle. "Our son. Thrace, Junior."

Fortunately, they looked like their father. "Congratulations."

Her face became less sour. "What question might only I answer?"

"May we sit?"

Her eyes narrowed, then she glanced at my cane. "Very well."

We sat across the round wooden table. I wondered how to begin.

"Well?" Gertie seemed most impatient. "What do you want?"

"How did you contact the *Golden Bridges*?"

Gertie turned white. "Get out."

Her baby began to cry. She picked him up and began jostling him in her arms as she walked around. "I said, get out!"

"I'm not asking for the Family. I don't want to get anyone hurt. How do you contact them? They have it all wrong about me."

"Do they now? All I've ever seen is that you're out for you and you alone."

"That hardly means I'm running a brothel."

She gasped, shielding her baby's ears.

"Did you know that's what they accuse me of?"

She shook her head, face pale.

"So I must contact them, before my husband or his father reads it! If Roy Spadros sees that, he won't rest until he's found them. And you know what he'll do! So if you care about these men at all, you'll help me. I don't want anyone else hurt."

Gertie held her baby close, just staring. Then she nodded.

"What do you do? How do you find them?"

She came to the table and sat. "You put an ad in the *Bridges Daily*: pork for sale, three pounds for a dollar —"

That was highway robbery!

"— that's so no one will answer but them. They contact you."

"And what happens once they contact you?"

"The man said they took all the pieces and put them together. So it wouldn't come out in the paper right away." Dismay crossed her face, and her words turned bitter. "He promised no one would know it was me who told."

I felt sincerely curious. "How did you know the code?"

She snorted. "We all know it, mum. Us Bridgers."

I nodded. It made sense that an underground group of religious fanatics would know such things. "Is that how your husband got his pamphlet made?"

She began to nod, then stopped, looking stricken.

"I'm not interested in that. Who contacted you?"

Her eyes and nose reddened. "A man my father knows by the name of Blackwood —"

Major Blackwood?

"— and he's dead now. Murdered." She shook her head, angry tears in her eyes. "I know the Families did it. I just know it."

"Major Blackwood was my friend," I said.

Gertie's head jerked towards me. "He was?"

"We had him to dinner at Spadros Manor last Queen's Night. I learned of Major Blackwood's death from my husband. He couldn't have killed him."

"Why do you say that?"

"Because I know my husband." Tony would never have a man killed who'd been at his house for dinner. And to strangle a man? "He's never done anything like that in his life."

But then what she might really be saying struck me. "How do you know the Families did it?"

"They've tried to ruin us. My husband can't get decent cases anymore, and other places won't see him. I know it's because I spoke out against you."

Her problems were of her own making. "I almost died because of you. A dozen Court guards are dead!"

She stood, clutching her baby to her. "I didn't mean that to happen!" Her face was red, her eyes full of tears. "You think I meant all those men to die? I just wanted people to know the truth!"

Little Harriet began to cry as well. She ran to her mother, falling onto her, clinging to her skirts.

And now they know. I handed Mrs. Pike my handkerchief.

She took it, trying to wipe her face with one hand.

"Here, let me take him for a minute."

To my surprise, she let me hold him.

I'd held babies many a time, and while this one had whimpered in his mother's arms, he settled in mine. I tucked him in my left arm and rocked in my chair, jostling him a bit to amuse the boy. "Why do they say such horrible things about me? It seems a change."

Gertie shook her head, her eyes not meeting mine. "I heard my father talking of it. I'm not in the Bridgers anymore — at my husband's command — but I do hear things."

"What things?"

Little Harriet held her arms up: Gertie set the girl upon her lap. "A new man joined the *Golden Bridges*, oh, two years back? No, it was three: they were talking of it at our wedding. But now he's been wanting more action against the Families. They almost came to blows over it." She sat staring glumly, arms around her daughter. "I don't understand why — they've been doing well up to now."

"Did the Bridgers start the *Golden Bridges*, then?"

"No, but we've helped. We don't agree with all of it. Most of it, really. But they want the truth, and they want the Families to end." She glanced up as if she'd forgotten who she spoke to. "No offense."

"None taken." I sat pondering all this as I rocked the baby.

"You're good with him," Gertie said.

I shrugged. Babies were abundant in the Cathedral. I'd cared for many such whilst their mother worked her trade; I had no desire to care for more. "Do you know anything of what this man is like?"

"I've never seen him, but the younger ones say he's fine-looking."

Interesting. "Is he now?"

Gertie gave me a sharp glance. "Beware of fine appearance. The Trickster may take the aspect of any of the Holy Cards, even a King, sheathed in the light of hope. Yet this light is false, and so he is as well. A fine-appearing man often possesses the Trickster's nature, and such have lured many a chaste woman and righteous man into disgrace and error." She nodded. "Thus saith the Grand-Master."

I had no interest in religious prattle. I handed over the baby. "I must go. Thank you for seeing me."

"If you really want to speak to the *Golden Bridges,* it's three pounds beef this month."

If they had any sense at all, they'd change the code as soon as they learned I was there.

So Major Blackwood was one of the Inside Reporters. Interesting.

I didn't know what I might do with the information, but getting more insight into how the city of Bridges worked was worth the extra penny.

There were so many things I still didn't understand. Why I, a Pot rag, had been forced to marry the Spadros Heir. I understood why my father Peedro Sluff had sold me — he'd do about anything for his own benefit. But why Roy Spadros took it so far was beyond me.

And why did Roy want me in the first place?

The Deception

When I got home, it was not yet noon. So I sat in my study.

It made complete sense for Major Blackwood to have worked with the *Golden Bridges*. I now understood his spending so much time at the parties of the high-born. I could even hear his voice in some of their articles. Yet now, he was dead.

And Mrs. Spade's neighbor. Dead, just days after referring Mrs. Spade to me.

I felt sure Mrs. Spade hid something about Maria Athena's letter. But what? And why? I needed to know, and soon.

Whilst Tony and Roy were both fluent in Italian, I couldn't bring Maria Athena's letter to them. Mrs. Spade had been incredibly brave to hire me in the first place.

A year prior, I'd gone to luncheon with Jonathan's sister Gardena. What had she said?

"My mother took me to Italy for a year ..."

I wondered if Tony's ban on Jonathan coming into the quadrant still held — or if he might be more willing to allow Gardena to enter. And of course, Jon would have to escort her.

* * *

I sent messages. Tony replied angrily, then an hour later relented. Gardena didn't reply at all.

But as we prepared for tea, the bell rang.

"Master Jonathan and Miss Gardena Diamond." Blitz had a wry smile on his face. "How did you know they'd show up?"

I smiled to myself. Gardena would visit anytime I called, whether out of real friendship or guilt, I never knew. And Jon had a way with their father, who was the main impediment to her doing so. "Seat them in the parlor."

"As my Lady commands."

I laughed, turning to Mary. "How do I look?"

"You look fine, mum. Let's get you round to the other door to make a proper entrance."

Jonathan Diamond and his sister Gardena sat on the sofa, rising to greet us. Gardena Diamond was five and twenty, sharing her brother's dark, dark skin. Her raven curls were loosely braided and up-swept under a hat covered in fresh flowers of deep purple.

Jon wore his navy uniform with silver buttons, and I suspected he'd come straight from his duties as Keeper of the Court.

Gardena said, "Your apartments are lovely! Nicer than Jon said."

I laughed at them both. "Please sit."

Mary brought in tea and our three-tiered stand, filled with small sandwiches. Once Mary left, I said, "I'm glad you could visit on such short notice."

Jonathan chuckled. "To be honest, I was glad to get away."

"Jon!" Gardena's voice was scolding.

"I arrived home at half past two and wasn't even allowed to change clothing before becoming embroiled in controversy. Father was determined to argue until it was too late to leave! I told him I'd have no more of it. We're full adults, and if he means us to take this Family one day, he must loose the reins."

Gardena chuckled. "Aptly put."

I leaned forward. "I hope Roland is well?"

All anger disappeared; they were both smiles. "He's very well," Gardena said. "Learning to read, and eager to write to his Daddy."

A wave of emotion swept over me, and my eyes stung. "I'm so grateful." I took a deep breath. "I did ask you here for a reason." I handed Maria Athena's letter to Jon. "What does this say?"

Jon glanced at the letter, then shrugged. "I was never interested in languages." He handed the letter to Gardena. "Jack and Dena are the only ones any good at them."

Jack? This was a side to my old enemy I hadn't known before. Heart pounding, I said to Gardena, "What do you read here?"

"It's a letter from someone named Maria Athena to her mother. Spadros men are still searching for her, and she can't put them in danger any longer. Then she says something strange."

"What?"

"It's — she says she's safe. But the way she phrases it is odd."

"In what way?"

Gardena frowned. "She uses the word secure. But it's like you would refer to a vault, or a property. Like she's behind lock and key. That sort of being safe." She hesitated. "She starts off with 'Mama,' so I assume she's writing to her mother. But this one sentence is so formal."

I sat beside Gardena, noting which sentence she referred to. "Could someone have forced her to write it?"

Gardena shrugged.

Mrs. Spade last heard from her daughter a year ago. Either Mrs. Spade never believed her daughter to be safe, so why contact me now? Or Mrs. Spade had thought her daughter was very safe, yet expected word from her long before this.

But if someone close to me wrote such an odd message, I'd be suspicious of it at once.

Which meant either they weren't all that close, or this actually said something else. A code? "Well, I appreciate your help." I took the letter, put it in my pocket, and returned to my chair. "I'm sure you heard about Major Blackwood." They'd been at that dinner, too.

Jon and Gardena nodded somberly. "It's terrible," Gardena said. "Why would someone do this?"

Blitz had thought Major Blackwood's death was connected with our Queen's Night dinner. Dame Anastasia had been there that night, and she'd consorted with Frank Pagliacci.

What did the Red Dog Gang stamp on the Major's body mean? Had he been part of the quarrel with that "good-looking man"?

Could Frank Pagliacci have infiltrated the *Golden Bridges* as well?

Jonathan said, "Jacqui, what will you do for the 500th?"

I shrugged. The Celebration for the 500th Anniversary of the city's founding was on Midsummer Night, almost two weeks hence.

Jon let out a breath. "I had to ask. Tony made it a condition of coming here today."

I chuckled softly, bitterly. "Which means Roy Spadros tires of my refusal to play the Lady of Spadros in public."

I didn't love Tony. I didn't like him most days. I didn't want anything to do with him. I didn't want to go back to pretending to be his wife, and I certainly wouldn't lie to everyone by appearing with him at events like we were some couple in love.

Gardena let out a sigh. "Jacqui, I have no idea what you've gone through. But we all have to pretend at one time or another. I play the virgin spinster —"

Jon flinched.

"— but it's not a lie, Jacqui. Not like that. I hide the truth. But I do it for my son's sake. For Anthony's sake. For everyone's safety." She glanced aside. "People may forget about you. But more likely, because you **are** the Lady of Spadros, the longer you remain separate in public, the more the rumors flow. The more people become obsessed with learning the truth." She peered out of the window. "Did you know four people watch this house right now?"

Jon snorted.

I'd been glancing outside all day and hadn't seen anyone unusual. Yet Gardena believed it to be true. "How do you know?"

Her face turned amused. "Protection of Family interests is taught to Diamond children from a young age. What people ask when they're after information. How they act when they're watching you. The patterns of movement and position most likely to indicate an ambush. I saw four men watching; I'm sure Jon found —"

"Six when we arrived," Jonathan said. "One saw I noted him, so he may have left."

I gaped at him. "Why do people care so much?"

"They have to care, Jacqui," Gardena said. "They don't know what's going on. Why did you leave Spadros Manor? Why did you break from the Spadros Family? Most importantly, why did Roy Spadros pardon you? Has he developed some new weakness? Is your quadrant vulnerable to attack? Or does it mean overwhelming strength on your part? Are you gathering a group around you in defiance? If so, what are your numbers? Who are your allies? Is another war about to break out? Whose side should they pick? Will they — or their children — end up in the crossfire?" She took a deep breath. "Anything you do is important to them." She gave Jonathan a meaningful glance. "Something else we're taught as children."

The implications of what she'd said were chilling. "He only meant to cheer me, Dena."

Jonathan winced. "I'm right here, you know."

I said, "If I'm so important, why wouldn't anyone hire me?"

For an instant, Jonathan gave me a look as one might a child. "And risk the wrath of Roy Spadros? What if this were some trick to see who humiliates his heir? He's seized hundreds already for rioting against you. They don't dare consider it."

"But they've been so angry, so rude."

Gardena said, "Jacqui ... they didn't know you were a P-" she stopped herself just in time, "- from the Pot. They didn't know you had your business. They thought you and your husband were happy. You're the Lady of Spadros. In their minds, they put you far above them. They feel hurt and betrayed."

I turned away, remembering the *Golden Bridges* article. *Why does this Pot rag not return to where she belongs?*

Once there was this beautiful flat rock outside the Cathedral. We played jacks on it, lay upon it in the sun. But one day, the men moved it, and underneath was a grave — all bugs and rottenness.

This was how they saw me.

I dashed away angry tears, feeling bitter. "They thought I was good, and clean. Like them. Better even. Now that they know the truth, I'm certainly not good enough for the likes of them!"

Neither of them spoke.

"Well, I have a job now. And when that ends, I'll get another. I don't need any of them."

"Oh, Jacqui," Gardena said. "We love you, truly, just as you are. Don't do this."

"I didn't know you had a job," Jon said, his tone falsely bright. "That's good! Is it about this letter?"

I nodded, too devastated, too humiliated to speak.

Jonathan said, "So you've put yourself on this woman's side against the Spadros Family?"

I wiped my nose with my handkerchief, smiling to myself. "Not exactly. These cases are seldom as they appear. Sawbuck knows the important parts."

"Good." Jon sounded relieved. "I've only spoken with the man once — when you fell in your rooms — but he seems steady."

I remembered my rage and grief, the broken glass, how drunk I was, falling. My face marred by tears and sweat. I touched the scar on my left temple: there must have been blood.

Sawbuck saw me like **that**?

I glimpsed how I must appear: some wild creature brought to a "civilized" land from an unfathomable place.

"Jacqui." Jon sat leaning forward, elbows on his knees, his hands clasped in front of him. "How can we help?"

Get me a drink?

I snorted bitterly. He'd never agree to that. What I most wanted was to leave here and never return. Jonathan offered that during the trial, but I'd refused. I didn't want to let the men who'd tried to kill me have their way. They'd been defeated in the courts. But they were still out there, and I wanted them dead.

"Whatever you need," Jon said.

What did I need? I peered at Jon, fiercely angry, and to my shame, I attacked. "I need the truth. Why don't you do something about Jack?"

Jon flinched back, shocked. "Jacqui, you don't —"

"I know he's your twin. You care for him. But he threatens my life! Why do you let him run loose when he should be in a ward?"

Jon's face turned stricken. "A **ward**?" He began to stand. "Is that what you —"

Gardena said firmly, "Jacqui, we will **not** discuss this. I'm sorry."

"Very well." I was a bit surprised by their reactions, but perhaps I shouldn't have been. I took a deep breath. "Then —"

Jonathan, almost standing, got this peculiar look on his face. "I don't feel well."

He collapsed full upon the table.

The Facts

I shouted, "Blitz! Amelia! Mary!"

They rushed in.

Gardena pulled Jon's arm. "Help me get him to the sofa."

Jonathan Diamond was a tall man: it took all five of us to lift and move him over.

Fortunately, the handle of the three-tiered sandwich stand had only given him a glancing blow. But his vest was ripped, as was his shirt, and a bleeding scrape lay upon his side.

I sat beside him, cradling his face in my hands. "Oh, gods, Jon, I'm so sorry." I looked back at Blitz. "Send for the doctor."

Gardena knelt beside me. "There's no need. He'll wake shortly. Put his feet up."

I stared at her, horrified. "This happened before?"

She glanced away.

"Uhhh." Jon's eyes were still closed. "Potatoes don't fly like that."

Gardena chuckled, then her face turned embarrassed. "He's done that before, too."

"My poor dear." I wiped sweat from his brow. His face was ashen, his lips deathly pale.

Blitz looked concerned. "Should I call for the doctor, or not?"

I said, "Bring supplies to bandage his wound." I cleaned and bandaged his side despite everyone's protests that it was "beneath my station."

Gradually, Jonathan's color returned. When he opened his eyes, I was applying a wrap around him as Blitz held him up.

Jon smiled at me. "The most glorious thing to wake to."

Heat rushed to my face. "You flatter me. Are you well?"

"Much improved." He surveyed everyone standing round, then the ruins of the coffee table. "I shall buy you a new table at once."

"That's not necessary," Blitz said.

"But I insist." Jon took a deep breath, then winced, touching his wounded side. A small amount of blood lay there. "What's this?"

Gardena said, "You're lucky that the sandwich stand didn't skewer you."

Jon's eyes widened. "Indeed!" He moved his hand to cover mine. "I've frightened you; forgive me."

I squeezed his hands, feeling overwhelmed. "There's nothing to forgive, save one: Dena says this happened before. When were you going to tell me?"

Gardena rose, turned to the others. "May I have a tour?"

They bowed or curtsied low. "Yes, Miss Diamond, at once."

Once they'd left, I turned to Jon. "No more lies, sir. You're always ill. You take tonics at regular intervals, 'for your health.' And now you collapse upon my table! Your sister says you have a 'delicate constitution' —"

Jon chuckled at that.

"— but I believe it's more serious. And it grieves me. This whole situation grieves me deeply! Not only do I fear some dreadful illness has befallen you," for an instant, I faltered, "but for years now you've hidden it from me." I drew myself straighter. "I am determined. I will not relent until you speak the truth."

"Jacqui, I —"

"Please don't hide from me any longer. I can handle truth much better than lies, especially from you." I smiled fondly at him. "Besides, you're not as good at lying as you think."

Jon laughed softly, then his face turned sad. "Very well. But I fear you won't like it."

* * *

Jonathan Diamond had been an exceptional athlete, skilled in sport of all kind. He'd won awards and medals for his achievement since he was a small boy.

His life was truly happy until the summer of his twelfth year. Jon and his twin Jack were to visit the countryside to camp with friends of the family. But on the day of the trip, Jon didn't feel well.

"How I wish I would have gone anyway," Jon said. "I wish that every day since."

For that summer, rheumatic fever swept through the quadrant, affecting both high and low. When Jon recovered, he went back to boarding school, yet was often sick.

He was taken to doctor after doctor, yet the verdict was the same: the fever had badly damaged his heart.

I felt horrified. "Is there nothing that can be done?"

Jon glanced away, shaking his head. "I wasn't even thirteen years old and I was sent home to die. But I've lived twice that, longer than anyone dared hope. So yes, I take tonics for my health." He gazed into my eyes. "And each day I wake is a gift."

I kissed his hands, feeling unsteady. "What will befall you?"

He chuckled, then pushed himself up to sit straighter on the sofa. "My poor broken heart will eventually fail, and I'll die." He took my hands in his. "But Jacqui, we all die."

"I don't want you to!"

"I don't want me to either. But just imagine if we never died. How would the children to come gain their cards?" He shrugged. "So that's the whole of it. Now you know."

"But why keep it from me? Why lie?"

He leaned close. "Your life has been **so** hard, Jacqui. How could I burden you with mine? Especially when there's no hope? I only wish I'd been stronger so you might never know this grief."

"Jon, listen. You've given me a gift." I put my hand beside his face. "We can get through this."

His face turned sad. "Jacqui —"

"You say you've lived longer than anyone dared hope. Could it be they're mistaken?"

Jonathan shook his head. "No, Jacqui, they're not mistaken."

"Well, then, I want to help."

"Jacqui —"

"No, Jon. Please. Listen to me. You've helped me so much. You've given me encouragement when I thought there was no hope whatsoever. Even through years of listening to me prattle on about Tony and Joe, you've never once berated me or made me feel the fool you must consider me. You've only ever helped." I gazed down at our clasped hands, then into his eyes. "Please let yourself be helped too."

That seemed to move him, and he sat for a moment in thought. "Very well, then." He touched the bandage at his side and smiled to himself. "I suppose if you'd like to help, someone should call my carriage. My father will want the doctor to look at this."

* * *

We got Jon and Gardena into their carriage with a promise to send word at once if they needed aid. Then I withdrew to my rooms, shaken.

Jonathan Diamond was ill. Really, truly ill.

I felt as if a support had been yanked from the foundation of my life. Jon was going to die?

But Jacqui, we all die.

I knew that.

They all died. Everyone I cared for, everyone I let care for me.

Jon knew everyone around me died. That he still wanted to be near both astonished and frightened me.

Then I understood: he had nothing to lose. His mother was maimed, his grandfather dead, his twin mad, his sister living in secret disgrace, and his own life ... *each time I wake is a gift*.

And I wept for the ill fate upon us both. The desperate need I had to both leave and stay, the dread that one day, whatever I did would kill everyone I loved. The terrible illness drawing Jon towards the Shuffler, no matter how hard he tried to keep it at bay. That doom approaching us both made me feel trapped. I had to go somewhere, anywhere. "Amelia!"

Her footsteps came down the hall. "Yes, mum?"

"I want to go for a walk."

I didn't take my cane, but my foot felt fairly well, and with the free breeze in my face, I felt numbed, quieted.

Amelia walked beside me; Blitz trailed several steps behind, hands in his pockets. At first glance, merely a man on a stroll, but his eyes swept the area.

If it were so dangerous, why did he leave Mary alone?

But then I recalled what Mary said: *I'm sworn to protect you in all things, with my life if need be.*

What had Blitz sworn?

He smiled, patting the holster at his side.

Surely he didn't anticipate attack on our very block?

I turned to face the wind. With these rogue Spadros men on the loose, who knew what might happen?

I must help Mrs. Spade find her daughter. And I must help Eleanora Bryce get her betrothed out of Clubb quadrant. But there had to be some way to help Jon. Something the doctors hadn't found that might help him.

I couldn't bear the thought of letting him die.

A man stood on the corner, smoking a cigar in the twilight, turning towards us as we approached. He wasn't that much taller than me, with a big bushy beard.

"Good evening, Mrs. Spadros," Mr. Eight Howell said. "Something I can do for you?"

"I'm just out on a stroll," I said. "My first, really, since the trial."

Blitz seemed to relax.

Mr. Howell's eyes held amusement. "And what do you think of our little domain?"

"Quiet." I glanced into the doorway behind him, which faced the corner. The room looked busy through the cut glass windows: well-lit, with men smoking, drinking, playing dice. I gazed at the amber liquid in their hands, and sincerely wanted to join them.

Mr. Howell snorted. "For once."

"What have you found?"

His smile turned smug. "Now why would **you** be interested?"

"Well, seeing as they were on **my** street, outside **my** apartments, cursing **me** ..."

Mr. Howell chuckled. "I'll allow you have a point. The usual dullards who wanted to speak their minds without giving the matter proper thought. They've been taken care of. But some ... some — well, most — were paid."

"Paid? By who?"

"None will say, even under duress. Even under threat to their families and friends!" He shrugged. "It seems they fear their master more than ours."

These men feared their leader more than Roy Spadros? What kind of man led them?

Mr. Howell glanced past me just as Blitz let out a cry of alarm. Amelia shrieked. Hands grabbed my arms, which I shook off.

"Your presence is requested," Mr. Howell said. Then he gestured towards the Backdoor Saloon. "Will you join us?"

* * *

Three of Tony's main men stood around us, glaring at Blitz.

Blitz glared back, hand resting on his revolver.

I turned to Mr. Howell. "You could have just asked."

Then I realized what was happening. "Mr. Roy's in there."

Mr. Howell grinned. "Pretty smart, for a gal. Come on in."

A warm blast of cigar smoke and hard liquor hit me. I forced my eyes onto Mr. Howell's back as we went past tables of men drinking and into a side room.

The room was paneled in dark brown, with a dark wooden table and chairs cushioned in black and silver. Roy Spadros sat there.

Amelia stood pressed against the wall, face white.

I faced Roy. "What do you want?"

"Is that a way to speak to your father-in-law?" He gestured at the chair across from him. "Please, sit."

I sat; none of the others moved.

Roy tossed a copy of the *Golden Bridges* onto the table:

THE LADY OF SPADROS PREGNANT?

Roy's ice-blue eyes bored into mine. "Are you with child?"

"No. Not that it's any of your business. Why would you ask me this," I gestured behind me, "in front of them?"

Roy let out a short laugh. "As Patriarch of this Family, it's entirely my business. You see, my Heir lacks an Heir of his own.

And until that changes, this Family, and by extension, this entire quadrant, is in danger."

I shook my head, exasperated. "I get carriage-sick once and suddenly I'm with child? But I suppose you believe I'm engaged in adultery. When would I have had the opportunity?"

"Why does a Diamond man frequent your home, then?"

I peered at him, confused, then a laugh burst from me. "Jon? I've known him since I was eleven. He's been a loyal friend to me and my husband, even when provoked." My cheeks burned at the memory of how I'd behaved in front of him before the trial. "You shouldn't doubt him. He defied his father to ally with your son."

But Tony wasn't Roy's son.

Our eyes met. He knew that I knew. And I realized I could reveal everything, right here to Roy's men. How Roy had lied to the quadrant. The truth about his heir. The secret of the cottage and what surely lay below it. Were the servants walking the halls of Spadros Castle silent because they had orders to be, or had Roy cut their tongues out too?

Roy froze. "Everyone, out!"

The others left. The entire time, his eyes never left mine. "What do you want?"

"To be left alone."

"I should think the incident outside the Courthouse would've cured you of that. What do you really want?"

I shrugged. A zeppelin ticket? That'd never happen. "A drink."

He shook his head. "Most disappointing. Well, since you don't know what you want, I'll ask this: What does Charles Hart want?"

Was all this just to get me to spy on him? "I have no idea." How Mr. Hart behaved at the racetrack flashed before me. "Well, I can guess, but —"

Roy burst into laughter. "We should meet more. They say laughing is good for you."

"Why do you hate him so?"

Roy recoiled, his manner icy. "I'll not speak of that, not to you." He rose, turned away.

Not to me? Why? Had my leaving Tony angered him that much? Could this sadist possibly be moved by Tony's torment? This was the first time Roy had come close to bringing it up. "My intention was never to hurt my husband. Or you. Or your precious quadrant."

Roy snorted, his back still towards me. "You asked what I want. I want the scandal to stop. I want these agitators dead and my quadrant under control," he faced me, "and that includes you."

I shrugged. Short of having me kidnapped, or carrying me back to Spadros Manor himself, he couldn't force me to return.

"How long will you continue this ridiculous situation? The Lady of Spadros, going door to door like a beggar —"

"That's over with. I have a client —"

"Who's suing the Spadros Family."

I'd forgotten. "I can ask her to drop the case, if that would help."

He rested a thick hand on the back of his chair. "It might."

But I hadn't forgotten how this discussion began. "I could have told his men everything. I didn't restrain myself because I fear you. I just don't want him hurt any further."

"Well, your actions aren't convincing. If you were serious, you'd return to your duty. Every day you're not in Spadros Manor invites more danger."

"Since when did you care?"

He sat, rested his elbows on the table, and leaned forward. "Have you forgotten your promise?"

"To help run the quadrant? I was twelve years old sitting next to a man twice my size who beat me on a daily basis. What was I supposed to say? No, I don't give a damn about your whining brat, your quadrant, or anything else? All I wanted was to get home to my mother. And saying what you wanted to hear got me there."

He leaned back. "Well played. Yet it's not up to you. I bought you, and you belong to me."

I stood, pushed in my chair. "You know, the Clubbs tried to coerce me, too. I'll give you the same answer. You have enough men to take me back there. But you'll have to keep me under lock and key day and night, because I'll tell everyone that I'm in Spadros Manor against my will. I won't be at your Grand Balls or your Yuletide spectacles or your gods-damned Celebrations, except bound and gagged." I leaned over to point at him. "You think you have scandal now? It'll just be getting started. Then you'll have a choice: kill me, put me in a ward, or leave me alone."

I straightened. "The next time you want to speak with me, instead of having your thugs grab me in the street, come to call. It's what an actual gentleman would do."

Roy stared at me, mouth open. "What's gotten into you, Jacq?"

I opened the door. Jonathan Diamond was going to die: nothing else mattered. "I got tired of men telling me what I had to do."

The Value

As we walked back home, I thought about what just happened. Roy had changed.

I confronted him, threatened him. Yet he made no move to hit me. He didn't draw his revolver. He didn't even shout. The only time he even became angry was when I asked why he hated Charles Hart so much.

I understood his position: Roy had to secure the Spadros quadrant's future. But Tony had an heir. Roland was illegitimate, yes, but if Tony claimed him as heir no one would say otherwise.

Why did they still need me?

* * *

After dinner, I sat in my room. Despite my words to Roy, I felt restless, frightened, shaky.

They didn't know you were from the Pot.

They thought you were happy.

Everyone thought I was happy except those who put me there. Roy Spadros, and by extension his wife, Molly. His staff.

And most of all, my father.

That wretched ruined former police detective turned assassin had much to answer for.

He abandoned me until I was twelve then used me to buy his way into Spadros quadrant. Since then, he seemed to have little use for me. Unless you counted trying to coerce me to give him money to feed his Party Time habit.

I wiped my eyes. I had use for him, though.

I crept to the door, listening.

Far off, I heard Blitz and Mary murmuring in their rooms.

The outfit I only used when on cases was widow's brown, with hat, shoes, ring, and handbag to match. I would become a poor widow, no one worthy of notice.

I eased out of the front door, taking the key from the hook beside it. My breath caught as the door quietly squeaked, and again as the lock clicked. But no voices raised on the other side.

Slipping the key into my pocket, I hurried down the steps, away from the Backdoor Saloon and the guards sure to be there.

The streets were empty at this hour. A few blocks over stood a taxi stand. The driver seemed surprised at a woman out this late, especially when he heard my destination. "Not sure they're open."

"That's not your concern. I paid you, now go." I wanted away before Blitz noticed the key missing.

But my mind kept returning to what Dr. Salmon had said. What Jon had said.

You must never drink again. Another poisoning would surely kill you.

I wasn't going to poison myself. I just wanted one drink.

Surely one drink wouldn't hurt, and I needed it. I wanted it, more than anything.

Roy asked me what I wanted. Jon asked what would make me happy. This was it.

I loved the way the liquor burned as it went down, the way it made me feel. In all my miserable useless life, surely one time, one night, I deserved to be happy.

Besides, my father would know if Clover still lived nearby, and how I might find him.

I asked the driver to wait, and went into Peedro Sluff's liquor store. The door didn't want to close, and I didn't force it to. The cold air felt good, clean.

The place hadn't changed. The same cracked tiles, dusty lighting, moldy smell, even the same bottles on the shelves.

To see so many bottles was tantalizing. It took an effort not to grab one and start drinking.

Peedro Sluff sat leaned back against a wall of the not-so-terrible stuff, snoring. I found a bottle with a bail-closed lid, and hands shaking, plunked it down on the counter. "Wake up."

"Huh?" My father jumped, bleary eyed, and focused on me. "What the hell you doing here?"

"How much?"

He laughed. "Never thought I'd see you coming in here to do anything but sneer at me and ask me to do your dirty work."

I thought I'd better ask before I started drinking. "I do need your help with something."

"Why am I not surprised?" Something about him was different. He was clean, with a proper haircut, although his black hair was thinner than before. And his pale skin had color to it. "You gonna actually pay me this time?" He gave a tight-lipped smile, tapping his temple. "I remember that clear enough."

I sighed. "I'm sorry. I'll pay you when I pay for this."

"So what do you want?"

"Clover still live around here?"

Peedro laughed. "Him again. He don't look like much. Was he good the last time?"

"He's in danger. And I need to find his friend."

My father shrugged. "Haven't seen him. But I'll ask around." He peered at me. "Your husband know you're here?"

A horse whinnied outside, and a carriage went past.

"He doesn't, does he? What if I told you he said if I sold you a drink he'd kill me?"

Tony said that? "I don't believe you."

"But I might be persuaded." He went for the bottle, and I snatched it back. "But you have to let me hold it first."

I didn't move.

"You want to drink that, or not? I need to see what the price is. My eyes ain't what they used to be."

Letting that bottle out of my hands was one of the hardest things I've ever done. "What happened? You're different."

He'd been to a dentist since I last saw him. "I quit Party Time. You should have asked before — I'd have given you the whole store for a hit."

He quit Party Time. I stared at him, astonished.

"I heard you'd gotten clean too. But I've had my bad days. Heh. It looks like you're having one now." My father picked up the bottle. "Also heard you came into some money."

He gestured with the bottle. "You want this? How much will you pay for it? A penny? A dollar? Ten?" He waggled the bottle just out of my reach. "A hundred?"

"That's quite enough." My husband Tony stood in the doorway, Sawbuck behind him.

What were they doing here?

"I had to see this for myself." It was after midnight, but Tony looked as if he'd walked out of a meeting on Market Center. His straight black hair was perfectly combed, his clothes flawless, his shoes shined. To this day I don't know how he got there so quickly. He had his emotionless public mask firmly in place. But his dark blue eyes were angry. "Just when I think you've discovered every possible way to disrupt my life, you come up with something new." In a few steps, he faced me, his skin even paler than usual, and he spoke in a tone pitched for my ears only. "Do you truly want to die? Because I can arrange that."

I recoiled in horror. "Tony!"

Shame flashed through his eyes, then his mask reappeared. "Ten, take her home. And have the locks changed so a key is needed to leave as well as enter. Blitz or Mary must wear the key at all times."

"So you intend to have me caged again."

Tony grabbed me by my upper arms. "I intend for you to stay alive!" Then he shoved me aside, but not far. "Although I don't know why I bother."

I don't know why I bother. Is that what he really thought?

"Come, Mrs. Spadros," Sawbuck said. "I'll take you home."

* * *

Sawbuck and I rode in his carriage, as far away from each other as two people might sit. For quite a while, neither of us spoke.

I'd never felt so humiliated in my life. The disgust in Tony's eyes ... how could I ever face him again? "Ten, I was only trying to —" What was I trying to do? "I was asking about a man who might be able to contact Master Rainbow."

"Not what it looked like to me."

Shame flooded through me, and bitter anger. "You don't understand what it's like."

Sawbuck was quiet for a moment. "I think I do."

Something in his voice told me to remain silent.

"It sounds insane," Sawbuck said, "but he's my drink. He's my drug. He's my death, should he learn any of this." The carriage passed a lamp post; his head hung over his clasped hands. "You know how hard it is not to speak, not to hold him?"

I bit my lip, eyes stinging.

But there came a smile to his voice. "Every day I tell myself that being close to him is enough." He sighed. "It has to be enough."

"Just think, one day I'll be able to leave Bridges, and who knows? Perhaps Roy will relent, or die, and then you can speak."

Sawbuck sat motionless for some time, then snorted bitterly. "Once long ago, he fell into despair, and I held him. I remember it as if it were yesterday. We sat upon the sofa in his study, and the afternoon sun was golden upon the far wall. It was one of the most beautiful moments in my life."

I felt a sense of dread.

"It took everything in me not to speak, to just let that moment be enough. But here he was, warm in my arms, his head lying upon my chest. Oh, gods, it was a sweet agony. I even dared kiss his hair. Then he looked up at me with those beautiful eyes, full and vulnerable and alive. He reached up and touched my face. And you know what he said?"

I shrugged, even though I was sure he couldn't see me.

"He said, 'Ten, I'm so grateful for you, more than anyone in the world. I feel you're the good father I never had.'" A short, bitter laugh burst forth. "How does one answer that? To speak now would be unfair. It would only bring confusion and pain."

"How can you stand it? Why do you stay?"

"Because he needs me, Mrs. Spadros. Because I love him. I considered leaving, once. I stood in the zeppelin station, ticket in hand. And I found I couldn't go. I couldn't leave him alone in this terrible place, not even if I could never speak."

That's exactly what I did. I left Tony where he was completely unsuited to survive.

That was why Sawbuck was angry with me most of the time.

As Sawbuck's carriage pulled up to my door, two of Tony's main men backed down the steps, blood on their upright hands.

Sawbuck leapt from the carriage. "What the fuck is going on?"

From the carriage, I saw straight into the hall. Blitz lay on the floor. Mary stood in the hallway, hair down, wearing a shawl and nightgown, with a shotgun pointed towards us.

I stared at her in astonishment. "Mary!"

Mary squinted in my direction, a wildness in her eyes.

I got out of the carriage. "Mary, stop! I'm here." I turned to Tony's men. "Did my husband order this?"

"Yes, mum," one said.

What the hell was Tony doing?

"You can go now," Sawbuck said, and the two left. "Mrs. Spadros," he said to Mary, "put down the gun."

The barrel of the shotgun shook.

"Mary," I said, "put down the gun so we can help Blitz!"

That seemed to reach her: she lowered the gun. We came inside.

Sawbuck helped Blitz up. Blitz rushed to Mary, who dropped the shotgun and began to weep in his arms.

The gun hadn't been fired. I cleared the chamber and set it atop my piano. "Go in the kitchen."

After Blitz and Mary did so, I said to Sawbuck, "Did you know he was going to do this?"

Sawbuck glanced away. "I would have advised him not to. But once he'd spoken to his men —"

I nodded. Going against Tony in front of the men would have been worse. "Nothing good will come from this."

"I had no idea they had a shotgun," Sawbuck said, "although I should have guessed."

"Go home, Ten," I said. "I can deal with this on my own."

Sawbuck tipped his hat. "Good night, Mrs. Spadros."

I waited until the lock clicked behind him, then picked up the shells from the floor and went into the kitchen.

Blitz had washed his face, and the two sat holding hands, staring at nothing.

Blitz looked up at me: his eye was blackened, his lip split. "I can't do this anymore, Mrs. Spadros. I have to trust that you'll value our lives enough — that you'll say something before you turn the Family against us!" His gaze dropped to the table. "Was whatever you did worth it?"

I sat heavily. Going to my father's liquor store in the middle of the night, even to get a drink, wasn't worth this.

"I don't know if I'll believe you anymore," Blitz said, "but will you promise to tell me you're going out next time?"

That hurt. "I'm so sorry. I don't know what I was thinking." At least I did get something useful done. "My father is going to —"

Mary blurted out, "I'm with child."

The Mistake

Blitz got this stunned look on his face. "Are you certain?"

She nodded.

"But ..." Blitz seemed at a loss for words.

His reaction amused me. "I think you're supposed to kiss your wife right now."

This seemed to shake him: he took Mary in his arms, eyes red.

"Congratulations." I rested my hand on his shoulder. "Why don't you go to bed? It's getting late."

They left for their rooms; I got a damp cloth and cleaned the blood from the hallway floor.

At the time, I didn't understand why I put everyone in such danger. Why I defied Roy, Tony, everyone. I felt almost as out of control as I did when I used to drink all the time.

But I kept thinking: Why couldn't they leave me alone? Why come here, beat Blitz of all people, who'd just tried to help me? It seemed so unfair.

While I cleaned the floor, something occurred to me. Mrs. Clubb had said last year at her hotel that this Black Maria had a ruthless nature. *Everyone fears her.*

People like that always made one mistake: they kept someone alive they thought insignificant, who hated them enough to talk to someone willing to pay. I had an idea who that someone might be.

* * *

The next evening found me and Blitz in a taxi-carriage picking its way through a tunnel in the Spadros Pot. The driver had asked five times his usual rate and drove with many pulls on the reins.

Through the thin curtain, rough men stood beside makeshift fires, eyeing us suspiciously. None prevented us from passing, but I wondered if it might not be so easy coming back.

Blitz said, "This is a mistake."

He'd said that six times already. Yes, we were in the worst part of the Spadros Pot. But there was no way to turn back, not in here.

We soon passed through the tunnel under the Main Road, and our speed increased. Then we stopped. The driver came round, opened the door. "Keycard Saloon. As you asked."

"Stay with the carriage," I whispered to Blitz.

"I'm not letting you go in there alone!"

"It's not a place for fine folk. Stay here."

He grabbed my arm, wincing as he did so. "I should never have agreed to this. Either I go with you, or we return home."

I gazed at Blitz, half-lit by the lantern the driver held in his shaking hand. *He's serious.* "Very well." I faced the driver. "It won't go well for you if you're stopped in the Pot without me aboard."

He gulped. "Yes, mum."

"Stay with the carriage," Blitz said to the man. "And if you have a weapon, keep it ready."

The Keycard Saloon was one of the worst places in the Spadros Pot: filthy, smoke-filled, broken-down. And it stank: sex and sweat, tobacco and Party Time. Most of all, it stank of booze.

Gods, I needed some booze right then.

Blitz put a hand on my arm. "Remember where you are."

The bartender said, "Whaddya want? You here for a threesome?"

"I'm looking for Tim," I said. "We want to talk to him."

"Gonna cost double."

Blitz looked exasperated. "Just get him."

The man called over his shoulder, "Kara! Go roust Tim. We got quality guests tonight."

I snorted. Anyone would be quality compared to the louts here.

The boy was dirty, ragged, and barefoot. But it was Tim of the Keycard Saloon. He glared at me. "You."

After paying the man his two cents, we went to Tim's filthy, candlelit bedroom, not much larger than a toilet room. I didn't dare sit on the bed — it was likely to have bugs in it.

Tim spoke with a sneering tone. "You wanna talk first or after?"

"Only," Blitz said.

I felt sorry for this kid. "So the deal didn't happen, did it? You know, the one where you got a place on Market Center?"

The boy spat, but his eyes reddened. "When the trial went well for you they took back the clothes and the shoes. They brought me to the Hedge and pushed me out the carriage. They had no use for me!" His face fell, and his shook his head. "Why'd I believe them?"

"Uppers always have use for ya, until it suits 'em," I said bitterly.

Tim sneered at me. "Even you?"

"I want to get back at this whole lot. They lied to try to kill me. They used you to do it. I want to get you someplace better."

The boy gave me a cynical glare. "Better? Where?"

I shrugged. "I have friends in the Cathedral —"

His little face went "oh".

"— and if not there, at least on the good side of the tunnel."

He didn't answer at first. Not that I blamed him. "I don't know." He sounded dejected. "What you want me to do?"

I said, "Just tell me what you know."

Tim was in the High-Low Split — all the kids were in it. He'd even gone on a few raids into the quadrants, not that he could go very often. It was a long way to the Hedge, and little boys were in big demand this side of the tunnels. His customers could show up any time after dusk.

But he'd never laid eyes on Black Maria. "The High Cards are scared of her," he whispered. "They say she's mean. She even thinks you're against her, you're dead." His eyes were wide in the half-darkness. "No one sees her do it. They call her the Death Card."

In the tales, the Death Card was the invisible spirit of evil come to destroy the unclean. A perfect way to frighten children living without running water into submission. "This is a woman like any other. Where does she stay?"

"All her Picture Cards —"

Surprised, I let out a laugh. "What?"

"Her Kings, Queens, and Jacks."

Black Maria was a fouled hand to be sure. She puffed these kids up to believe themselves rulers as she exploited them. "Go on."

"They live around the Plaza. You know —"

"Yeah." I remembered not the Plaza on Market Center but the mile long, quarter-mile wide grassy area two miles away. The crumbling statue of Benjamin Kerr, the broken fountains. All surrounded by weeds and the ruins of 'scrapers. Where Joseph Kerr and I made love for the first — and last — time. "I know."

Blitz said, "What guards are there?"

He shrugged. "Never been." He seemed to draw back into himself. "I don't like the tunnel."

Blitz pulled me aside. "We can't leave him here."

"Why not? I can get him a place in a few days."

"What if he's accused of spying on them and is killed? Besides," at that, he shuddered, "look at how he's living!"

"Blitz, I grew up in the Pot." I glanced at his room. "This is a bad place, to be sure. The worst. But he'll be fine. I just need to —"

"I don't believe this! We can help him right now. Or do you only want to help the Pot when it benefits you? Don't ever speak to me again about wanting to help this city if you can't be bothered to help one child."

I snorted. "You're what, thirty? Did you care when I was the Pot rag being beaten in Spadros Manor?" No one gave a damn about what happened to little girls. "You look after him, then."

Tim stared at us, eyes wide.

Blitz said, "Do you have a coat, or shoes? It's cold out there."

Tim wrapped rags around his feet and put a dirty poncho made from two blankets over his head. "They won't let me go with you unless you buy me."

He grabbed a small sack and stuck it under his belt, tying it so it wouldn't jingle. When he saw us watching, he looked afraid. "Don't tell 'em, or they'll take 'em away."

He didn't get to keep tips? "Won't hear it from me," I said.

We went out to the bar. Blitz said, "Who's in charge here?"

"Depends on who's asking."

"I am," said Blitz. "How much for the boy?"

"Our boys ain't for sale."

An older man sat at the bar. "Come off it! He eats as much as he makes since he got back. In a year or so he'll be too old anyway."

"Shut up," the bartender said. He turned to Blitz. "Two dollars and not a cent more. That's how much the other man gave us."

"I'll give you 25 cents, and I won't report you for a slaver."

The man's eyes narrowed. "Make it thirty and we have a deal."

Blitz handed over the thirty cents. "Anyone who follows us," he pulled out his gun, "I shoot." Grabbing Tim's hand, he strode to the door, and I followed.

"This is a mistake," I murmured.

When we opened the door, the carriage was gone.

The Walk

I looked around. "Now why did I not anticipate that?"

Blitz said quite seriously, "Why would he leave?"

"The same reason you couldn't stay with the carriage." He was afraid. I gave even odds he and his horses ended up feeding the tunnel rats, both men and beast.

Sure enough, the sound of horses whinnying and men shouting echoed from the tunnel.

Blitz said, "So what now?"

"We walk." I started towards the Hedge.

Blitz caught up to me. "How far is it? What about your foot?"

I retrieved my pistol from its calf holster. "My foot isn't what you should be worrying about."

"It's not far," Tim said. "A mile, maybe."

The brightly-lit statue of the first Acevedo Spadros poked its head over the quadrant point's Hedge behind us. "More like three. Come on."

The streets in the Pot weren't often straight like those in the quadrants: they wound and curved. Tim was right about taking the tunnel, dressed as we were. And we couldn't get to Main from here; the Hedge lay in the way, guarding the uppers from the likes of us.

But as long as we kept moving away from Acevedo Spadros, we'd find the quadrant.

Blitz said, "They bought you the last time?"

Tim said, "Yeah."

"Then you're a free man twice over," Blitz said sharply. "Don't let anyone slave you again."

While the glow of the quadrant lay ahead, around us was dark at pitch. As the quadrant grew closer, shapes moved at the edges of our vision in the mist.

"Ignore them," I said.

Blitz jumped a bit.

I smiled to myself in the darkness. "They won't attack unless they have the advantage."

"There's only two of us," Blitz whispered.

"Yes, but we have guns."

Tim said, "I have a knife."

I doubted this boy had ever used a knife to cut someone. "That's good to know." I'd trained in knife fighting with the best, but I'd never cut anyone until the year prior.

The glow from the quadrants moved to our right as we went, falling behind the darkened buildings. "Once we get to the corner," I said, "we go right. It's straight on from there."

The dark shapes flanked us. A few more feet, then it would be light enough from the quadrant's glow to see them.

If they mean to ambush us, I thought, they'll do it now.

"Whatever happens," I whispered, "stay together."

Just as we turned the corner, the dark shape of a huge man stepped in front of us, back-lit by the city.

* * *

Tim screamed. His knife clattered to the ground, and he ran.

"Get the boy," a deep voice said. "Good gods, Jacqui, it **is** you."

Blitz whispered, "You know this man?"

The man chuckled, stepping aside to show himself. Tall, muscled, brown-skinned, he wore a blanket poncho much like Tim's, but it was clean. His hair, straight and black, pulled back to a braid which dangled beside his hip. Not so much clean-shaven as he'd never grown a beard.

I said, "Benji? What the hell are **you** doing here?"

"I could say same." He called out, "Bring the boy."

A smaller man had Tim in a fireman's carry, slinging him over to stand upright. "You owe me, Benj. He bites."

"I d-didn't know ya," Tim said. "Ya not from this side."

Benji chuckled. "Tis true." He gave Blitz a hard stare. "Why bring quadrant-folk here?"

Anything I said would upset someone. "None your concern."

Benji rolled his eyes. "Not changed one hair. Well, come then, before your Family spins to pieces."

"Wait," I said. "My husband sent you?"

Benji took my arm, and we began walking as his men melted into the shadows. "Family men came all a-flurry." He let out a short laugh. "The Cathedral ignores Spadros dogs —"

Blitz flinched.

" — but I offered to find my small sister."

"Sister?" Blitz looked astonished.

I patted Benji's hand. "Different wombs birthed us. But we grew up together." I looked up at him. "You got so big."

Benji shrugged. "And you, dressed so fine."

I wore my shabby widow's garb that I only used on cases. I squeezed his arm. "I've missed you."

He stopped then, glanced around. The Hedge lay straight ahead in the distance. "You should not come here, Jacqui. It's not safe for any, but you have the greatest danger."

"Why?"

"It's not like when we were small. The High-Low Split's changed. They wish the ruin of the Pot upon the entire city."

"The Red Dog Gang," I said.

He twitched, surprised. "Yes. They try for information. What you like and hate. Who you trust. They spy upon the Cathedral!"

"Our Inventor told me he sent spies as well."

Benji nodded gravely. "Don't trust the Inventors."

Certainly not if they would try to force the Cathedral to treat with them. I rose on tiptoe to kiss his cheek. "It was good to see you." I turned to Tim and Blitz. "There's a small gap ahead, and the river's not far. We can flag down a taxi-carriage on Promenade."

Tim drew back. "I'll go with him." He looked up at Benji. "I work hard. Day and night. I won't say no, whatever the men want. And I'll find food. Whatever you say. I don't want to go back."

I gaped at Tim, horrified at the implications.

Benji snorted. "The Daughters will flay me, but I'll speak for you." He knelt before Tim. "No one compels the Cathedral. You can always say no. We have food." He glanced up at Blitz. "And we don't beat ya." He offered Tim his hand, and the boy took it. "My advice, small sister, is to return to your duty." He smiled to himself. "But you never will take it."

I could never go back to Spadros Manor. "Until next time."

He shook his head, turned away, yet one arm flung into the air in farewell. And they were gone into the mist.

* * *

My feet hurt by the time we got to the Promenade. One of the plain carriages pulled up. A footman I didn't recognize opened the door: Sawbuck sat inside. "Get in."

Blitz climbed up in back with the other footman, apparently not part of the invitation.

I got in and arranged my dress around me. "How did you know we'd be here?"

"When the men the Cathedral sent found your driver outside the tunnel, they reported back to my men."

I raised an eyebrow. "Surprised he's still alive."

Sawbuck snorted. "Whipped, stripped, and branded for a traitor, but alive."

"And the horses?"

Sawbuck shrugged. "I hear they pulled the carriage back through the Gap themselves. What was so important as to go gallivanting into the Pot in the midst of night?"

"I know where the Red Dog Gang hides out."

The Code

Cold air spilled down my neck as the small window behind me opened. "We know where this High-Low Split gang hides out," Blitz said. "We don't know they're the same."

Sawbuck glared at him, and the window shut.

I remembered what Benji just said. "They're allied. The leader of the High-Low Split is a woman! She consorts with Frank Pagliacci and is the one who shot Marja."

Sawbuck's eyes widened. "Is that so?

"Mrs. Clubb has a witness. This woman is the Black Maria you're searching for."

Sawbuck leaned back, crossing his ankle over his knee, his arm along the back of the bench. "And yet you've taken money from Maria Athena Spade's mother to find her."

"I don't think that this girl is Black Maria. I think that either the Spadros rogues or the Red Dog Gang have taken her to lure us into a trap." It certainly fit the pattern the Red Dog Gang's leader had followed so far.

He put both feet on the floor. "Then you need to stop. We need to figure out what their trap is before doing anything else. These are dangerous people. You can't just go charging into their stronghold without being sure."

"I ran in the High-Low Split as a child. These are people I grew up with! I don't believe they'll harm me." I searched around for something to sway him. "I promised this woman's mother I'd find her. She's spent a great deal of money already. I know where Black Maria is. I believe that's where we'll find Maria Athena as well."

"And if you're wrong, you could be killed, or worse, captured, used as a discard in whatever game they're playing." He leaned forward, eyes fierce. "I won't have him put between two terrors!"

Everything came back to Tony and his fear. Fear of me coming to harm, or fear of defying Roy. If faced with both, I wasn't sure which would win.

Just one of many reasons I walked away.

Having Family connections was an advantage, but my business had to stay separate from the Spadros Family. "There is no 'we,' Ten. This family lives on Market Center for a reason. I won't jeopardize their well-being because my husband feels anxious!"

"What will it take for you to understand?"

"This is the Pot. It's the High-Low Split." How did he not grasp what I said? "You grew up there. You never ran with us?"

"Aunt Molly took me from there to spare me that life."

I stared at Sawbuck as if seeing him for the first time. He wasn't really from the Pot at all, not in his mind. My mother-in-law Molly grew up in the Pot. Why would she take him from his people? Never teach him our way? "Pot rags don't hurt other Pot rags, Ten."

A scoff burst from him. "They don't hurt children. But you're a full woman. You're the Lady of Spadros. Do you not understand the danger you put yourself in?"

When Tim testified at my trial, he had it right: these quadrant-folk were all soft, frightened of their own shadows. "Very well: I'll get more information before I proceed. I have contacts I haven't heard from yet. But you must let me do my work! I can't have you barging into a situation you clearly don't understand." If Maria Athena were still alive, I'd have one chance to rescue her.

"I understand well enough," Sawbuck said. "You're determined to ruin us all."

"That's not true. It has never been true. I don't care about your Family schemes, or how you run your quadrants. What I want is to be left alone to help this girl! My husband promised he wouldn't interfere with me again —"

"He's not —"

"That's not how it feels."

He seemed to withdraw into himself. "Then I apologize. I've overstepped." He turned away to lean on the window edge. "I will say no more."

I felt astonished. "Mr. Anthony doesn't know you're speaking with me on this matter, does he?"

Sawbuck shook his head, still turned away.

He'd directly defied Tony's orders: for that, Tony could have Sawbuck killed. "And I'll not tell him of it."

"Thank you."

Now I had an advantage. How to play this ...? "I want a private carriage. I can't go walking the streets anymore."

Sawbuck nodded, but wariness lay in his eyes.

"And I want my footman to attend me. I don't know your men. I trust Honor to guard me."

"If Honor is available, certainly."

I almost asked for Tony not to know about it, but if he did, perhaps that would ease his mind as to my safety. "And no more attacks on my home!"

"You know I had nothing to do with that."

"If Spadros men attack my home again I will confront my husband about your interference."

He leaned forward, face angry. "Now see here —"

"These are my servants, not his, not yours. Your men may not beat my butler and terrorize my housekeeper. Is that clear?" Perhaps now he'd be more interested in managing Tony than me.

"Very well. But this is where it ends. Are **we** clear?"

I got more than I hoped for. "We're clear."

Wariness and anger still lay in his eyes, and I hoped I hadn't pushed him too far.

* * *

When I returned home, a message sat on my desk from my friend Vig. I felt so happy I exclaimed, "He found Clover!"

Blitz, stood in the darkened hallway. "Who's Clover?"

"Clover might know where Master Rainbow is."

"Ah," Blitz said, clearly not understanding.

"Don't you remember? Master Rainbow stayed with us for a while last February."

"Oh, the new man, the one who got injured. Didn't he run off?"

"Testifying at the inquest would have put him into danger. My husband understands the matter."

Blitz nodded slowly. "Thank you for saying what you did. Back there in the carriage."

I smiled. "So you were listening."

Blitz chuckled. "The window was behind my head."

"You're my responsibility. And since it was my fault Mr. Anthony's anger fell upon you, it was mine to make straight."

"Mary's been anxious of our safety."

"More the reason to set things right."

"That's very kind," Blitz said. "And I'm sorry. That I didn't help you at the Manor." He glanced away. "I could give excuse," he shook his head, "but there's none."

He would've been seventeen, maybe? Living under the same roof as Roy Spadros? Perhaps I'd been too harsh, expecting him to defend some Pot rag he didn't know. "How did you end up here? If it's not too personal a question."

Blitz drew back, his face confused. "Like I said last year, we decided to leave, and —"

"Before that. How did you come to live at Spadros Manor?"

Blitz chuckled. "Oh, that. I grew up on East 3rd. Six kids, each with a different Pa. They all sort of watched out for us. Mine was a Family man — you don't know him, he's dead now."

"I'm sorry to hear that. What happened?"

"Shot near the end of the Spadros-Diamond war."

"Is that how you got into the Family?"

"In a way. My Pa got me hired on as a messenger boy for East 6th. I learned to read and count from there. He got me started delivering Party Time with the messages when I was eleven."

"Were you very close to your Pa?"

Blitz shrugged. "All Pa cared about was being with my Ma when he came over. But we always had Family men around the house, and they all knew me. After Pa got shot, they told Mr. Roy how I never sleep. I was fifteen when they moved me into the Manor."

"Did you like being there?"

"Wasn't the most interesting job I've ever had. But as long as I patrolled every so often, I could do as I liked. And I had all day to do as I liked as well."

"And do you like it here?"

He gave me a wry grin. "Now I won't get pounded on, it's fine."

"Have you heard about Major Blackwell's funeral —?"

Blitz stopped me. "They don't want you there."

I blinked. "They don't?"

He looked away. "They mainly don't want reporters there. The family feels you being there would bring too much attention."

Did his family know he might have died because he defended me? "Thank you for telling me true."

He chuckled. "If it makes you feel any better, they didn't want Mr. Anthony there, either."

* * *

The next morning, I asked Mary where she'd bought the sandwich stand. Later that day, Amelia and I went there.

It was a small shop on 31st Street to sell items people donated to the poorhouse. I had a coat for my widow's outfit, but I wanted an old cloak with a hood as well.

I didn't like that Sawbuck saw me dressed in my widow's garb. Yet I didn't want to buy another full disguise. I needed to keep the widow's garb for when I didn't want to be recognized by anyone. So I planned to use this cloak when there was a chance to be recognized — as when I made my excursion to the Pot. Then I might wear my regular clothing, yet keep my identity somewhat hidden.

After I selected a threadbare black cloak a bit too large for me, Amelia and I ate luncheon at a nearby street vendor. Surely I could spare a penny a bowl, now I had pennies to spare.

"Mum," Amelia said, "will you be getting a dress for the 500th?"

I sighed. Despite what Gardena said, I still didn't want to go. "I hadn't considered the matter."

"It's not far off. I know it's too late to have one made. But we have money for you to buy one. You can't go in any of the dresses you have — it would look as if you were in mourning."

I had the four dresses I went to court in — all charcoal, with various white lace embellishments in the neckline. They did look as if I wore mourning. "Perhaps I still am."

"Oh, mum," Amelia said, "I'm so sorry. Your mother —"

"All is forgiven." I didn't mourn my mother: she still lived, although I let everyone think she was dead for her safety.

No, I think I mourned the lives I'd meant to have. Traveling the world with Nina Clubb. Married to Joseph Kerr. A long, happy friendship with Jonathan Diamond, growing old together.

But it seemed none of these were more than fantasy. Everything I'd hoped for had been lost somehow. I felt in a bewildered daze, trying to understand where my life had gone so very wrong.

Amelia put her hand on mine. "It gets better, mum. Time doesn't take it away, but it does soften the blows when they come."

I'd found this to be true as well.

"The new table's to be delivered today," Amelia said. "And Master Jonathan sent a new tea service as well."

"That was kind of him."

How might I learn about Jon's condition? "Amelia, when we return, would you call Dr. Salmon?"

Her face turned concerned. "Are you ill, mum?"

"Not at all. At his convenience."

He arrived that evening. We sat in the parlor.

"Is your foot well?"

"Entirely."

Of course, he didn't believe me. But after pushing and tapping upon it, he judged I might be right. "So how can I help?"

"I suppose this may sound odd," I said, "but I wish to learn about," what had Jon called it? "Rheumatic fever, and the heart condition it brings."

Dr. Salmon nodded. "Master Diamond."

I felt entirely surprised. "You knew of this?"

He shrugged. "I only know of it in passing. We took a zeppelin together once when I visited my sister in Azimoff." His eyes grew wistful. "Not even their technology can forestall death, I'm afraid."

"I'm so sorry for your loss, sir."

"You're very kind." He sat quietly for a moment, then said, "I'll have some books on the matter sent over."

This solved one mystery: where Jon had been during the trial.

I felt glad that he'd been seeing the doctors in Azimoff. Whether they might forestall death or not, it was said they had the best doctors in the world.

If anyone could find a way to help him, they could.

After he left, Mary went past with a vase carrying Mr. Hart's roses. I stopped her. "Send them back. And don't accept more."

Mary gaped at me. "Are you sure?"

Mr. Hart had been the only one to send me flowers since the trial. Flowers sent by men were specifically mentioned in the *Golden Bridges* article. Could the article have been another way for Mrs. Judith Hart to attack me? "Yes, I'm sure."

Major Blackwood died after a "very good-looking man" agitated for harsher action against us. Then the *Golden Bridges* attacked us about a matter which only Mrs. Hart would ever care about.

What did it all mean? How did these pieces fit together? What were the Red Dog Gang really doing?

* * *

The next day, a package arrived with three books inside.

I never learned to read until I was brought to Spadros Manor at twelve, but I did enjoy it. And I particularly had interest in learning about Jonathan's malady.

My dictionary got a great deal of use that day. But the more I read, the more I understood.

The tonics. His quiet disappearances, when he'd fly to Azimoff for treatment. Jon's frequent fevers. Why he often used a cane.

Jon had suffered all this, alone.

He wouldn't have burdened his younger sister with his illness, his fears, not when she already had her child to care for.

Who did he turn to?

Jon had sent me a letter almost every day since the trial's end, including that day. He'd promised I should never feel alone.

Now I understood this as well.

So I wrote to him:

Dear sir,

I have begun to understand the calamity you face. I wish to
stand with you. There's no longer need to hide your woes
from me. I find it most helpful when I can be of support.

I look forward to our outing. I hope today brings you joy.

Several times, I had to remind myself that others might intercept
the letter, so I couldn't reveal too much. We planned to go boating
the next day, though, and I wanted him to know I hadn't forgotten.

When Mrs. Spade came to call later that day, I said, "I'm sorry
about your neighbor."

"How you know this? Yes, she shot a dead. Police say robber."
She appeared glum.

I brought out Maria Athena's note and pointed at the line in it
Gardena thought odd. "What does this really mean?"

Mrs. Spade smiled to herself as if remembering a happy moment.
"It about a something I say when Maria Athena small girl. 'Safe in
my heart as lock and key.' It our saying."

"So no one else would know this."

"No," Mrs. Spade seemed surprised at the question. "Not even
my boys, unless they listen at the door." She chuckled. "But no,
Giovanni read a to them same time."

I nodded. So unless she'd told someone about this happy time
with her mother, the note was from her.

Mrs. Spade looked anxious and hopeful. "Have you learn
anything about a my girl?"

I shook my head. "None of my people has heard anything." At
her grimace of dismay, I said, "This is a huge city. It may take time."
But then I remembered Roy's request. "I must ask something."

"Anything. What it is?"

"Stop the lawsuit against the Spadros Family."

"What? No!"

"The men at your home were not Spadros men. The Family
wants to help. They can help find Maria Athena, but not if you send
lawyers to hurt them."

She nodded, eyes downcast. "I understand. Mafiosi. We should
never have move here."

To avoid any hint of scandal, Jonathan and I thought it best to take Amelia along on our sailing trip the next day.

As we approached Jon's carriage, Werner Lead came running up, his two brothers close behind.

I handed Amelia my parasol. "Get into the carriage."

Jon and I went to greet the boy.

Werner panted for a moment, bent over, before he might speak. "Urgent," he finally said. "From Mrs. Regina Clubb." His older brother rested his hand on the boy's back, and Werner straightened. "The witness: matters intersect now, today."

I peered at him. "And?"

Werner looked up at me. "I don't know what it means either."

I smiled. Doubtless that was the intent. "Well, then, I suppose I must use my brainpower." I handed him a dime tip. "Well done."

He beamed at me, still panting. "Thank you, Mrs. Spadros!"

I got into the carriage, Jon sitting across from me. "What do you think it means?" Jon said.

I shook my head. "I don't know."

I pondered the question for the entire trip to Diamond Marina, an elegant study in black, silver, crystal and white.

Jon's yacht sat in its moorings. A white boat trimmed in black and silver, it had a white sail and gray lines. The deck was white, trimmed in dark wood. "This is lovely, Jon."

The deck was large enough for a party, with benches and even a few tables bolted to the deck. Jon and I sat at one, surveying the marina as the boats passed. A man not so dark as Jonathan approached. "Where to, sir?"

"Once round then back should be sufficient," Jon said.

"Yes, sir." The man moved towards the bow. Another cast off the lines. Amelia went below to see how she might help.

Jonathan smiled at me. "I know white and gray are your least favorite colors."

I took a deep breath, let it out. "It's different, here with you. I don't know how else to say it. I think any place would suit, so long as you sat with me."

Jonathan smiled to himself.

I opened my parasol. "I read about your condition —"

Jon raised a hand. "Please, don't. Not here. Not today."

"But I just —"

"I know you want to understand, to find some way round it."

At his insight, I felt abashed. "Yes, well —"

"But could we not speak of this? I wish only to enjoy the day."

When had Jon ever asked me not to speak on a topic?

He faced me. "I know you're afraid. I know you want to help. But the best way to help is to trust me." He took my hands. "Jacqui, I want to live. I've consulted the best doctors in the world. Taken every treatment. What I want is to live. Not to spend life scrabbling after false hope like some frightened old man."

I hadn't considered this aspect of the matter.

Jon let go of my hands and sat gazing over the water.

The day was bright, and the breeze cool. The shores of Diamond fell away. Hart quadrant appeared in the distance as we turned downstream towards Market Center.

I didn't know how to feel, what to think. I wanted to help Jon. He thought I didn't trust him?

Yet I'd seen more than one frightened old man "scrabbling after false hope," as Jon put it. And I remembered how without question or hesitation, Jon saved my life outside the Courthouse.

No, Jonathan Diamond wouldn't give up on life without a fight.

The island of Market Center loomed closer, and the boat kept to the Hart shoreline to avoid the Suction. A pale-skinned freckled maid with finely coiled yellow hair came on deck. "Tea, sir?"

Jon nodded, not even glancing her way.

Matters intersect now, today ...

It was obviously a code of some kind, something Mrs. Clubb thought I'd know.

I'd first asked Mrs. Clubb about this witness a year ago. Why was this message so urgent? What had changed?

Matters intersect now ... "Something's happened."

Jonathan nodded sagely. "Mrs. Clubb is not known for her urgent messages."

The maid set a tray down holding two silvery gray wooden cups and a matching teapot. She began to pour.

The aroma of the tea ... I glanced up at her. "This is mint!"

She put the teapot down and curtsied low. Her voice shook. "Yes, mum. Would you prefer some other?"

"No, this is good. Thank you."

She poured our tea and hurried below.

Of course. The code. It was right there in front of me.

Matters intersect now, today. M-I-N-T.

Something about mint ... what was it ...

The whole world became silent.

"Jacqui?" Jon was staring at me. "Are you well?"

"**Morton's** the witness?"

Morton ran up panting, eyes wide. "I saw her. The woman I told you about. She just shot at me!"

It came to me. "I know why it's urgent. Morton's in trouble."

Jonathan appeared perplexed. "Who's Morton?"

I laughed, then lowered my voice so none but he might hear. "You know him as Master Blaze Rainbow."

"How do you know Master Rainbow's in trouble?"

Morton and Gardena said that Morton was friend to Julius Diamond, her father. Jon's father. I leaned over to speak in his ear. "He loves mint tea. It's his favorite."

Jon gaped at me for a long moment, then his face changed. "Ah." He pondered for a moment. "And only you know this?"

I shrugged. "And a few others in Spadros Manor. He stayed with us for several weeks last spring." Who was there when he said it? Myself, Mary, Amelia, and Tony.

For Mrs. Clubb to know this, Morton must have stayed with the Clubbs for a while as a guest. And told her he'd told me of it.

He'd led me to believe he was a hired man. Or had **he** sent the message in her name?

Jon nodded. "He did say he stayed with you. He'd been injured."

Indeed he had been, quite badly, when someone exploded his yacht as he slept in it. "He said the Feds tried to kill him. I don't know if I believe that, but —"

"Someone tried, most certainly. Do you recall the night we came to you at the zeppelin station? Someone tried to kill him earlier that day. In Diamond quadrant! We were in the park: my parents, my brothers, Gardena, Roland. We had guards around us. Someone drove by and shot at Master Rainbow. If he hadn't dropped his fork and bent to retrieve it, he would have been killed. My father was mortified for a guest to be put into such danger." Jon paused for a moment, head down, and I felt more had happened than what he told me. "My brothers and their men chased the carriage, but —" He shook his head. "The whole thing was dreadful."

"I imagine."

"But Jacqui, why send this to **you**? Surely he could call on my father, or Tony. Or Mr. Charles Hart. Or even the Clubbs."

That was odd, to be sure. "Suppose he doesn't want anyone to know the nature of the trouble?" What had he said in Clubb Hotel the night I left Tony? *I've done work for them all at one time or another.* "If he happened to be with Mrs. Clubb and asked her to send the message, she might not have known what it meant."

"Are you certain it's from him?"

Was I certain? I recalled Morton doing a crossword puzzle, of all things, as our train raced to rescue hundreds of people from death. "He does love a puzzle. And he knows I do as well." Then something occurred to me: what if the Clubbs — or one of the other Families — were part of the danger? "And he knows I'm free to help. Or he must believe I am."

"But what could you do?"

I smiled, putting my hand on his. "I could discuss it with you. And I could call in those I felt trustworthy, without any of the Families becoming involved."

Jon's eyes widened. "Master Rainbow places a great deal of trust in you."

Or he was desperate, with nowhere else to turn.

The Reunion

A few nights later, me, Blitz and my friend Vig Vikenti gathered in my large upstairs room.

Vig was a former bouncer who owned the Pocket Pair saloon down on 19th and Broadway. Before Vig's piano was destroyed along with most of the rest of his saloon by Roy's men, Blitz used to be Vig's piano-man.

It had been a while since I'd seen Vig for more than a few minutes, and I missed talking with him.

Looking back, I'd have to say that Vig was my Sawbuck: as devoted to me as Ten was to Tony. Vig refused to work for the Family, though, and I can't say that I blamed him.

The windows were covered with bedspreads. A lantern sat on the floor, turned low. I sat hooded and cloaked at the edge of its light. Blitz and Vig stood in shadow.

Clover had been invited to join us. He sat facing me, his hands tied behind him, a black cloth sack over his head.

Clover was gangly and nineteen. Since our last meeting, his light reddish beard had grown in. He dressed better now, and he had a new eye-patch. When Blitz pulled the black cloth sack off of his head, Clover blinked his good eye at me. "What do you want now?"

I peered at him through the thin material of the cloak. "A meeting with Morton. Tell him I received his message and wish to take tea with him. I'll make sure to have his favorite."

"Why do you think I know where he is?"

"Because you saved him once already. Perhaps you've helped him again."

I sat in silence.

"All right, yeah, miss, I seen him. I got him hid for now. Where and when?"

I glanced at Vig, who nodded.

I didn't want to risk Roy Spadros destroying Vig's saloon again. But Blitz insisted it was the one place we could keep this quiet. The many exits could be useful if the rogue Spadros men — or whoever else was after Morton — should try to ambush us. "The place he was shot at in the street. The same time. Tomorrow."

"Okay," Clover said.

"The other boy in your trey. Besides Stephen. Is he well?"

"Don't know, miss. He's run off."

Run off? I hoped the boy was still alive. "If you see him, tell him to be careful."

"Can you not tie me next time? The ropes hurt my hands."

"Very well," I said. "Thank you for your help."

Blitz came up behind Clover and put the sack over Clover's head. Vig hoisted Clover onto one shoulder and carried him down the stairs, off to his waiting horse-truck.

* * *

The next day after tea, Mary let me out of the side door. I wore my widow's outfit I only used on cases, without a corset, and padded to make myself look wider, fatter. I grasped my cane, and wore old stockings sporting a worn hole or two. My hair was floured, I was veiled, and I used a trick from Dame Anastasia's stage makeup book to look like a very old woman.

I went down the narrow alley, away from my front door. When I got to the street, I slowed my pace, bent over a little, gave myself a limp. I was old, tired.

It took me a half hour of wandering this way and that before I felt sure I wasn't being followed. During this time, I stopped in a few markets, letting my hand tremble as I handed a penny over. None of the places remarked on my appearance, or treated me as anything but an old woman.

People did treat you differently when you were thought to be an old widow. Instead of the great deal of attention I garnered in my usual garb, men barely gave me a glance. Instead of curtsies and jealous awestruck glances, women treated me with great gentleness and care. As if I were fragile, possibly ill, or perhaps a bit crazed.

By the time I reached a taxi-stand, I felt certain that I wasn't being followed, and that my outfit withstood scrutiny in daylight.

I didn't know where the danger to Morton came from. If he truly was in trouble, I wanted nothing I did to lead his enemies to him.

The taxi-driver got down from his perch to help me inside, and I leaned heavily upon him as an old woman might. "The florist on 18th by Broadway, if you please, sir," I croaked.

"Right away," the driver said. "Will you need me to wait?"

"Oh, no, no," I said. "My daughter lives right near by, today's her birthday! It'll be so good to see my grandchildren again. You know, I have six now, and —"

"Very good," the driver said, closing the door in my face.

The driver came round to help me out. I waved good-bye to him as he drove off. "Lovely man," I said to no one in particular. The others around me smiled to themselves, glancing away. I bought a small bouquet for a penny, putting it into my sack with the rest. Then I limped up a side alley and around the corner to the back of Vig's saloon.

I rounded the corner onto Broadway and stopped, hand on the wall. I suppose it might have looked as if I were tired, but in truth I watched the way the lamp shone on Marja's dying body. The blood was gone, but I saw it there even still.

I limped to Vig's side door and triple-knocked, then rattled it, stopped, and rattled it again. Then I gave two thuds with my fist.

Natalia peered out. She was a bit shorter than me, with dark hair and eyes. "Who am I?"

"Natalia of the Romani."

"Would you care for tea?"

"Only if you have mint."

"Good." She looked me up and down. "You look good." She opened the door; I came up the few steps and inside. She shut the door behind me and locked it. "I didn't recognize you!"

I smiled, taking her hands. "How are you?"

"Well enough," she said. "He's already here."

I stopped limping and followed her down the hall to the room we'd all hidden in during the raid after Marja's death. As before, Morton sat there.

Morton's eyes widened, then he rose to greet me. He looked his usual self: in his middle thirties, light brown hair, nattily dressed, all in brown. He wasn't much taller than me, and I wouldn't have called the man handsome even before the scars from the injuries he'd gotten along the way. "You look terrible, Mrs. Spadros. In a good way. I only recognized you by your eyes."

We sat. "Tell me everything," I said. "What's happened?"

His teeth were his best attribute: he had a beautiful smile. "Everything would take all day."

Morton fled Spadros Manor right before our appearance at the inquest, leaving only a note. But he'd gone in search of his informants. They were all dead but one: a former police detective — now Spadros enforcer — named Albert Sheinwold.

"But now he's disappeared," Morton said. "Which is bad, Mrs. Spadros. He claims Zia killed them all. And I've checked his story — Zia's killed a dozen men that I know of already. Before he got dismissed from the force — which he swears was a frame-up — Zia tried to kill him too. I fear she's succeeded."

This seemed like sloppy work. "How did she know about your informants?"

He glanced away. "We worked together. We shared the list. Most of them I got from her." When our eyes met, his gaze held real distress. "I had no idea she would murder them."

"Sheinwold. The Spadros Family can't find him either?"

Morton shook his head. "Nor his friends, nor his family. Worst yet, no one knows whether this is a hit on the Spadros Family until they find him. Or at least his body. They don't know how to react."

"And people still try to kill you."

He chuckled. "Indeed. You see," he tapped his temple, "I know their faces. Frank Pagliacci, that so-called detective with him, the woman Birdie — or whatever her name is."

I nodded. The one they'd been calling Black Maria.

"Everyone else who does is dead, assuming the worst. But I have enough friends in this town that so far I've been able to keep ahead of them."

"Can you tell me anything about these people? Anything at all."

Morton pondered this. "Frank Pagliacci was young, not much older than you. Tall, brown hair, reasonably good looking. But the best liar I've ever seen." He shook his head. "I don't understand it: the women — and many of the men — fawned over him. Every time I saw him, he had a different woman on his arm. The detective — for the life of me, I can't recall his name — he was dark, like your young friend Master Diamond. Come to think of it, he reminds me of him. Older, though — I'd say forty. And I told you about the woman in my letter."

I nodded.

"Sheinwold is tall, a year or so older than me. Tanned, with graying hair and pale blue eyes."

None of this was particularly helpful. And in my eagerness to disguise myself, I'd forgotten to bring Maria Athena Spade's portrait. "Were you by any chance at the Grand Ball last year?" I hoped that Morton had seen Frank Pagliacci there.

Tony had asked Sawbuck to go over the guest list from the Ball almost a year ago. Did he? What had he learned?

Morton laughed. "Me, invited to that? Hardly. I may be from a good family, Mrs. Spadros, but as far as the Four Families are concerned, I'm little more than a lackey." The thought seemed to dishearten him.

"A pity. It was a good party." I leaned forward. "You called for me. How can I help?"

"I have to find Sheinwold. He's the only other witness to what she's doing! The Feds still think I killed her — I need his testimony to clear my name. You've said you're good at finding people. Can you help?"

I leaned back, crossed my arms. "That depends. You never paid me for helping you the last time."

Morton's face twisted in disbelief. "You can't be serious."

When he helped me, I wanted to find David Bryce as much — if not more — than Morton did. But pay was pay — if he did get anything from his employer and I didn't get it from him now, I likely never would. "You promised me a forty percent share of what your employer paid for finding the boy. That was our agreement. If you want me to even think about helping you again, you pay me that first."

His shoulders slumped. "Oh, very well." He reached into his pocket, counting out four dollars into my hand. "There. Now what will it take for you to help me?"

I gave him the same rate as I did Mrs. Spade, and he handed over another seven. "That's about all I've got left," he said. "But if you can find him, it'll be worth it."

"Just so you know, I always find them. But sometimes I find them dead."

He grimaced. "If Albert Sheinwold is dead, I'm in a lot of trouble. The Feds don't know me. They don't believe I didn't kill her. They don't believe she's gone rogue. Even if I can produce Sheinwold, and he's willing to talk to them, I'm not sure they'll believe me. Without him, I may not have a chance."

"I'm looking for Birdie too," I said. "Mrs. Clubb claims you saw her shoot Marja."

Morton's eyes went wide. "You knew the woman she shot?"

Melancholy swept over me. I'd gone to meet Marja to learn who meant to kill my Ma. "She helped raise me."

"I'm sorry, Mrs. Spadros. I had no idea."

Marja died in my arms that night, but as far as I knew, Ma was still alive. I hoped she was well.

"Don't trust the Clubbs," Morton said. "They may put on a good show, but there are some of them who are not, let's say, out for the good of the city."

"What do you mean?"

"Your young friend Miss Gardena and Master Lance. Not all in the Clubb Family are in agreement with this alliance, especially when it could mean putting a bastard boy over their own children."

I gasped. "How do you know about this?"

"I listen, Mrs. Spadros. I watch what people say, and how they say it. How they react. It's one of the ways you survive in a place like this."

I felt stunned by the implications. If Morton knew about Roland, others did as well. From that it wasn't far to learning who his father was. Worse yet, if there were dissension in the Clubb Family, what was Gardena walking into? She had to be warned. "Do you think they might harm the boy?"

"I have no idea, Mrs. Spadros." He glanced away. "I have no children, but I've seen how strongly people react to theirs being slighted. And these husbands of the Clubb daughters — some are near sixty without chance of ever moving up in the Family. They feel more than ready to take command. They mutter, asking when Alexander Clubb will die. They knew it was coming, but now that it's here, they don't like young Master Lance being named Clubb Heir one bit."

This was bad.

I promised not to hinder Gardena and Lance's courtship, but the trial was over. I would not let Gardena and her son — Tony's son — walk into a trap.

The Trip

Natalia agreed to smuggle Morton out through the tunnel under the street we'd gone out the last time. I left the way I'd come in, at the last minute remembering to limp as I walked down the steps.

Twilight had fallen, and the streetlights were being lit as I went to the taxi-stand across the way.

As I returned home, I thought how strange things had gotten. Spadros men in open defiance of their Patriarch. Mrs. Hart leaving the racetrack the Hart Family had owned for over a century, after openly defying her Patriarch. The split between Cesare Diamond and his Patriarch over the handshake on the courthouse steps. The *Golden Bridges'* sudden attacks on the Four Families. And now, what sounded like a civil war brewing in Clubb quadrant.

I got home in time to wash, change, and have dinner. But the questions still lingered. And I had much to do.

I needed to talk with Gardena about this in person. Should I ask Gardena to go on an outing? Somewhere public, but not so open as to put her in danger. Or cause further controversy.

The Spadros Ladies' Club was no longer an option after the time Roy Spadros barged in there. They'd had a great debate about allowing armed men to guard their ladies, and had settled on armed maids. Yet still few of the uppers would visit there, and there were rumors the Club might be forced to close.

Tony and I had stayed at the Rim for our first anniversary. The hotel was quiet, refined, and few stayed there this time of year.

I needed a trip. And it had an excellent restaurant.

I made a note to myself to have Jonathan extend her an invitation the next time he came to visit. He'd been writing, most discreetly, every day.

Perhaps it would be best to write to Gardena directly. So I did so, putting the letter aside for Blitz to post the next day.

And then I realized something: Morton wasn't the only one who could identify Black Maria.

If Black Maria had visited Madame Biltcliffe's shop last Yuletide before the break-in, then Madame could identify her too.

* * *

The next morning, I wrote asking for the plain Spadros carriage so I might visit Madame Biltcliffe. An hour after tea-time, the bell rang. Blitz came in looking surprised. "You asked for a carriage?"

"I did! But no one ever replied."

Blitz just stood there.

"Have Honor wait for me in the parlor," I said, thinking he might have some news. "And call Amelia —"

"I'm right here." She pushed past Blitz. "Out — the Lady needs changing." Once the door shut behind him, she said, "Are you getting a new dress, then?"

After she put one of my charcoal walking dresses on me, I shook my head. Tony dismissed Madame Biltcliffe over a year ago for not informing him of my business. "I need to speak with her, though, and I don't know who might intercept messages."

"Very good, mum." Amelia began redoing my hair, which usually I hated. But today I needed to look presentable. And I made sure to put Maria Athena's portrait into my pocket this time.

My former day footman — now somewhat of a spy — Skip Honor simply bowed when I entered the parlor, then gestured to the door.

As we approached the carriage, he said quietly, "He's made a deal with the Acey-Deuceys. You'll have no more window rocks."

"Oh." I felt impressed. The Acey-Deuceys were the most violent young men in the Spadros Family.

"Or if you do, they get to play with the thrower."

I chuckled. That in itself would be a deterrent.

Most of these young men were like Roy — causing pain and destruction was fun. If any of the Acey-Deuceys survived, most became enforcers, so it worked well for everyone. I went up the steps, drawing my dress inside. "Thank you."

"My pleasure, mum."

* * *

There were two ways one might travel to an address in mid-Clubb quadrant from where I sat, none of them speedy. One might travel over the "city" bridge, which crossed the river at 6th Street, or over the "betters' bridge" at 190th. And of course, there were various ways to get to each bridge.

The driver chose to go directly to Promenade then down to the 6th Street bridge. I liked going to Clubb quadrant, but it was a slow trip: we crept along in traffic. But police — and more importantly, Family — presence was greatest on Promenade.

The carriage stopped in front of the shop. Much like her shop in Spadros quadrant, Madame Biltcliffe's had an oak exterior with large glass windows showing her wares. The door, as it often did, had the sign turned to "Closed — entry by appointment only".

It was early still, not even seven. And although the shop looked empty, the lights were on. I didn't have an appointment, but I knocked all the same.

I got no answer, and I had a strange feeling. So I tried the knob — and it opened.

I turned to Honor. "Something's wrong. She doesn't leave her door unlocked."

Honor drew his revolver, and we entered the shop. "Madame," I called. "Are you here?"

A gasping noise, off to the left. "Madame?" I began to feel alarmed. "Marie?"

Madame Marie Blitcliffe lay on the floor of her office, slumped against her desk, gasping for air. Blood lay on her dress, on the floor around her.

Terrified, I said, "Honor, get the doctor!"

He didn't move. "We can't. They can't find you here."

"Get the doctor, now!" I knelt beside her and took her hand. "Oh, Madame. What have they done to you?"

141

"It was her," she gasped. "The young woman."

A shock went through me. "Oh, no." The woman at her shop before the break-in? The one we thought was Black Maria?

Madame Blitcliffe looked down at the blood on her dress, her face puzzled. "She shot me!"

Her forehead was cold, her lips pale. Frantic, angry, I said, "Honor, why haven't you gone? We have to do something!" I turned to her. "Oh, please, Madame, don't die."

Madame Biltcliffe raised a blood-streaked hand to my face, recognition dawning in hers, as if just now realizing it was me who knelt beside her. Tears lay in her eyes. "Oh, ma cherie. I'm so glad you're here."

Honor whispered, "We have to leave! If they find you here, the trial you just had will be nothing in comparison."

Madame's eyes were closed, her body limp. I don't know if she was breathing, but there was so much blood.

Honor grabbed my arm, hauling me to my feet.

As he dragged me from the shop, a bullet whizzed past from our right. Maria Athena Spade stared at me in terror from behind a tree, a gun in her hand, as several men pulled her away.

"Wait!" I lunged towards her. "I'm here to help you! Your mother sent me!"

Honor pulled me back. "We have to go!"

People cried out, running towards us. Police-wagon bells came from the direction of the Promenade.

"Get in!" Honor half pushed, half lifted me inside, then jumped on the runner-board as the driver started off. We took a different route, barreling along the streets without stopping once.

I wept the whole way home.

*Oh, Madame, Madame ... how could you be **dead**?*

* * *

Blitz opened the front door as we climbed from the carriage. "You were gone so long — good gods, you're covered in blood!"

I ran up the steps to him. "It was the Red Dog Gang," I sobbed. "They've murdered Madame."

I glanced back. Honor nodded, eyes wide in the lamplight.

"Get inside," Blitz said, so we went in. He took hold of my shoulders. "What happened?"

"Her door was unlocked. She was shot in her office. She said it was the young woman, the one who came before the break in. The one we thought was her. There was s-so much b-blood ..."

"Someone shot at us outside the shop," Honor said. "A woman. Several men were with —"

"It was her," I said. "Maria Athena Spade. It was her."

The Guests

Mary stood nearby, hands to her mouth. Blitz took a step back. "She **shot** at you?"

I'll never forget Maria Athena's face, half lit in darkness.

She looked terrified.

She shot at **me**!

I'd done nothing to her! Why was she so afraid?

"Let's get you out of these clothes," Mary said.

Someone rapped on the front door.

"Come on," Mary whispered. She pulled on my arm. "It could be the police."

I let her pull me along into my room — which fortunately had the curtains shut — then I looked down. My charcoal walking dress was smeared with Madame's darkening blood.

Mary closed my door at the same moment Blitz opened the front door. "Okay," Blitz said to whoever it was. Then his voice turned inside the house. "They want you back at the Manor."

"Will she be well?" Honor sounded concerned.

"We'll take care of her," Blitz said.

But who would take care of Madame? She had no one. I looked over my shoulder at Mary, who was undoing my buttons. "I want her taken care of."

"Mum, you can't be involved with this at all. If someone comes looking for donations, then by all means give. But if they even **think** you killed her —"

I felt aghast. "That I killed her?"

"Did anyone see you come out of there covered in her blood?"

I stared at her. "I don't know."

Mary let out a breath. "Thank the gods you went in the plain carriage. We might be able to claim you were here the whole time."

My legs felt weak; I leaned on a chair for support. "They're trying to frame me for this, too."

"It's likely, mum."

"But why? I don't even know who these people are. I've never seen this woman in my life. Her mother sent me to help her!"

"Come on, mum," Mary said. She turned me gently towards her. "Let's get you out of this dress. Then we can decide what to do."

How could Madame be dead?

Mary wiped down my face and hands, and got a house dress on me. As she put my house shoes on my feet, she said, "There's a group of girls to see you. They arrived just before you did."

I blinked, confused. "Girls?"

"Well, one's older than that — a maid, I think. She helped before the auction? She said her name was Tenni."

"Tenni? Why is she here?"

"I don't know, mum. They came to the door out of breath like they ran. And they won't say what they want. Something's frightened them badly."

Tenni was nineteen. She used to be Madame's shop maid before Madame moved to Clubb quadrant — as well as my double when I needed to go out on a case. She looked like me from behind: the same reddish-brown curls, the same light brown skin. We used to be the same height.

She'd grown now, so pretending to be me from afar was no longer an option, but —

Horrified, I stared at Mary.

Mary stared back, her face concerned. "What's happened?"

"I think I know why they're here."

* * *

Tenni and her five sisters huddled together on my parlor sofa, their faces streaked with tears. Tenni stood when I came in.

I said, "What's wrong?"

Tenni's hair lay loose around her shoulders. She wore a house dress with a shawl, and her boots were untied. "Men came to the house. They —

The other five ranged from fifteen to eight. They burst into tears, all speaking at once:

"They banged on the door!"

"They had guns!"

"They shot our windows!"

"They tried to break in!"

Tenni's eyes reddened. "I didn't know where else to turn." Then her face turned suddenly alarmed. "Did I do wrongly?"

I put my arm around her thin shoulders. "You did well. Have you eaten?"

All six shook their heads.

"Mary," I called out. "We have guests for dinner."

* * *

I sent Blitz to a messenger stand to hand out anonymous messages to the girls' employers. They couldn't go to work until we had some idea whether they'd be safe there.

After dinner, I sent the younger ones to the back room next to my study. I took Tenni to the parlor, and told her about Madame.

Tenni leaned upon the sofa's arm, head on her arms, sobbing.

I'd cried so much already that I felt numb. I saw Madame die in front of me. But it didn't seem that she could possibly be dead.

I'd known her for almost six years. Madame Biltcliffe had made my engagement dress. She'd made my wedding dress. Most of the clothes I'd had in Bridges were made by her. Stunning works of art.

She'd been one of the first to help me get cases. Her becoming the person to screen those wishing my help meant I could reach other owners, merchants, women of class and worth.

I owed everything to her.

She loved me, not as a daughter, but as a woman.

She loved me.

And because of me, she was dead.

Tenni's sobs slowed, quieted. And I showed her Maria Athena Spade's portrait. "Have you seen this woman before?"

Tenni held it nearer the lamp. Then she handed it back to me. "No, mum, never."

Tenni could have been running an errand for Madame Biltcliffe at the time the young black-haired woman came to the shop. As Madame's shop maid, Tenni had seen many thousands of women coming and going over the years. She might just not remember her.

Or Maria Athena might never have been in the shop at all.

But why was Maria Athena in Clubb quadrant? Why was she outside Madame's shop? Why did she shoot at me? And why were men terrorizing these girls? "How did you escape?"

"There's a passage I'm not sure the landlord even knows about," Tenni said. "It's in the basement. It comes out in a boarded-up shop on 25th. The door opens onto the alley and you can lock it. We leave and enter that way when men are about."

I glimpsed what life must be like for these orphaned girls. Forced to walk the streets alone to jobs paying them a pittance, never safe from kidnapping or worse. It amazed me that they'd survived so far. "Don't you worry. I'll take care of everything."

* * *

Having sold all the extra furniture, it took a while to get places for six girls to sleep.

The back wall — the one joining the two sides of the duplex — had framed pictures upon it, with a large, heavy dresser below. The bed was big enough to fit three. So I pushed it to the other wall, then put heavy bedding under the window with light coverlets atop. That would do until we could buy a second bed.

Late the next morning, the police arrived. I'd told the girls to stay in the back room and keep the curtains shut until we felt sure they hadn't been followed.

Blitz put the officer in the parlor.

"Detective Constable Leone Briscola, mum." He showed me a well-worn brass shield clipped to the inside of his jacket. "Might I have a word?"

"Of course." I sat, gestured to the sofa. "Would you care to sit?"

Detective Briscola was not yet twenty, with dark hair and eyes. He had an attractive face, yet his navy suit was old and too large for him. He stood to my right across our new coffee table, beside the sofa. "No, thank you, mum." He stared straight ahead. "I regret to inform you that your former dressmaker, Madame Marie Biltcliffe, has died." He peered at me. "Her notes indicated you should be contacted in case of emergency."

Me? I felt astonished. But I had enough presence of mind to answer the question he must have if anyone thought they'd seen me there the previous night. "She's dead?"

He relaxed just a bit. "Yes. We're regarding it as suspicious."

I let my gaze fall. "So you think someone killed her?"

"That's possible. Do you know anyone who'd want to hurt her?"

I shook my head. I knew exactly who killed Madame. But this man surely wouldn't believe me. Besides, Tony had declared anything to do with the Ten of Spades or the Red Dog Gang a Family matter. Which meant I couldn't speak to the police about it even if I wanted to. "I thought she lived in Clubb quadrant. Is that where you're from?"

Detective Briscola let out a small snort of amusement. "Apparently Clubb police aren't allowed in Spadros quadrant."

He took a notepad and pencil from his pocket. "I realize she was your dressmaker. Yet I'm learning that Madame Biltcliffe had a certain —" he hesitated. "Um, reputation."

I nodded. From her own words, she'd had many liaisons since moving to Bridges, none of them with men.

"So I feel curious as to —"

This amused me. "Our relationship?"

"Well, yes, if you put it that way."

We were in the room, yet it felt empty. "I looked to her as a mother. You may not know, but I've not been with my mother for many years. I lost her last March in the zeppelin explosion."

"I'm very sorry to hear that."

I did love you, Madame, if not as you wished. "So I'm grieved at Madame Biltcliffe's passing, more so if someone has hurt her." My eyes stung, remembering the wound she'd taken. The blood.

Detective Briscola nodded. "This explains her wishing you to be contacted, then," he said to himself. "Rather than her husband."

I blinked, taken aback. "Her husband?"

This seemed to confuse him. "Yes, mum. Did you not know? He followed her here, many years ago."

"I — I knew she'd been married, but —"

"But what?"

I shook my head, puzzled. "She believed he thought her dead."

The detective's eyes widened, his head tilting a bit to one side. "Now that **is** interesting."

"Do you think perhaps he did it?"

Detective Briscola let out a short laugh. But then he sobered. "We're looking into all possibilities, mum."

"I don't understand. What could possibly be funny about this?"

He seemed abashed. "Forgive me, mum." For a moment, he stood silent, head down. Then he straightened. "So you didn't know her husband is your — Spadros Manor's —"

I peered at him. "What?"

"Mum, her husband is Monsieur Tongo Sabacc. The chef for Spadros Manor."

The Arrangements

I gaped at Detective Briscola, stunned. Monsieur — a giant bear of a man who terrorized most of the kitchen staff — was Madame's **husband**? She'd described him as "stodgy" and I'd pictured a small, meek, timid sort, not this. "I'm astonished. I had no idea."

"Well, I go next to speak with him. Hopefully he can shed some light on matters."

After he left, I sat pondering all this. Did Madame Biltcliffe know that her husband was in Bridges? Did that influence her decision to leave Spadros quadrant? Had she feared him?

Monsieur was big, loud, and petulant. But I couldn't see him killing anyone.

* * *

Once the police detective left, Mr. Eight Howell came to call. When I told him of the six girls in my back room and how they got there, he shook his head. "The men running that street should have had patrols out to come to their aid."

Mr. Howell wanted to speak with Tenni, and she came out with some hesitation. After giving the address — on 26th Street — she said, "They broke the door, sir, and frightened my sisters badly. I'm not taking them back there."

"But where will you go?"

Tenni turned to me. "We'd like to stay here, if we might."

I blinked, confused. "But you'll have a higher Family fee, and rent, and your room is so small."

Tenni laughed. "It's bigger than what we had, mum, and we don't have to go down the hall to the bath. Plus there's board. We always had to eat at the street vendors. And it's closer to work for all of us." Her face turned determined. "We all talked about it last night. We have the chance to move up seven streets! It's more than we could have ever hoped for." A hint of desperation entered her voice. "Please, mum. We'll be neat, and quiet. You won't know we're here. We're willing to pay whatever you ask."

I glanced at Mr. Howell, but his face showed nothing. I said to Tenni, "Very well, then. Will you need help fetching your things?"

She nodded.

"I'll let you know when we're ready to go over there."

After she returned to her sisters, Mr. Howell asked, "Why were these men after them?"

"That's the thing," I said quietly. "I don't believe they're safe here, nor even at their jobs."

I told him in very general terms of the Red Dog Gang and how they seemed to be killing off anyone who might identify them. "I hadn't considered it until now, but they might think Tenni can identify one of them. A friend was just murdered last night for the same thing."

Mr. Howell stood quietly for a moment. "We're aware of this Red Dog Gang. Stay here. I'm going to make some arrangements."

I nodded. If I understood how this worked, he'd speak to the man he reported to, who'd probably bring it to the Button Man for the area. Who'd likely kick it up to Sawbuck. "Thank you."

After he left, I thought about Tenni walking from her secret exit on 25th all the way to 42nd every day, just grateful for the chance to make a better life.

* * *

Sawbuck arrived later that day. With him were a horse-truck and three men, who brought in several boxes full of the girls' things. I followed them into the girls' room.

"Make sure nothing's missing," I told Tenni. "We don't know what they were looking for, but if something is gone, that may help us understand why they did this."

151

That set the six girls heartily to work, and after the men returned to the truck I pulled Sawbuck into the kitchen. "We need to talk."

"Indeed we do. The Clubbs haven't figured out that you were there, but they suspect something."

"Black Maria shot Madame, Madame said so. And they've got Maria Athena so upset that she shot at me." I'd thought about it for a while, and that was the only conclusion I might reach. "I believe she thinks I mean her harm!"

That set Sawbuck into some thought. "If she's working for them, this plan of yours becomes even more dangerous. You must wait."

I shook my head. "I can't wait, Ten. Her mother is depending on me to find her, get her free of these people."

"How will you do that when she's shooting at you?"

"If I can just talk to her ..."

Ten threw his hands up in the air and stalked away. "All I want is for Mr. Anthony to be safe! You're going to be the death of us all, if you don't throw the entire city into turmoil."

I snorted. He obviously thought more highly of my importance than warranted. "Whatever happened to your looking over the guest list from the Grand Ball? It's been well over a year now."

Sawbuck looked surprised. "I gave that to Mr. Anthony the very next week. Did he not tell you?"

I shook my head. "What did you determine?"

Sawbuck glanced away. "A man with brown hair and a dark suit? The room was filled with them."

"A very good-looking man."

"Yes, well, that all depends on your tastes, I suppose, and I don't know what sort of fellow Crab fancied. Well, perhaps I do: Bull and Duck come to mind."

I recalled the large, foul-mouthed, drunken man at the Grand Ball and the painfully thin, frightened one kneeling bound in Tony's study. Two men who couldn't have looked more different. "Did you ask if anyone had seen such a man speaking with Crab and Duck? That might narrow the list."

"Several hundred men and women were there, Mrs. Spadros. Most from other Families who wouldn't take kindly to their people being questioned. But before I gave the list to Mr. Anthony, I spoke with those I could. Six men were mentioned by name."

"And."

He got a stubborn, defiant look upon his face. "The one most frequently mentioned was Joseph Kerr."

"That's ridiculous. I'm sure —"

Sawbuck took hold of the chair beside him with one huge hand, gripping it so hard that I heard the back of it crack. "What will it take for you to see reason? The man is a Kerr —"

"Which is no fault of his —"

"And a vicious scoundrel to boot —"

"You don't know that —"

He growled, taking a step forward; the rage in his eyes made me take a step back. "I do know that. He's destroyed the only person I've ever loved. And when I find Joseph Kerr, I'll kill him." His voice lowered to a whisper. "It's only because of Mr. Anthony that you're alive right now. But one day you'll be the death of him. I just know it." He reached up, moved my hair over to rest his hand on the side of my neck, but gently, trembling, like a lover's caress. Or like a man restraining himself from doing what he most wished to. "And on that day," he stroked the back of my head, "I'll have this pretty neck in my hand, and not you or anyone else will stop me."

I jerked away, appalled. "Are **you** the one killing those boys?"

Sawbuck gave me a puzzled look, the anger draining from him. Then he let out a short, disgusted laugh, shaking his head as he let his hand drop to his side. "Good night, Mrs. Spadros. You obviously need your rest."

I stared after him, heart pounding in fear.

Blitz came into the kitchen just as Sawbuck closed the front door and rushed over to me. "How could you speak to him like that? We need him on our side."

Normally, I would have said I wasn't afraid of Master Ten Hogan. But that was no longer true.

I went into the hall. Tenni's littlest sister stood there outside her door, face pale, eyes wide.

"Hello," I said.

She curtsied. "Hello."

I went to her. "What's your name, sweetie?"

"Emma."

"Is all well, Emma?"

She hesitated, then nodded.

The girl had gloves on. "Tenni told me you braid twine for the Bridges Daily."

"Yes, mum, I do." She glanced away. "I best get back to work." She rushed into her room and shut the door.

That was odd, I thought.

Speaking of the danger I was in, the danger everyone around me was in, made me realize: I had to see Gardena at once. This had gone on long enough.

* * *

After some messages back and forth, Gardena Diamond agreed to meet me at first light at a small park in the Business District of Spadros quadrant. Which surprised me, given the history between Gardena and the Spadros Family.

Her arrival in what appeared to be a taxi-carriage — without outriders — surprised me even more. The driver was the same dark-skinned, white-haired old man who'd helped us twice prior. When he saw me, he smiled, pushing his goggles up, and he tipped his hat.

Jonathan Diamond got out first, revolver in hand, and surveyed the area before gesturing to Gardena to exit. They had no footman with them, so he helped his sister from the carriage.

"Come," I said. We hurried to a small grove of trees, which hid us from the street on three sides. Blitz stood watch near the fourth, tipping his cap when Jon and Gardena appeared.

Once we drew into the grove, I turned to them. "Jon, what's going on?"

Jon holstered his weapon, watching everything but me. "Let's say matters are unsettled. And neither my father nor brothers have approved this meeting." He glanced at Gardena, then at me. "So what is this urgent message?"

I said to Gardena, "I hoped to spend the day together."

Her face fell. "I hoped so too."

There was no way to tell this without causing pain. "I had a disturbing discussion with Master Rainbow. He believes you and Roland are walking into a trap."

Gardena gaped at me. "How does he know about Roland?"

I took hold of her hands. "The plans for your betrothal to Lance has caused controversy within the Clubb Family. The husbands of Alexander and Regina Clubb's daughters wish to move up in the Business." I glanced aside. "More to the point: they wish Mr. Alexander dead. They want to rule Clubb quadrant, and Lance is in the way. They know about Roland — I suppose from Lance, or even Mr. Clubb himself — and don't want Roland someday placed above their true-born sons."

Gardena's head drooped. "And if they're speaking of it in front of a hired man, more know even still."

"Master Rainbow is discreet," I said, "but yes, others may not be. I fear you're both in danger."

This time, Jon didn't make a joke of it.

Gardena looked horrified.

"I have no ill will against the Clubbs," I said, "not anymore. But I won't have you or Tony's son put into harm's way."

"And Lance!" Gardena seemed ready to cry. "His own brothers-in-law plot against him, men who watched him grow from a boy? This is monstrous!"

It was. Yet from what I'd seen so far in the Spadros Family, not entirely surprising. "So you wish to marry Lance? Do you have feelings for him?"

She shrugged, glanced away. "I want to be settled. I want my son to have a future. I want another child." She blushed, smiling to herself. "Many, if the gods will it."

Oh, Dena ... "Don't make a rash decision."

She gave me a fond smile. "I have learned something from my life, foolish as I may appear."

"Well," I said, not really knowing how to answer that. "I'll let you decide what to do with this. But I thought you should know."

Jon seemed ready to go. "Thank you, Jacqui."

I put a hand on his arm. "My husband won't let Jack into the quadrant. But visit Roman Jewelers on 42nd Street, Spadros quadrant and tell Mr. Roman I sent you. Hopefully he can confirm that Jack wasn't the one who tried to blackmail him."

Realization dawned in his face. "Because I look like him."

"Exactly."

He put his hand on my arm. "You could have said nothing. This means a great deal to me, Jacqui. Thank you."

I felt suddenly humbled. What a life Jon must have had, sharing his face with a madman, ever suspect for Jack's crimes. But I shrugged as if it were nothing. "I hope you find it helpful."

The sky had begun to lighten; the sound of traffic moved around our grove. "We must go," Gardena said. "Our servants mustn't find us missing."

We hurried to their carriage. Before they got in, I took their hands. "Be safe."

Jonathan grinned. "We'll do our best."

As we watched them go, Blitz said, "So Master Rainbow is still with us."

I nodded slowly. "So far."

We walked back to our carriage, which sat on the other side of the park. A Spadros outrider had joined us; the man stood by his horse speaking with the driver. Honor had been sitting on the steps yawning, but snapped to his feet when he saw us.

Blitz stopped me perhaps ten feet from the carriage. "Your husband should know of this."

"Are you certain?"

"I am."

"So you listened at the door even then." Skip Honor and Tony's manservant Jacob Michaels had secretly pledged to my service the year prior. Or, it seemed, not so secretly.

Blitz grinned. "It's my job to know of your alliances." He waved Honor over. "Say this to Mr. Anthony: the Clubb sons-in-law wish no bastard rule."

Honor stared at us, uncomprehending. When he next spoke, he sounded offended. "I'm to play the messenger, then?"

I said, "You do us great service. This is much too important for a Memory Boy to hear."

* * *

Without explanation, the carriage let us out at the Backdoor Saloon. A couple of Spadros men stood out in front, tipping their caps to me and Blitz as we passed.

The sun hadn't crested the buildings. Yet even for this early in the day, the narrow street seemed less populated than usual.

A man wearing an overcoat a bit too heavy for the day stood a few paces from my door. But he stood almost touching the building, so Blitz and I had plenty of room to pass. When he tipped his cap, his eyes reminded me of Mr. Hart's.

Another man stood the same distance past my steps. I stopped to stare: if he hadn't been the same color as I was, I'd say he was Jonathan's father Julius Diamond. He nodded, tipping his hat.

When Blitz unlocked the door, Mary stood there. "You're back!" When she shut the door behind us, she said, "Mr. Charles Hart and Mrs. Rachel Diamond are here to see you."

The Offer

At that moment, I felt dumbstruck. *Rachel Diamond?*

Mary led me in to take my hat and touch up my hair. She took up the necklace Mr. Hart had given me. "Here, mum, wear this."

Before her marriage, Rachel Diamond had been an Inventor's Apprentice. Yet a terrible accident had left everyone thinking her mind had gone. I'd stumbled on the truth: her mind was whole, yet she hid this from even her children, for her own protection. This woman held the secrets of both the Inventors and the Diamond quadrant, in a body barely able to walk, much less defend herself.

How had her husband allowed her to come here, of all places? And with Mr. Hart, of all people?

Mary said, "Let's not bother with changing." She took a damp cloth and scrubbed a bit of mud from my hem. "You should see them at once."

I stood. "Very well." Heart pounding, I went into the parlor.

Mr. Charles Hart and Mrs. Rachel Diamond sat on my sofa. Neither of them rose, and I stood there, unsure what to say.

They both looked well. Mrs. Diamond was an attractive woman of eight and forty, sharing the dark, dark skin of her Family. Mr. Hart was portly and seventy-one, a pale man with silver in his red hair. Gardena's cousin Octavia, a woman of nineteen with grayish-blue eyes and golden curls, stood beside Mrs. Diamond.

"Close your mouth before something flies in," Mrs. Diamond said. Her voice was strong, yet slow, as if speaking took effort.

I felt alarmed. "My servants. My boarders —"

"Have been warned," Mr. Hart said. "A man is upstairs with them to ensure they listen beside no doors."

"Yet I fear for you both." How did Mrs. Diamond trust Mr. Hart with the knowledge she had faked the severity of her illness for so many years? That alone could mean her death if the wrong people learned of it. My hands shook at the danger this woman put herself in. My knees buckled, and I fell to them. "I beg you, leave here at once. Don't put yourself in such peril, dear Queen, not for me."

Mrs. Diamond smiled warmly. "Come sit, my Lady."

Mr. Hart rose then, helping me up.

I sat across from them, heart pounding, feeling close to tears. "Thank you for saving my mother."

Mrs. Diamond said, "It was my pleasure."

"But what is she to you? Why help us? We're just P- I mean, from the Pot. I don't understand —"

"Mrs. Spadros," Mr. Hart said. "We have little time."

"Yes, sir," I said with a sudden chagrin. "I'm sorry, sir."

He smiled. "I'm glad you enjoy my gift."

I touched the heavy pendant he'd given me during the trial.

"I'm here to warn you," he said. "These two ladies are here to help you listen."

A laugh burst from me. "Am I so unreasonable?"

"At times, my dear," Mr. Hart said. "And you must listen." He glanced at Mrs. Diamond. "Matters are becoming very dangerous."

"Dangerous? In what way?"

"All is yet unclear," Mrs. Diamond said. "But we don't want you here if the worst happens."

I blinked, confused. "What do you mean?"

Mr. Hart leaned forward. "Men have risen in rebellion against your Patriarch. You're being publicly slandered. You've been shot at. Bombs have detonated within a block of here. Rocks are thrown at your window. Your retainers are being hunted down and murdered one by one."

Madame. Tears blinded me, ran down my face.

"I'm sorry, my dear," Mrs. Diamond finally said. "But you can't stay here any longer."

"But why? This is my home!"

"Spadros Manor is your home," Mr. Hart said. "And if you won't return there, you have a place with me. Always."

So this was how he planned his seduction. "Mrs. Diamond, I'm surprised that you would countenance this. His wife has left him, yet he offers **me** his home?"

Mrs. Diamond and Mr. Hart shared a glance.

"Nonsense," Mr. Hart said. "I don't know what lies your father-in-law has whispered about me. But this is nothing of the sort. You may bring your maid. You'll have your own suite ..." His words trailed off, as if he felt unsure how to continue. "There will be nothing unseemly about it. You must trust me."

"But what will you do about your wife? That matter seems —"

Mr. Hart snorted in amusement. "My wife is the very least of your worries."

I felt perplexed. Surely his wife's actions were the very center of the problem!

Mrs. Diamond sighed. "My dear, if you find Mr. Hart's offer unsuitable, you're welcome to stay with us."

"Would your husband allow it? Or am I to be kept in a bedroom the rest of my days?" This sounded much too close to what the Clubbs had suggested.

Mrs. Diamond glanced aside. "My husband is a stubborn, unyielding man. Yet your defense of our sons and your kindness to our daughter has softened his stance. At least in this matter."

"I'd have to consider it —"

"But you must say nothing to Jonathan," Mrs. Diamond said.

"How would you keep it from him?" I didn't understand what was going on. "Has my husband consented to this?"

"Mrs. Spadros," Mr. Hart said, "we don't have time —"

"No. I'm sorry. If my husband and my best friend must be kept in the dark about such a drastic play, I need to know why. I don't wish either of them to feel anxious for my safety."

"Then come with us," Mr. Hart said. "You can appear at the 500th with your husband and leave from there with us. We'll tell them you're safe. But no one must know where you're hidden."

"I have a cottage you might stay in," Mrs. Diamond said, as if she'd not considered it before then. "It's on the Diamond Manor grounds, yet far from the Manor itself. No one goes there anymore and you never need be bothered. You'll be free to do as you wish. I think you'll like it: it's quite lovely."

I recalled the cottage in the Spadros countryside and the hideous secrets it held. What secrets lay within this one?

And even if it were just a lovely cottage, I hesitated to take either offer. Living alone, abandoning Jon, Tony not knowing where I went? Or if I went to the racetrack with Mr. Hart, how could I live with myself, knowing I'd consented to interfere with a man's marriage? "What about my business? My property? My servants?"

"Oh, my dear," Mr. Hart said. "Is all this really so important to you? It surprises me. You're better than this. You deserve so much more than," he gestured around him, "this."

Octavia Diamond froze, staring forward, color high on her cheeks. Either she didn't approve of me, or she didn't approve of what Mr. Hart had just said. I couldn't tell which.

Something was wrong. "What are you not saying?"

Alarm crossed Mr. Hart's eyes for an instant. "Nothing, my dear. Well, there is something, but it's not for me to say. Not here."

I shook my head. "Then the answer is no. I'll not alarm my husband, hide from my friend, and betray my quadrant —"

Mr. Hart raised a hand. "Mrs. Spadros —"

"— by fleeing when they all most need stability! This quadrant may hate me, they may even despise me, but I'm their Lady, and to just disappear would hurt them. Deeply. It would make them fear for my life and theirs." I recalled what I'd said to Mary a few weeks past. "And fearful men do things outside their nature. I'll do nothing to bring about the turmoil you dread!"

And then I understood: Mr. Hart feared for me. Yet why was Mrs. Diamond here? Why risk so much to sit on my sofa in support of a man by all accounts she barely knew? "You need not fear for me. Despite my unseemly display when the verdict was read, I'm no fainting ingenue. I'm a woman of the Pot. I've survived war, famine, and more than one attempt on my life. Yes, people slander me. Yes, there is danger." Then I recalled Jonathan's little joke, and I grinned fondly at the memory. "But I'm also a Spadros. There's always danger."

Mr. Hart looked dismayed.

"I appreciate your concern, your support, and your offers. Truly and sincerely I do. But I can't just think of myself. I may have left my husband. But if the future is as dire as you fear, I won't abandon and betray my people, not when they need me most."

Mr. Hart gazed at me as if seeing me in a completely different light. "I bow to your wishes then, madam."

I looked at them both. "I intend no disrespect. I hold only the deepest gratitude for your offers of concern and support. And I hope you'll understand. This place, my business, it may seem like nothing to you, but to me, it's freedom. I must be free. And I must be free in my way."

This statement affected Mr. Hart: he seemed to collapse into himself a bit, become less sure of his position.

Mrs. Diamond said, "We don't wish to pry, or to compel you. But if you find yourself in need, we offer two ways to safety."

I smiled at her. "Thank you." At least she didn't mention the third: returning to Spadros Manor.

If I needed any of these ways to safety, matters would have become much worse than I might ever imagine. I rose. "Thank you so much for calling. I do appreciate it."

Octavia Diamond looked at me as if she'd had a revelation. Yet she never spoke, and the three of them left.

I didn't dare tell Gardena's mother about what Morton had told me, not with Mr. Hart listening. I knew nothing of the Hart quadrant's alliances. I didn't want news about the danger to Tony's son to get back to the very men plotting against him.

* * *

Despite their frightening experience two days earlier, the girls insisted they had to go to work. "They'll be fired if they don't," Tenni said. So after a bit of rushing around, we got everyone into a plain carriage and off.

When I returned to my room, my mail sat on my tea-table.

On the bottom was a flat envelope, but larger and thicker than a normal letter. Inside was an illustrated pamphlet:

HOW FAR WE HAVE STRAYED!

Did you ever sit with your grandmother beside the fire and listen to stories she learned from her grandmother?

We did.

Our elders brought us the wisdom of the past as we nestled in their laps.

With all the love in their hearts, they gave us accounts of the beautiful and gentle life we once had.

The bridges made of gold!

Clean streets, healthy children, and work for all.

Days of ease and freedom, before the dark and ugly times to come.

Today we celebrate a dream our ancestors took part in ending!

But all is not lost.

We are here to tell you these stories are true.

The Golden City was real.

You can make it real again.

Help return Bridges to the glory of old!

Join us, so we can rebuild our homeland together.

Paid for by People For A Better Life

Underneath it was a note:

My father knows nothing of this. — GP

Gertie Pike. So the Bridgers weren't part of this "People For A Better Life" group.

Who were they?

At the time, I supposed they could be a wholesome influence, people wishing to help the Inventors fix things around the city.

Yet something about this pamphlet disturbed me.

* * *

I got ready to leave for my luncheon with Karla Bettelmann. Without asking, a plain carriage appeared at my doorstep. Blitz grinned at my reaction. "We can't very well have the Lady of Spadros go to luncheon with one of the Clubbs alone in a taxi."

The ride to Clubb quadrant was uneventful. Since the Clubb Women's Center was in the uppers' area, we took the betters' bridge over the river between Spadros and Clubb. Then we drove down Promenade, which lay along the waterfront.

Instead of the wrought iron and gray stone cobbles of Spadros quadrant, the lampposts and street signs in Clubb were of brass, the cobbles, sandstone. Polished oak or golden mahogany storefronts passed by, with signs in yellow or brown.

I always enjoyed driving into Clubb quadrant, mostly because it had so many outsiders. Tourists, they called them. But their clothing! Their hair! The curious things they brought with them! It spoke of other places, other ways of living. I wanted that, more than anything. To ride the zeppelin, go through the Aperture and outside the dome, to see other cities.

And yet the last time I'd driven into Clubb quadrant, I'd found Madame dying. What should I have done?

A young girl walked beside her mother, her thick brown hair loose. And I was poignantly reminded of Nina Clubb, how we'd longed to run off together and travel the world.

My eyes stung at the memory of our first — and only — kiss. If only I'd kissed her when her mother wasn't around to keep her from me. We could have found a way to leave, had whatever time we might before she died, if that were her fate.

If I'd been by her side, she would have had hope. She wouldn't have fallen into despair, taken her own life.

I'd failed Madame. I'd failed Nina. But I had another chance. I would not let Jonathan Diamond suffer and die alone.

164

The Clubb Women's Center approached on the left. A grand building of polished oak, trimmed in brass. Golden carpeting ran down oak steps; yellow roses bloomed.

Honor helped me from the carriage. The guards in their golden-brown livery opened the doors. Inside was an oak-paneled hall carpeted in gold. A man stood behind a stand painted yellow. "Welcome, Mrs. Spadros. Mrs. Bettelmann awaits you."

The dining room was filled with tables draped in pale yellow, set with cream plates edged in gold. Maids moved to and fro. Perhaps half the tables were occupied, and many already sat eating. A maid brought me to one of the private tables in the back of the wide room, pulling aside the sheer curtains for me.

Mrs. Karla Bettelmann was as Werner described: brown curly hair, brown eyes, perhaps thirty. But she was tall, slender, with fine hair, small wisps going to and fro in a most elegant manner. She wore a walking dress the color of new grass, with a large feathered hat. She rose. "Welcome, Mrs. Spadros! Please, sit beside me."

I offered my hand, which she took briefly, then I sat to her left. "It's a pleasure to meet you, Mrs. Bettelmann."

"Oh, please, call me Karla. I do so hate formality."

I smiled at her, yet felt some anxiety about what to say. "I don't believe I've ever eaten here before."

"The roasted ham is excellent."

So she knew my tastes. This didn't make me feel any better.

The maid stood waiting. "Would you care to order drinks?"

"Just water for me, please," I said.

The maid went to a sideboard, returning with a carafe of water.

"Bring tea," Karla said. She handed me a menu. "Order whatever you wish."

"You're very kind."

"I was surprised to receive your invitation," Karla said. "It took me some time to learn of the topic." Her eyes flickered to her right.

So these private dining rooms weren't so private. I nodded, hoping my voice didn't shake. "I'm quite grateful for anything you might have learned on the matter."

"The main reason for my surprise **was** the topic. I wasn't aware —" For an instant, she hesitated. "— you were interested in such matters."

Nicely done. Not only was my status in question, but both "Pot rags" and Spadros Family members didn't deal with police. I smiled warmly. "I believe that while the past is important, striking a new path is of highest priority, if only to ensure freedom for all. Especially when it's to aid a dear friend."

Karla beamed. "I agree!"

The maid brought in the tea.

"I think we're ready to order," Karla said. She ordered fish; I ordered the roast beef, well done.

I said to Karla, "But what price freedom? Many have died to secure it. And goodwill is of high importance to us all."

Karla nodded, eyes far away. "I heard an amusing tale the other day. Well, my cousin Lori Cuarenta —"

The Clubb Family's Inventor. Oh, dear.

"— told it to me."

I took a sip of water. "Do tell."

"What is of higher value? A sheet of paper, or a dollar bill?"

I chuckled. A test. If I answered the question, she'd know I wasn't worth dealing with. "I couldn't possibly guess."

"Why, the dollar, of course."

"And why is that?"

"Well," Karla said, clearly pleased with her tale, "whilst you can make several dollar bills from one sheet, you can buy many reams of paper with the dollar!"

"That **is** amusing." So her husband cared nothing for what the Inventor wanted — my map. Or whatever secrets Inventor Cuarenta believed the Cathedral held. He only cared for Constable Trey Highcard's money. "I'd never considered the matter. How many dollar bills could you make with a sheet of paper?"

Karla chuckled. "After she told me, I measured it out. Ten. Just think, to be able to cut a dollar from the sheet whenever you liked!"

I nodded. They wanted a tenth of what Constable Highcard had brought with him to settle here. "I'll have to tell my friends this tale to see how they like it!"

Karla's face changed, as if she'd come to some decision. "I didn't know you cared for roast beef! I should show you the stockyards sometime. Just lovely animals, and so amiable."

I stared at her. Why did she bring this up now? Could she possibly know about the private discussion I'd had with Mrs. Spade in my study? "I do like animals, as it turns out. I should enjoy spending the day with you."

The maid brought in my food, which smelled delicious.

Karla made the sign of the Board over her plate, crossing her arms to grasp her shoulders. I hurried to follow suit. "We give thanks to the Floorman who provides us this bounty," she murmured, "and to the Dealer who blesses us all."

They did this in Spadros Manor. But we didn't pray like this back home, where all could see. Which seems odd, now I tell it. But our prayers were for the Dealers' Daughters alone. We always met together before the Cathedral opened for the night.

The food tasted as good as it smelled. "Thank you for suggesting this place. The food is excellent."

The men and boys always left when we gathered to pray, down to the tiniest babe in arms. Where did they go?

"I'm so glad you're pleased," Karla said. "My grandmother so hopes you'll return a second time. Or perhaps even a third. It's a charming place."

I chuckled. So Mrs. Regina Clubb did get my message, and knew Karla would be meeting me. "I hope your grandmother is well?"

"Quite. Rather busy." For the first time, Karla seemed to be speaking plainly. "My cousin's wife had a boy last week, and the child is sickly. My grandmother has been in attendance day and night. The things she knows about caring for sickness!" Karla shook her head in astonishment.

"I suppose that comes with great age," I said. "It must still have been quite a turmoil when she was a small girl."

Karla's face grew pensive. "I never considered that."

Something had changed. Karla Bettelmann wanted to be my actual friend. "Your dining hall is more beautiful than I imagined."

She nodded slowly. "I've never been to the Spadros one. Or anywhere in your quadrant, to be perfectly honest." Then she gave me a real smile. "But I imagine it's lovely."

* * *

When I returned to the carriage, I said to Honor, "I'd like to go to Bryce Fabrics, please, before I return. It's in Spadros, on 2nd Street near Book." Eleanora shouldn't get this news in a message.

"Right away, mum."

On the way there, my mind felt all a-flutter. Somehow, what I said in my study reached Mrs. Clubb's granddaughter.

My study had one window, which opened onto a narrow alleyway. But the window was high, and kept closed. Could someone have been able to listen to us?

It seemed doubtful. Besides, anyone learning that Mrs. Spade and I met could visit Market Center and find out what her husband did. And if Mr. Giovanni Spade only died a year ago, the Clubbs probably knew him. The stockyards were in Clubb quadrant, near the zeppelin station.

So what was Karla Bettelmann trying to tell me?

I felt glad Mrs. Regina Clubb received my messages, and now knew that someone diverted her mail. That sort of thing had given me grief I'd never wish upon another woman.

We made our way far down the Clubb Promenade to the "city bridge" at 6th Street, then over the river into Spadros quadrant.

The west Spadros slums was a dismal place: ramshackle homes, ragged children playing barefoot in the street. A weary woman with several toddlers around her sat on a tiny porch peeling potatoes.

We turned onto the Main Road, then again at 2nd Street, a narrow, barren thing. Boarded-up shops, a few homes, then we came to Bryce Fabrics. Honor helped me out of the carriage, and I went inside.

The white wooden door still squeaked; the gray-green paint on the walls still flaked; the room still smelled of mildew, although not as much so. But new cloth sat on the battered shelves.

Two shabbily-dressed women browsed through the stacks. Eleanora stood behind the rickety counter. She looked up when I

168

came in. "Mrs. Spadros!" She and the other two women curtsied low. "Please, come in."

I hurried to the counter. "I have news."

Eleanora glanced at the women, who'd returned to their browsing. She whispered, "Is it about the Constable?"

"It is." I kept my voice low. "I've just met with the Clubbs. They want ten percent of what he's brought. Then he can go."

Eleanora gasped, and her face turned angry. "That's unjust!"

I suppose I could have negotiated further, but it was my first time at such things. I did the best I might under the circumstances.

Her face fell. "He'll be most disappointed: he spoke of buying us a home, or perhaps even a new shop, if I wanted to continue."

"Are his finances that slender?"

"It cost a great deal to come here, and on a constable's salary ..." She sighed. "I never wanted to cause him grief."

I put my hand on her arm. "You haven't. He loves you. That's worth more than anything." I looked towards her back room. "I hope David is well?"

She peeked in. "Lying down. He sleeps quite a lot these days."

"Sleep can be healing," I said. "Remember when he used to rock so at the slightest noise?"

Eleanora nodded. "Perhaps he is improving." Her eyes reddened. "I truly hope so."

* * *

Mrs. Spade visited later that day to bring her payment. "What have you done to find a my daughter?"

"I found her in Clubb quadrant. But she shot at me."

Mrs. Spade stared in shock. "Maria Athena never own a gun. Why she shoot at you?"

"I don't know. Someone has made her afraid of me. Can you think of who might do that?"

Mrs. Spade shook her head. "She never a know you, other than the portrait in a paper."

Maria Athena Spade had written a note to her mother, with details proving the letter was from her. She felt she was as safe as if under lock and key, but her known friends claimed they couldn't find her. So either they lied, or Maria Athena Spade had made a new friend. Or perhaps both. "Did Maria Athena have any suitors?"

Mrs. Spade broke into a smile. "Yes. Very nice boy. Beautiful Italian boy, such gentleman. Not with mafiosi, he hate them. And money, too. He treat her so nice." Her head drooped. "He offer her the marriage. They to marry after a Midsummer."

This made me suspicious. "Has he seen her?"

"No, Signora, he not see her. He look and her brothers. They say he work hard to find her."

"How long has it been since **you** saw him? This boy?"

She frowned slightly. "Many weeks now." Then her face turned alarmed. "Could something happen?"

Now I felt sure something was wrong. "What's his name?"

She beamed. "Franco Pagliacci."

The Rebuke

A young, sheltered spinster offered sanctuary from ruthless "Spadros men" by a "very good-looking man"? One who paid her attention, flattered her, promised to marry her. Her mother loved him, her brothers trusted him. "I fear this man is the one who took her," I said, almost to myself.

"No, Signora, Franco a good boy. He like my own son."

I nodded. Just like the rest. She was convinced of it. "I think I know where she's being held. I'm going to see some people who may be able to help. I hope we can have her home soon."

She clasped her hands in front of her. "I hope so too."

The thought that Frank Pagliacci might have taken this woman chilled me. Not only was she in danger from the man I felt almost certain to be the Bridges Strangler, but from all the other women who believed Frank only loved them.

Sawbuck had been right in one thing: rushing into the Plaza without knowledge of what I faced was risky. I needed to learn more about this group camped out there and their numbers.

The one place I could learn more was the Cathedral.

The Cathedral — well, more to the point, my Ma — had only given the briefest replies to my messages, and that late. And from what Mrs. Clubb told me that day in her hotel, she was full aware of me sending them. If she was, others likely were too.

So I must send no more messages. Despite Benji's warnings, that night, I must go there myself.

* * *

The girls arrived home safely before tea, but fifteen-year-old Oma was in tears.

"There was traffic," Mr. Howell said, "and she was late."

"I was reprimanded!" Oma hid her face in her hands. Mary put her arm around the girl to console her, while little Emma threw her arms around her older sister's legs.

I felt confused. "Have you been late often?"

Oma said, "I wouldn't dare! The manager said if I'm late again I'll be fired. He has a whole list of girls waiting for my position."

Tenni looked concerned. "We need her job to pay fees."

I turned to Mr. Howell. "Can we start them off earlier?"

He nodded, and made plans for them to leave a half-hour earlier.

"Don't worry, mum," Tenni said to Mary. "I'll get up and make sure they're fed."

Mary smiled warmly at her. "Let's do it together. I'll show you where everything is."

* * *

Blitz insisted on going with me to the Cathedral; I insisted on being let out of the carriage at the Gap. "Benji is always out front nights. He knows your face. If he sees you, the Cathedral won't talk to me, and this trip will be for nothing."

"He won't see me," Blitz said.

"You're right, because you'll be here in the carriage."

"At least take Honor with you."

I laughed. "He screams 'quadrant-folk'."

Honor drew back, face dismayed.

I said, "When will you people learn? This is my place, not yours. I'm in no danger. I'll return in two hours, or send word if this takes longer. But I shall be vexed if you come in here after me."

Neither of them liked it, but I was the Lady of Spadros, and they were sworn to obey.

It was a couple of miles from the Gap to the Cathedral. Revelers from the quadrants filled the darkening streets, and lamps lit the way. Tonight, I wore my regular clothes and my black cloak.

172

Dressed as I was, it was easy to move along with the crowd, behind a group, alongside a couple, as if I were part of them.

Soon the Cathedral loomed before us, light spilling from the broken windows of stained glass. Pieces had been broken from a column and dents marred the walls, yet the frame itself seemed untouched by the centuries.

The Cathedral was a dome set atop an immense round wall. In the back I knew there to be other areas, square or rectangular, where business of a more sensitive nature was done. One room, I'd shared with my Ma, before everything went wrong.

Benji wasn't there. I didn't recognize either of the men who stood taking weapons and sizing the men up.

It was the first step in the process. Once they — mostly men — passed this first round, they'd be brought one group at a time to the left of the lobby, where preferences were asked and payment taken.

Then they were brought under the Cathedral dome to choose their partners for the night. Those ready to serve would stand outside the open curtains in front of their area. Once chosen, they'd undress and bathe the men, then examine them for disease.

If the men didn't pass, they'd be taken to the herb women's building behind the Cathedral, their payment returned to them. The herb women had their own way: no one was denied aid, even those kept from entering the Cathedral's front door.

Guards stood ready in case there was trouble, but usually the men were more shocked and afraid then angry. Many refused to take back their payment, especially if the bath was enjoyable.

If they passed the test, their clothes were taken, and returned to them clean and dry. For a while, I did that.

Business ended when the sky began to pale. All who remained were roused and sent on their way. I was always told: *no outsider must be under the dome when dawn rises*. I began to suspect why.

When he saw me, one of the men gestured to a boy beside him, leaning over to speak in the boy's ear. He might have been six. The boy ran up the cracked, chipped white marble steps and inside the large, door-less entryway. Then the man fixed me with an unfriendly glare, returning to his work.

Benji told me not to come back. He probably spread the word. But everyone here had to learn I was no longer a child.

After twenty minutes, the boy returned to the doorway. He came down the steps and reached out his hand. "They want you inside. Come with me?"

I smiled and took his little hand, letting him lead me just inside the entryway. A woman I didn't recognize stood there. "Thank you. I'll take her now."

The boy's sandals flapped down the steps as I followed the woman off to the right, where a wall stood directly in the way. But she took hold of a lever behind the thick curtain there and gave it the barest touch towards the wall.

A part of the marble, a foot thick, moved inward. Placing her hand upon it, she pushed gently and it slid aside to the left. We hurried through; it returned to its place with barely a sound.

The room was full of candles, a place where negotiation could take place without the rest of the world knowing. The next group to enter the lobby would believe I'd merely moved into the Cathedral.

What I saw next surprised me, although I'm not sure why.

The room itself was as it always was: paneled in warm brown. Bookcases covered the walls, filled with documents and ledgers of various kinds. Leather and brass-bound chairs sat forming a circle. A wide thick woven rug patterned in red, gold, and brown covered the marble below.

This didn't surprise me; the room had been there since the Cathedral was built five hundred years past. What did surprise me was who sat there.

Her leathery face, lined and scarred beyond imagining. Her hair, long, straight, and white as snow. Her eyes, bright blue. She wore not one of the whores' shimmering silk gowns, but the white wool robe of an Initiate to the Dealers, now gray with age. Its long flowing sleeves covered the arms of her chair.

The Eldest did not rise. I was astonished she still lived. I knelt, my forehead touching the floor, then rose, taking a step back. "You honor me above all women."

Her ancient face turned amused. "Such was not my intent." She gestured with a hand sunken by age. "Please sit."

I glanced back; the other woman stood at the door, which had disappeared into the wall. Feeling uneasy, I hurried to obey, sitting several seats to the Eldest's left.

She nodded. "You have chosen wisely."

I blinked. "I have? In what way?"

Her voice turned stern. "This is what you are here to learn."

"I wish to learn of the men infesting the Plaza. The woman with them may have captured —"

"That group, that woman ... this is not what you're here to learn, Jacqueline Kaplan."

I hadn't heard anyone refer to me by that name in a long time. "So what is it I'm here to learn?"

She rested her hand on the armrest. "I sit here. You sit there."

"I'm sorry, Eldest. I don't understand."

At that, she smiled. "That's your problem. You don't understand. Yet you insist on acting without knowledge."

Very well, I thought. "So what is it I'm supposed to learn?"

"I sit here. You, on the other hand, sit there."

She sat in the place of the host. Without her signal, hidden somewhere in that chair, anyone leaving this room would be killed. Even Benji would be obligated to kill me. "You have control."

"I do. But it's more than that, little Jay."

No one had called me that since I was a tiny child: four, or perhaps five. "Eldest, I understand. You're so old that I look as a child to you. But I'm no child. I'm the Lady of Spadros, and with one word I can have this place —"

"You may not threaten me," she snapped. "You do not threaten me. Not you."

I sighed. "I wasn't. I can help you. I want to help you. But I need your help in return."

She didn't answer.

I looked up at her. "Is my mother well?"

"She's in hiding because of your betrayal."

"What? I would never betray her."

"Yet you did." A flash of anger went through her eyes. "You told our greatest enemy that she lives, and even now men plot to take back what it took us a hundred years to gain. That is how you've 'helped' us so far. I pray you 'help' us no further."

How could this be? I'd told **no one** that she lived!

Stunned, I said, "Whatever you think I've done, whatever someone told you I've done, it's not true. I would never betray you. I've given up everything I've ever wanted to keep from betraying you." At this, I felt grieved, angry. "I would think you'd be grateful!"

She shook her head. "You still don't understand. I sit here. You, on the other hand, sit there." She let out a small laugh. "You chose wisely, to sit there, even without knowing why." A small bemused smile flashed past. "If only you might for once just sit, and learn."

I glanced back; the other woman, this woman who I didn't know, stood staring ahead, refusing to meet my eye.

"She is reliable, oh Lady of Spadros," the Eldest said. "Ever so much so than you."

My eyes stung. "Why am I so wretched in your eyes? I was sold to the Spadros Family. I had no choice in the matter."

"That is not what I refer to, young Lady of Spadros. And from your own lips, so you name yourself. To me, that says everything."

What had I done? I leaned forward, gripping the armrests in terror. "No! I'm one of you! I'm one of the Dealers' Daughters!"

"And so you once were, until the day you betrayed us. And yes, you did: not once, but twice." She leaned back, crossed one leg over the other. "You don't even know who I am, do you?"

"You're the Eldest Daughter."

"I was a daughter, true. Long ago." Her eyes grew misty, unfocused. "But not the sort you mean.

"I was once a young girl, my little Jay, much younger than you are now. The legends of the past, the tales of the Holy Writ, the stratagems of the Holy Cards, it all fascinated me. I was not only gifted in game play, I had a fire to play the Cards better than anyone." She snorted, amused. "I was much like you. No one could ever teach me.

"I was betrothed into a good match, which would have let me live out my days in peace and comfort. Yet I defied my mother, just as you did the night you were sold. I defied her to come here. I wanted to be one of the Dealers! And I determined that no one would stop me." She gave a knowing, one-shoulder shrug. "And I got my wish, so far as it went."

She let out a long, wheezing breath. "I was fifteen when I walked through that entryway. It had the most beautiful doors back then. And soon after, I was sent to the cloister to learn about becoming one of the Dealers." Her eyes turned wistful. "I did so love that time. I wanted to learn everything!" Then she straightened. "Yet no one could tell me what to do even then. When the call came for those to choose: stay or flee, others urged, nay, begged me to flee. But for me there was no choice other than to defend the Cathedral. I who am now Eldest was Youngest back then." At that, her head bowed. "I didn't tell anyone, but the red firework rising above Market Center marked my sixteenth birthday."

I stared at her in horror.

"They say some women don't remember. But I remember every man. One hundred and one years later, I see their faces before me. Their lust to dominate, deface, destroy. There was no tenderness in their eyes, nothing approaching love. Only the use of their bodies as weapons. Only hate."

At that, she let out a sigh. "We were supposed to be dead. We were supposed to not care. But after they left me broken in front of the altar, it was hate that kept me alive. But the other women helped me learn pity for the brokenness of their minds, and later, the child I bore from that night and all the nights of suffering to follow taught me love." She raised her eyes to meet mine. "That was your grandmother, little Jay."

I shrank back, aghast.

"You sit there. Your mother sits beside you. Her mother, may she receive better cards next time, sits beside me." Then she patted her armrest. "And I sit here."

She took a deep, wheezing breath, let it out. "So I hope you can see how this ... knowledge ... has value? Yes, you can help us, really help us, if that is what you wish. Or you can help your quadrant-folk — if that is what you truly wish. But all I see before me is a mad rush to destroy yourself, the last remnant of my line, and that I can't stand by and idly watch." She took a deep, wheezing breath.

"Not just because you're my kin. Because you threaten to take us all with you, not just us here at the Cathedral but the entire city, which I have given everything to defend. Do you understand now?"

I didn't, not really, not like I do today. But I knew how to answer instruction. "Yes, Eldest."

Her shoulders sagged; a light left her eyes. "I hoped to move you gently, as is our Way. But I see you're not ready." She shook her head, made a small motion with her right hand, under her sleeves. "You may go, Lady of Spadros. But I fear I will never see you again. Do you understand? You must not return until the time is right —" She gazed off to the side, falling silent.

I nodded, vision blurring. I thought I knew exactly what she meant. *Only if the question is asked, the woman provided, and the room cleansed, should the sacred Heart of Bridges ever be exposed.*

Of course, back then, I didn't know anything, not really. At the time, it felt like such a day would never come. I was banished from the Cathedral, from my home and family, not for a while, but forever. Bitter remorse tore through me: I'd ruined everything. I'd not only received rebuke, but I was named enemy. Enemy! I wasn't worthy even to be with them — and I didn't know why!

"— and I don't have long now before the Dealer collects my cards." She smiled at me warmly. "Come, my Lady, give me your hand."

So I knelt before her, weeping, and kissed her hand as she stroked my hair. "Farewell, dear girl," she said, and it was gentle, full of regret. As was custom when leaving the Eldest, I knelt to kiss her bare lined foot, then rose and bowed, backing away past the chairs before turning to go.

She spoke once more. "If you want my advice, it would be to return to your Manor and trust yourself to play the cards you've been dealt for the good of us all. Make yourself worthy of my sisters' sacrifice." Then her head drooped. "But I fear you still have much to learn."

The marble slab opened in front of me. I took one last backward glance at the Eldest Daughter: she had her face buried in her hands.

For a moment, I deeply regretted hurting this woman who had gone through so much.

The woman beside me put her hand on my shoulder. "Come, Mrs. Spadros," she said, but her tone was kind. "It's time to go."

* * *

I stumbled through the open entryway, down the steps, past the men waiting in line, and across the wide, cracked boulevard.

An old barrel sat across from the Cathedral's entrance. I leaned upon it, numbly watching the line of men move along.

My own great-grandmother had named me enemy. Without proof, without trial, without recourse, she cast me out!

How dare the Eldest judge me! Sitting there like some goddess in comfort while the Pot lay in ruins around her. From all accounts, her precious Dealers were offered the chance to rebuild the Pot, more than once, and turned it down.

I suddenly hated them, the Cathedral and the Families both, with their inhumanity and schemes, their lies and their desire to control my life. All I wanted was to be free.

But first I had to survive. And I had to get Maria Athena Spade away from the scoundrels who held her.

Someone grabbed my arm from behind. "I told you not to come back," Benji said.

I turned to face him. "I'm not a child for you to command."

"I don't command, Jacqui. I ask. I beg."

Something in the way he said it moved me. But I pushed that aside. Fear for myself was what got me in the predicament I was now in. Against my better judgment, I'd told Mr. Doyle Pike that Ma was alive. But how could a lawyer on Market Center be such a fierce enemy to the Cathedral that they would cast me out after he saved my life? What possible harm could he do to them? "I don't understand what's happening. But I want to. Why are you here, instead of at your post?"

"The Daughters rebuked me —"

I gaped at him, shocked. The rebuke was bad enough for a woman to earn, but for a man ...

" — and refuse the boy to come under the dome —"

The Cathedral's dome. They called this Pot boy an outsider.

" — because he helped our enemies."

"What? He's a child!"

179

"He's old enough to know the difference between quadrant-trash and the True City," Benji said. "He left not out of any desire to serve, but only to gain for himself."

"But isn't that what everyone wants? To get out of the Pot? My Ma called it 'true freedom.' Is she a traitor, too?"

Benji shook his head. "You claim the Pot yet you understand nothing of it. Why leave your kind just to become one of them? We encourage exile to gather aid, to turn the quadrant-folk from their folly. To help our Sisters who labor as we do. Not to thrall themselves to the traitors who ruined Bridges!"

"But he didn't want to go back."

"That's why I left," Benji said. "The Daughters' words dismayed him. He's run off."

"Did he return to the Keycard Cafe?"

Benji shook his head, then glanced behind him. "Come inside."

The building was abandoned, fallen-down, but in one area the roof was mostly sound. Several shivered there, peering up as we entered. Benji went down a hall to the right, to another room which opened to the stars. A corner of roof still remained, and a sleeping mat lay upon the weeds under it.

"You're staying here," I said.

Benji nodded. "The Cathedral used to own it — perhaps still do. I'll make a place for these people. And for Tim." He gazed up. "If I find him."

"Have you learned any more of the High-Low Split or the Red Dog Gang?"

He shook his head.

"Then I must go."

He led me to the street. "Until next time, small sister. But please, let it be the Day Foretold."

Only if the question is asked, the woman provided, and the room cleansed ... I snorted bitterly. In other words, don't come back. "I can't promise that, Benji. I have others to consider than myself."

He nodded, turned away.

When I returned to the carriage, Blitz asked, "Did you learn anything useful?"

Did I learn anything useful?

The Eldest seemed to think I'd betrayed the Cathedral by telling Mr. Pike my mother was alive. Which meant he had to have told someone else who threatened them. Because on his own, I couldn't see old Mr. Pike being much of a threat to the Cathedral.

The whole of my trial, he'd been fiercely opposed to Mr. Freezout and by extension, Mrs. Hart and the Red Dog Gang. So the Eldest's accusation truly confused me. Was this yet another thing that the Red Dog Gang had framed me for?

"I don't know if I learned anything useful or not," I said, "but I think I know what I need to do to get Maria Athena Spade back."

The Link

Could Maria Athena Spade still be alive? It was almost too much to hope for. With her in the hands of the Red Dog Gang and the High-Low Split, she might be anything from a new recruit to a bone of contention to a target. At this point, there was no way to be sure.

And Maria Athena knew much more than I'd thought.

She'd seen Frank Pagliacci's face and could identify him. When Madame Biltcliffe was shot by Black Maria, Maria Athena was with her. So she could identify Black Maria as well.

After the girls left for work the next morning, I asked Blitz to find Sawbuck and bring him here. "I want it done quietly. I believe we have spies."

Blitz nodded. "I'll pay a visit to Mr. Howell."

"Have a pint for me," I said.

Blitz gave me a fake smile. "Don't you think it's early for that?"

I shrugged.

He returned an hour later. "On his way! What's all this about?"

"Nothing which should harm you." I thought about what I'd said to Mr. Hart. "I'm sorry for all the trouble I've caused you and Mary."

He gave me a real smile. "Never to fret. Mary's so happy about the baby coming she's forgotten about everything else."

This was true. The house had never been so clean; our little gardens, immaculate. She hadn't even been sick.

We had breakfast, then I went to my study to wait for Sawbuck and Amelia to arrive whilst I made my plans.

The doorbell rang as I lay my pages out on my desk. Blitz knocked on my bedroom door. "Mrs. Spadros?"

"In here."

Blitz came in. "Monsieur Sabacc is here to see you."

"Oh!" I'd never spoken directly to the Chef of Spadros Manor before. I went to the hallway where he stood, top hat in hand. "I'm pleased to see you."

The man was almost as tall as Sawbuck but wider and at least fifty, with black hair and brown eyes. "Might we speak on a business matter?"

"Of course." I'd only ever seen him shout at the kitchen staff, so this changed demeanor gave me great interest. "Would you care to join me in my parlor?"

"I would."

I wondered at the formality: normally Blitz would have put a guest in the parlor at once. "Would you care for some tea?"

"That's very kind of you, but I won't be here long." Monsieur handed his top hat to Blitz.

We went into the parlor, and I gestured for Monsieur to sit on the sofa. I sat across from him. "I wanted to thank you for your kindness to Pip Dewey."

"It's no trouble," Monsieur Sabacc said. "He's a good boy and a hard worker. He has real talent; I think he'll do well for himself."

I recalled Pip's little face turned up to me there in my gardens back at Spadros Manor. "How may I help?"

"I'm sure you're aware of my wife's demise."

Oh, Madame ... "I'm very sorry for your loss, sir."

"Thank you. Yet I lost her many a year ago."

"I'm glad you came to call. Your wife meant a great deal to me."

He drew back. "Oh?"

"Not like that, sir. But she told me about the troubles between you. I never imagined —"

"That you had me right within your walls?" He shook his head. "My Lady, I was a fool. I married in haste. When that ended in disaster, I married again, to a much less suitable woman." He shook his head regretfully. "When one is of a certain age, intelligent conversation holds the greatest value. I missed our talks together." He gazed at the floor. "I hired detectives, Mrs. Spadros. It seemed I'd searched everywhere. So I returned to Paris, where Marie and I met, hoping to find her. Yet I never did." He shrugged. "Instead, I decided to change my life." He raised his head and smiled. "I learned to cook. And here I am today. I never considered she might take her maiden name. If I hadn't overheard the servants speak of her passing, I'd never have known. Of course, I immediately informed the police. To imagine, all this time, in the same city. The same quadrant!"

"She loved being here."

He smiled fondly. "She would." He let out a breath, his eyes reddening. "And that makes me quite happy." He leaned forward, clasping his hands, and gazed upon them for a moment. "I shall come to the point. My inquiry has to do with her business."

"I'm not sure I understand."

"She has put me in a bind. By law, her business goes to me upon her death. Yet in her will, she states it is to go to you."

"To me? Whatever might I do with a dress shop?"

"I suspected you might feel this way, my Lady. I've spoken with my lawyer, and there's a simple way through this matter. You sell the business to me, and I dispose of the property in it."

"Why can you not sell it yourself?"

"Because of the conflicting law." He shook his head slightly. "Who actually owns it? The matter of whether a last will supersedes marital law is a thorny one. It may cost more than the business is worth to settle."

"I see. And I would be most happy to oblige." Extra money was always good. Very good.

Then something occurred to me. "Would it not be more beneficial to have someone manage the shop? The day to day use would bring profit beyond merely its sale."

"Very smart thinking, I must say! I suppose you have a candidate for the position?"

"I do: a fabric shop owner of long acquaintance. If you would allow me to consult with her, I could bring you her answer at once."

"Very good!" He rose, as did I. "I'm most glad to have this settled. And it's a pleasure to speak with you."

"And you, sir. I'm sorry it's taken so long to finally converse."

He smiled. "Not at all, mum. Thank you for seeing me."

* * *

A message came from Spadros Manor: Amelia's daughter was ill, so Amelia wouldn't be here that day. Which was fine: I had nowhere in particular to go.

I wrote to Eleanora Bryce, asking when it might be best to meet with her. Now that she had customers — and her wedding was no longer being delayed — I wanted to disrupt her as little as possible.

Sawbuck arrived after luncheon, his manner on the chilly side. He sat in my parlor, just where Monsieur had, and spoke in a biting, sarcastic tone. "How may I help you, Mrs. Spadros?"

"I believe both the Ten of Spades and the High-Low Split are hiding in what you call the Old Plaza. I know they're aligned with the Red Dog Gang."

"And how do you know this?"

"I've spoken with the people who live in the Pot." Tim and the Eldest both agreed the High-Low Split was there. "Madame Biltcliffe told me the woman leading the High-Low Split shot her. I saw Maria Athena Spade with her. Maria Athena's mother told me she'd had a suitor named Franco Pagliacci."

Sawbuck stared at me, mouth open.

I said, "So this links the High-Low Split and the Red Dog Gang. I believe Frank Pagliacci is the go-between for the two groups."

His tone became less chilly: more a snap than a bite. "And how do our rebellious men fit in?"

"When Tony's man attacked me, it was just like the Red Dog Gang's attack on my husband. Lightly done. If they'd killed either of us it would have been incidental. Neither brought sufficient firepower to do the job properly. Your man killing all those Court Guards was sheer luck! I believe both attacks were meant to distract from other matters." What had they been distracting me from? "This tactic indicates to me that one person leads them both."

Sawbuck leaned back, hand to his chin, a small frown upon his face. "So someone has lured our men away to their cause," he shrugged, "whatever it is."

"They're likely seen as hired guns," I said. "I can't imagine any group entirely trusts the others."

"So what do you suggest doing? I hear no plan here."

"Storm the Plaza now, before they have chance to split up again."

"Tomorrow is the 500th! Don't you have preparations to make?"

"This is the perfect time to strike! No one would ever expect it."

He quickly stood. "I must consult with Mr. Anthony."

"We don't have a lot of time, not if we're to do it tomorrow night." We walked towards the door. Blitz unlocked the door, and handed Sawbuck his hat. I followed Sawbuck to his carriage. The breeze was cool; I wished I had my shawl. "I only want to help."

He turned to me. "You want to help, stand with him. A dress is being delivered for you —"

"What?"

"— so you'll have no excuse. Your maid will be here tomorrow night at seven. A carriage will arrive at eight. The show begins at half-past nine. Dinner will be served there." He tipped his hat. "Good day."

Standing on the sidewalk by the street, I turned towards the building. Blitz stood in the open door at the top of the steps waiting for my return. Before I got to the steps, a young girl perhaps seven years old dressed for a party approached me, her manner easy. "Are you really Mrs. Spadros?"

She was a pretty little thing. I bent over to greet her. "Yes, dear. How can I help?"

She drew an envelope from the back of her pink ribbon sash, handing it to me face up. The surface was blank.

Did she want to play a game? "What's this?" I turned it over: the seal of the Court lay embossed there.

"You've been served." She smiled back at a proud beaming man standing ten feet off, then skipped over to take his hand.

Tricked! I stared at the envelope with horror.

Blitz rushed down the steps. "Is that what I think it is?"

Once inside, I tore the envelope open. "They say I must give up all documents or information about the Cathedral or the Magma Steam Generators." I peered at it, puzzled. "But I have no documents or information, save what I gave Inventor Call."

And I realized what the Eldest meant when she said I'd betrayed the Cathedral twice.

No outsider must be under the dome when dawn rises.

I'd shared my map with Inventor Maxim Call!

I only wanted to help our quadrant, to help him fix the Magma Steam Generators. Could he have told someone else about the map, someone who wanted to harm the Cathedral?

"Then they must think you have more," Blitz said. "And how could you prove you didn't?"

I walked to my study, paper in hand. This was devious indeed. If I didn't provide what documents they believed I had, I could be jailed until I did so.

This stank of Mayor Freezout.

When I refused to help Inventor Maxim Call, the man must have felt he had nowhere else to turn. Was Mayor Freezout the enemy who the Eldest believed I'd betrayed her to?

Not only had I hurt the Cathedral, I'd put myself into danger. I had money, yes, but not nearly enough to hire an attorney to fight this summons — not unless I wanted to add to what I already owed Mr. Doyle Pike.

I went to the kitchen; Blitz and Mary stood holding each other, eyes red. I asked, "What's wrong?"

"Oh, mum," Mary said. "I've lost the baby."

The Risk

How could this happen? "I should have let Tenni do more here."

"It's not your fault," Blitz said. "This was a misdeal. There's not any blame to be had."

Mary pressed her face into his chest, weeping.

I felt lost. "Should we call the doctor?"

That seemed to move Blitz. "Yes, I'll send for the doctor."

"Here," I said to Mary, "let me bring you to bed, just until the doctor arrives."

Mary nodded, face downcast. I'd never been in their rooms since they moved in, and it was cozy. She'd done up the back area with pastel patterned wallpaper. "My mother said it brought bad fortune to paper the baby's area before it was born," Mary sobbed, sagging onto their bed. "How I wish I would have listened!"

I sat next to her, put my arm around her shoulders. "You heard your husband: there's no blame here. I'll strip the wallpaper myself if it'll make you feel better."

"It would." Tears flowed down her face. "I'd see it and weep all again. My baby! It's so pitiful a thing. So red and small."

"But you loved it, Mary. And you grieve its passing. Surely that means something."

Mary sat quiet. "Would you call one of the Dealers for me, mum? I'd like to see her."

"Of course."

Blitz stood in the hallway, head bowed, his face a mask of grief. I went to him, grasped his upper arms. "All will be well."

He shook his head. "It feels the opposite."

"I know." How might I help? "She's in bed. I'll strip the wallpaper tomorrow. She wants to see one of the Dealers, and —"

Blitz made to go to the door, but I stopped him, spoke gently. "I'll send for the messenger. Tenni will be here soon and can get dinner. You don't have to do anything but go to your wife."

A mixture of shame and anguish came over him. "I can't let her see me like this!"

"You're wrong. Grief is best done together. Give me the key."

He took the door key from around his neck and handed it to me.

"Now, go." I pushed him towards their rooms. "Grieve with her. This is how you can help best. Trust me: she will love you for it."

He moved down the hall, and I waited there until he'd rounded the corner and the sound of him entering his rooms faded.

Back when I was taken into house arrest, Tony had the house wired to shine a light at the door when we wished for a messenger. Now other houses were doing it as well.

When the boy came, I sent a message to the poorhouse asking for the Dealers' aid. I sent another to Jonathan Diamond, telling him I wished to see him at his convenience. Jon might know some way to help with the summons. It was dated a month hence, so there wasn't any rush to be had.

So I was surprised to see Jonathan arrive before one of the Dealers did. Not only that, but he was dressed as a servant on his day off might: white shirt, gray tweed vest and pants, with matching cap. And his eyes went wide when I answered the door. "Why do **you** answer the door, Jacqui? Is all well?"

"No, it's not. Please, come in." I drew him inside, closed the front door quietly behind him. "There's been ... medical trouble. We're waiting for the doctor to call."

"Jacqui, if it's serious, I can come back."

"Well, it's serious. But not contagious. Let's go into the parlor." I closed the door, drew him to the sofa. "Please sit. Some tea?"

"Not if it'll be a bother."

We both sat. I looked him over. "Why are you dressed like that?"

"I meant to bring you to see something. And where we're going, I thought it less conspicuous than to appear in top hat and tails." He chuckled to himself, then fell quiet.

"Did you get my letter?"

Jon appeared surprised. "No. When did you send it?"

"A half-hour ago."

"I haven't been home for twice that. Is something wrong?"

I took the summons from my pocket and gave it to him. "I don't have anything to do with this."

Jonathan shook his head. "Freezout again." He handed it back. "Let Tony's lawyers take care of it."

Probably best. "I don't understand why he keeps pestering me."

"You did say you thought he worked with your enemies — what were they called, Red Dogs?"

"The Red Dog Gang, yes."

Jonathan's eyes narrowed. "Are these the people framing my brother as well?"

He did that on remarkably little information. I'd never had the chance to tell him everything. "I believe they are."

He sat quietly, head bowed. "What is the connection here? Why —? Ah." His head rose. "As we thought."

"As who thought?"

Jon hesitated a long moment, gazing aside. "These men use Jack's reputation, his ... behavior. If they might cause suspicion to fall on him, everyone believes it. They fix attention upon him." He chuckled to himself. "As Mr. Hart once said: a sleight-of-hand," his jaw tightened, his eyes narrowing. "But one using my brother. And to do so believably," he glanced up at me, "which they have, they have to have had spies upon him." He gave the tiniest shake of his head. "This is bad, Jacqui. Spies within Diamond quadrant?"

I assumed everyone had spies on them. "Is that so surprising?"

A soft laugh burst from him. "Well, yes, it actually is."

The bell rang, and when I answered it, Dr. Salmon stood there. "Come in," I said, "right this way." I went towards Blitz and Mary's rooms, and the doctor followed.

Once I got the doctor settled with Blitz and Mary, I set the kettle on, in case someone might want tea. Then I returned to Jon and sat across from him. "I'm surprised you dared come here alone."

Jon blinked. "Why?"

"According to the *Golden Bridges*, there are 'unsavory rumors' about me."

Jon rolled his eyes. "Yes, well you must consider the source. Why would anyone believe it?"

"Because I have men coming and going, and I'm from the Pot, so of course —"

Jon held up his hand. "You mustn't read such things, Jacqui."

He'd never spoken to me in such a direct way before. "I need to know what people think of me, if only for my own protection."

"Then have a servant do it, one who can bring anything important to your attention. Like when Amelia took care of your mail during the trial."

Perhaps Amelia might do that. Or Honor, if she found the *Golden Bridges* too distressing. "So what is this something I must see?"

I thought Jon might smile, but he didn't. "It'd be better if you saw it, rather than hearing about it from me."

"Well, now I'm intrigued! Whatever could it be?"

Jon didn't answer.

A soft knock on the hall door: Dr. Salmon peeked into the parlor.

I went to the door, leading the doctor into the hallway. Then I closed the door behind me. "How is she?"

"Grieving," he said softly, "but her body is well. All seems to have passed, and she has no fever or weakness. So I think she'll recover. Of course, it's a terrible blow, but she's still young. Give her a week without duties. I'll return to see her then. If she worsens, particularly if she runs a fever, please send for me at once."

"Thank you for seeing her," I said. "What do I owe you?"

He smiled at me. "I'm on my way to an appointment. It was no trouble at all."

"Thank you. But this must be the last time. We have money to pay." I unlocked the front door for him.

One of the Dealers, a middle-aged woman dressed in a forest green robe and matching headscarf, came up the steps. Behind her was one of her Apprentices, dressed the same but in pale green. I opened the door wide; the doctor moved outside to let them enter.

"Welcome, Blessed Lady." I curtsied low. "This is Dr. Salmon."

"Thank you, Mrs. Spadros," the woman said, ignoring the doctor entirely. "Where is the woman?"

Dr. Salmon smiled to himself, tipped his hat to their backs, and went down the steps.

"She's with her husband," I said. "Follow me." I closed the door, bringing the two women to Blitz and Mary's rooms.

The kettle had begun to whistle, so I made tea for myself and Jon. Then I returned to Jonathan with a tea-tray, leaving the door to the kitchen open.

Jon smiled. "I've never seen you with a tea-tray before."

I smiled to myself. "I suppose I'm a woman of many talents." I set the tray down and poured him a cup. "How far is this place you want to take me? How long will I be gone?"

Jon shrugged. "Depends on traffic. But it's early yet. No more than an hour."

"I shouldn't leave them until Tenni and the girls return from work, which won't be until just before tea-time." Tenni's littlest sister was in her room braiding twine. But I couldn't leave an eight-year-old to guard a household.

"There's no need, Mrs. Spadros," Blitz said, coming in from the kitchen. "I've been banished from the room." He seemed sad.

"I'm sorry, Blitz," I said.

Jonathan seemed surprised, but he held his tongue.

I said, "What would help?"

Blitz considered the matter. "I have no idea." Then he held out his hand. "I do need my key back, before Sawbuck returns and sees you with it."

The Dealers' footsteps rounded the corner from Blitz and Mary's rooms. I went to the door to the hall, Blitz following. "Thank you for coming," I said as they passed.

The two ignored us as thoroughly as if we weren't there, halting at the closed door.

Blitz hurried up, fumbling the key a bit, then opened the door. "My apologies, Blessed Lady."

She looked up at him. "You're the father?"

"I am," Blitz said.

"The Dealer's blessings upon you."

"Thank you."

The woman nodded and left without a further word.

Blitz closed the door. "That was very odd."

Suddenly afraid, I hurried to Mary's room, and Blitz followed.

Mary lay quietly on the bed, turning her face towards us when we entered. "Thank you for calling her for me."

I smiled at her. "You're quite welcome."

Blitz and I returned to the front hall. "If you need to go somewhere," Blitz said, "I can manage until the girls arrive. Will you be back for tea?"

"Let me make sure." I went into the parlor, and Jonathan rose. "Can we be back by tea-time?"

Jon glanced at the clock. "I don't think so."

I returned to Blitz. "Master Diamond and I will wait until after tea-time to go. You stay with your wife. Rest. We'll get the girls settled and dinner ready."

"Are you certain?"

"I am. And if Master Diamond wishes to do this another time, so be it. You and Mary are more important than some outing."

Relief crossed his face. "Thank you, Mrs. Spadros."

"But I'll probably need the key to let the girls in."

He chuckled, taking it from his pocket and handing it back. "I suppose you will."

I put the key in my pocket and went back to the parlor, leaving the door to the hall open. Jonathan still stood by the sofa. "Jon, can we go after tea? I don't want to leave them alone here."

Jon's eyebrows rose, his head drawing back a bit. "Of course. It might be better. Jacqui, come sit down." After I did so, he said, "What's going on?"

Should I say? "It's not for me to tell, Jon."

"But the Dealers were here. Has someone died —? I see. Your housekeeper was with child, and is no more. I'm so sorry."

I felt astonished. How did he deduce this?

"Should I go?"

"No, Jon, you don't need to go, unless you must."

"Good gods, you must have thought me mad. You said you had medical trouble, yet I came in anyway. Please forgive me."

"All is well. Be at peace. Drink your tea."

The bell rang, and I answered it. Tenni and her sisters stood at the doorstep, a plain carriage driving off behind them. "Come in, but quietly," I said.

I brought them into the parlor. Jon rose when they came in, and I closed the parlor door. "This is Master Diamond," I said.

All the girls curtsied.

"You're dressed funny for an upper," one of the girls said.

Jon's hand went to his mouth as he turned aside, stifling a laugh.

I said, "Master Jonathan is here to help. Mrs. Mary's fallen sick, and Mr. Blitz is with her. We must take care of things until she's well. I've already set the kettle on."

Tenni nodded, then turned to her sisters. "Put your things away and get changed, but quiet, then come to the kitchen. I'll see what we've got for dinner."

The girls scattered. Jon and I followed Tenni into the kitchen.

She glanced uneasily at Jon. "Will Master Diamond be cooking with us, then?"

"It's all right, Tenni. He's done it before." We'd had a lovely dinner to celebrate my reprieve from the gallows.

I pointed to the loaf sitting on the counter. "Jon, would you slice some bread for the sandwiches?"

He cast about for a knife, and found one, peering at the loaf as if it were some exotic and possibly dangerous creature.

I said, "Have you never sliced bread before?"

"I haven't."

"Well, then," I said, "now's your chance to learn." I took the paring knife from him, replacing it with a long serrated bread knife. "Slice it thin. Use a very light hand, sawing it gently, like so," I demonstrated on the end piece, "so as not to crush the loaf." Amelia had taught me that in those first months after I moved here.

I can't say Jon's tea sandwiches were the most elegant I've ever seen, but they tasted just fine. "I'm quite proud of you," I said. "It's not often a man will attempt something new, especially in front of a bunch of giggling girls."

Jonathan grinned. "I'm the youngest of seven brothers, all who wished to prove themselves superior."

"Including you?"

"Especially me, when I was younger. If I never tried anything new for fear of ridicule, I'd be quite useless now."

After tea, I put on my cloak, then followed Jon to his plain carriage. We crossed the bridge onto Market Center as the sun dipped below the horizon. The carriage turned left, drove half round the island along the Promenade, then crossed the bridge to Hart quadrant.

We finally stopped at an empty field in the Hart slums. "Come, let's walk," Jon said, so we did so.

Jon was quiet, somber. What could he have to show me here?

The homes were small. Windows showed families preparing dinner. The narrow streets were full of shop maids and day laborers. The air rang with good cheer, the sounds of men coming in to greet their families. Mothers called in their children, giving us curious glances. As we walked, the noise died away, the streets became silent.

Jon pulled me out of the light of the lamppost. He pointed across the street. "Look there."

A young woman sat upon a window-seat, back-lit by the lamps inside. Her face, downcast and streaked with tears. Thick curls draped about her shoulders. An older woman who had to be her mother bustled about, setting a table behind her.

"This woman," Jon said quietly, "met a man. He promised her love. He promised her marriage. He gave her gifts. Nothing too high for her station: flowers, a shawl. He even gave her an engagement ring. Once she'd succumbed to his kisses, though, she never saw him again."

A small child, three or so, came to her, gazed up, pulled on her skirts. The woman set the child on the window-seat beside her, yet continued to look out of the window.

"Every day she sits there," Jon said. "Until well into the night. Hoping he'll return, I suppose." He turned to me. "Her father took his life from the shame of it."

"Why are you showing me this?"

"Because I want you to see what I see. Look at this woman. Look at her child."

The light was dim, but still enough to see. Brown curls, light brown skin on them both. A carriage went by, and in the lantern's light, I saw the child's big green eyes.

He reminded me of someone.

"Who fathered this child, Jacqui?"

I blinked, confused. "How should I know?"

"The answer's there, right in front of you."

The eyes, the shape of the chin. I peered at the young woman, removing her features in my mind.

Jonathan said, "She's one of the women whose family came forward with the complaint against Joseph Kerr."

I stared at him, then at the boy. "I thought they went to the Pot."

"All these lawyers want are their court fees. They care nothing about what happens to these women and their children afterward. Fortunately, I got to her in time, dissuaded her mother from making formal protest."

He slumped against the wall. "This family used to live twice their current station. To keep her out of the Pot, after much searching, the mother found a man to sign that he'd wed her daughter. But it cost the family their life savings.

"This woman sends messages to Joseph Kerr every day, to every place she's ever heard rumor of him. She's posted bills. She's sworn the tenants at her old home to send word should he appear. But he never has."

"I don't know what you want me to say."

Jonathan took my hand. "I don't want you to say anything. I just want you to let go of some fantasy that Joseph Kerr is coming back for you. He's not come back for any of them. He got what he wanted and now he's gone."

"So this boy looks like him. It doesn't prove anything."

Jonathan shook his head. "Come on, then. I'll take you home."

But the little boy's eyes haunted me all the way.

Could this possibly be Joseph Kerr's son? Why would he not tell me of him? The boy was at least three. Had Joe been getting letters from this woman at his grandfather's home this entire time? When we planned to leave the city together, would he have just left this woman and their son behind?

"There's something more," Jonathan said. "All the children born to him were girls, save this one. She calls him Joey, but the name on his birth certificate is Polansky Joseph Kerr."

The first Polansky Kerr — Joe's ancestor — had been our King before he was betrayed by his own men. The Spadros Family financed the coup which murdered the King and destroyed the Pot of Gold. Of course, there were many justifications given for this betrayal. Then they locked my people away in the Pot, without food or water, to freeze and starve.

How could things ever return to the way they were? Yet hearing the name of the King on a living, breathing child was thrilling.

One day this place could be good, like he made it. No more cold, no more rags.

Joe said that long ago, before I'd been forced to marry Tony. He'd been speaking of Benjamin Kerr, the Inventor King, who'd built the dome which covered our city today.

Was this child somehow part of Joe's plan?

As the carriage crossed the river, Jonathan Diamond rubbed his face with his hands. "The city of Bridges will not — cannot — tolerate another Polansky Kerr. Not even the boy's great-grandfather uses his real name here. Why would she name her son this if Joe hadn't urged her to do so?" He hid his face in his hands for a moment, then straightened, not looking at me. "What Joseph Kerr has done is reckless. No, it's heartless. I fear for this child. I fear he'll not live to become a man."

"Well, then we must help them. I must go to her —"

"No, Jacqui. No! I put them in enough risk just bringing you to their street! If the Lady of Spadros were to visit a woman's home in the Hart slums, it would fix everyone's attention on her. A woman who's put out so many notices, with a son looking like Joseph

Kerr ... it wouldn't be difficult for a determined man to learn the boy's real name."

"But I must speak with her to learn the truth!"

Jonathan recoiled. "Do you not believe me? Jacqui, I spoke with her almost four years ago, when her mother first brought claim. After she was found with child. I myself investigated the matter. She has a portrait with Joseph Kerr, the portrait they had done when he gave her the engagement ring."

He looked out of the window. "Jacqui, I wished to keep scandal from your home. That's why I helped her. Perhaps I should have told you about it earlier, but I never imagined the situation would go this far! Your servants — and Mrs. Clubb — have kept your meetings with the Kerrs secret for now, but if word of this should appear elsewhere ... if the two of you should be linked together —!"

I nodded, feeling dismayed. Leaving Tony with the intent to flee with Joseph Kerr would become the top headlines. Tony and I would never get a moment's peace: we'd be hounded everywhere we went. Scandal would never leave Spadros Manor, ever, even if Tony divorced me and took another wife. Even Tony's grandchildren would be pointed at, whispered about.

And Roy would finally be forced to do what the Ten of Spades had agitated for all this time: kill me.

Knowing him, he'd probably force Tony to do it.

I felt humbled, and sincerely grateful that the Red Dog Gang hadn't learned of this. If they really wished to destroy the Spadros Family, they'd surely use it against me. The *Golden Bridges* would salivate over such a story. "I'm sorry — I don't know why I would ever doubt you." I reached over to take his hand. "Thank you."

He gave me a quick glance, then squeezed my hand. Then he drew his hand back, blushing as he looked away. When he next spoke, it sounded an effort for him to do so. "What I want is for you to be safe and happy and well. That's all."

"Jon, there's something — personal — I'd like to ask."

He hesitated, just an instant. "Anything at all."

"I spoke with Dr. Salmon. He said you'd been going to Azimoff."

"Yes, that's true."

"And I'm glad. But you said you wouldn't leave Bridges again without me. There's something I don't understand. Shouldn't the doctors still see you?"

Jonathan faced the seat across from him with a thin smile. "There's nothing more they can do. My tonics are as strong as they can be. They dare not give me higher doses, for fear the medication itself might poison me." Still not looking at me, he grasped my hand. "The doctors here can tend to the rest."

Anguish filled me. I squeezed his hand. "How can this be?"

He smiled to himself. "A question I've asked myself often these past years." He leaned back, stared at the ceiling, still grasping my hand, yet his eyes were red. "I regret not telling you of this before. I see now that I need to — to make plans. For what I might do with the life that remains to me."

I wasn't sure why, or even how, but at that moment I finally understood: nothing would keep Jon from death. And my desire to talk about it, to find things to do for it ... it caused him pain.

"I won't leave you, Jon. No matter what happens. And if you wish it, I'll never speak of this again."

He kissed my hand. "I could think of much worse ways to greet the Shuffler." Then he smiled. "I'll be glad to have you along."

The Detection

When I returned home, the Spring dress Madame Biltcliffe made for me last year lay draped across my bed.

It was beautiful: green shantung silk with black embroidery. I'd last seen it amongst the other items I sold at auction to pay Mr. Doyle Pike's fees.

Seeing the dress was bittersweet. I so enjoyed trying it on last spring, yet now it reminded me too much of Madame. I hung it in my closet.

I still didn't know if I wanted to go to the 500th Celebration.

I loved fireworks, but they reminded me of my dead friend Air. We'd watched them together every time the quadrant-folk put on their shows.

I felt grateful for the founding of Bridges 500 years ago. But I hated the cost of such events: the endless reporters, the crowds, the glares from the other women. And I'd have to deal with Tony the entire night, either sniping at me or begging me to return. The thought of enduring another such ordeal made me weary.

After dinner, Mary's parents arrived: John and Jane Pearson. Mr. Pearson was the butler for Spadros Manor; Jane, its housekeeper.

I'd been looking forward to their visit. While at Spadros Manor, I looked up to them as parents, Mr. Pearson particularly.

I expected them to visit as soon as they heard the news. I didn't expect them to rush past without even a greeting. They stayed with Mary and Blitz, never once emerging.

Eventually, I told Tenni I was going to bed. I must have been tired, as I never heard the Pearsons leave.

* * *

The next morning dawned bright and clear, perfect weather for a fireworks display that night.

I felt surprised to see Tenni in the kitchen. "Aren't you supposed to be at work?"

"I told her we had a death in the family." She stirred the bowl of batter in her hand. "She's not nearly so unreasonable as most."

"Well, thank you. I hope you didn't have to walk back?"

"No, I had the driver deliver the others then come back for me." She gave me a sly smile. "I think he likes me."

"Good for you," I said. "How can I help?"

"Stir this; I'll bring Mrs. Mary her tray." She set the bowl down and picked up a tray with tea and toast already prepared.

"Knock quietly: Mr. Blitz is likely still asleep."

Blitz opened the kitchen door from the hall. "No, I'm not." He looked as if he hadn't slept, but he took the tray from Tenni. "I'll be right back."

I said to Tenni, "How late were Mrs. Mary's parents here?"

"Well on to midnight," she said. "I didn't want to disturb them."

Feeling melancholy, I poured myself some tea, put two slices of buttered toast on a plate, and returned to my bedroom. The Spring dress Madame made for me last year hung in my closet.

Oh, ma cherie, I'm so glad you're here.

Would I ever forget that scene? I'd never gotten to say goodbye.

I wanted to feel that my being there gave her some comfort at the end. But each time I forced myself to think the words, grief and guilt blocked my path to believing them. I felt as if just like with Marja, my going there led them to kill her.

I knew the Red Dog Gang were cunning, and bold. I knew they had spies. But they seemed to know me so well, down to where I would go and when.

I was clearly missing something.

But what?

The bell rang, and before I could get there, Blitz rushed to open it. "Ah," he said to whoever was outside. "Thank you."

201

I went back into my room, feeling relieved: it was just the street's messenger boy with our mail. Blitz would sort it and bring it in once that was done. But it was Tenni who brought my mail in, along with my breakfast tray.

"You didn't have to do that," I said. "I could eat in the kitchen."

"It's not right, mum," she said. "Besides, I was bringing trays anyway; it was no trouble to bring yours."

"You might do well as a lady's maid."

"I've tried. They won't take my sisters, and I won't leave them alone, not here."

There was always that. "How are your sisters?"

"Emma's been having nightmares about men threatening. And she keeps saying there's ghosts in the walls." Tenni shook her head. "But it's to be expected, what with all that's gone on."

A wave of compassion came over me for the poor child: cooped up all day working for the newspaper, then going through this. What kind of life was it for a young girl? "I suppose so."

"Mrs. Dewey won't be here until time to dress you for tonight," Tenni said.

"So her daughter's still unwell?"

"Mr. Blitz didn't say." Tenni spoke as if distracted; she'd been gazing at my Spring dress. "Madame so loved making that. Every bit of it delighted her."

My eyes stung. "I wish we might have settled things."

"Begging your pardon, mum, but she held you nothing but good. I got to sit with her at the inquest. And again at the trial, though I was never called up for that one. She missed you something fierce." Her eyes reddened. "They'd told her to have nothing to do with you, mum, not even to look at you once when she spoke. And never to see you again. Your lawyer-man feared if she came a-calling, it would cause scandal."

Oh, ma cherie, I'm so glad you're here.

Grief choked me then: I put my forehead on my arms, sobbing. Tenni put her hand on my shoulder. "All will be well, mum."

I shook my head. How could anything be well again? "She was like a mother to me."

Tenni stood there silent for a moment. Then she said, "I suppose she was like a mother to me, too."

* * *

Mary looked better when I went in to check on her: her cheeks had color, and her eyes weren't quite so red. I sat beside her, took her hand. "I'm so sorry this has happened to you."

She clasped my hand in hers. "I know, mum." She brought out the moonstone I'd given her, still on its chain around her neck. "You've done everything for us and more."

"My mother told me once the first is the most difficult, for many reasons." Which was odd, as I had no true brothers or sisters. Perhaps she merely spoke of observing other women. "Your husband was right: next time should be better."

She gazed at our hands. "I hope so, mum. I so wanted a child."

I looked over at the wallpaper. "Would it disturb you too much for me to take that down today? I did promise I would, but it can wait until you feel well enough."

"Take it all down. I don't want to wake to it another day."

At this I felt sad, not only for her, but for the expense she went to in purchasing it. "I'll fetch the kettle and start steaming it off."

It took me a good part of the day, stopping for luncheon, and by the end of it all I had a headache and didn't feel well. I picked up the big basket with the scraps of wallpaper in it. "I'll wash the walls tomorrow," I said. "I may lie down before tea."

"Thank you," Mary said. "I'm so grateful for your kindness."

A commotion of feet went up the stairs. "What's that about?"

Blitz came in. "Let me take that for you," he said, and I handed over the basket. "Sawbuck and his men are here."

"Here?"

"That big room is perfect for planning. They've brought tables and lamps."

I'd ordered curtains for the room after hosting Clover there: bedspreads would be most conspicuous during the day. "As long as the men aren't tromping up and down all evening."

Blitz glanced up. "I'll remind them Mary's in here."

I followed him out to the hall. One of Tenni's sisters stood there. "You know we can hear everything they're saying."

Blitz set the basket on the floor.

I said, "You can?"

Blitz and I went into their room. Three of the littlest girls sat on the beds braiding twine, and indeed you could hear the men upstairs speak. The words were very quiet, but in the silence of their braiding, plain to hear. "They won't be there long," I said. "If you'd rather sit in the parlor and do that, you're welcome to."

"Poor design," Blitz said. "There must be some way to dampen the sound. I'll look into it tomorrow."

Remembering the summons, I handed it to Blitz. "Would you give this to Sawbuck?" Sawbuck could give it to Tony, or do whatever he wanted with it. I went to lie down, head pounding.

I woke at Tenni's knock. "Tea's ready, mum."

I felt bleary. "I'll be right there."

The men were taking their tea upstairs, so I sat in the parlor — Tenni insisted on it — and drank my tea in silence.

I didn't want to go to this Celebration. But I supposed there was no real reason I could give not to. Gardena had been right: once people saw us together, maybe they'd stop obsessing over us.

I'd give Sawbuck Maria Athena's portrait, so he'd know her if he saw her. He of all people knew how important she was to finding the Red Dog Gang.

Did Maria Athena have a portrait of Frank Pagliacci? That could be useful, if only to get a better idea of who we faced.

I pictured the disgust in Tony's eyes the last time I'd seen him. Tonight, I'd stand beside a man who despised me and watch fireworks in the midst of strangers who despised me.

How I wished that I'd gone with Jonathan Diamond the year before, when he asked me to leave Bridges with him!

But Jon had worked so hard and traveled so far to find a life he could live for the time he had left. He obviously wanted to be here, or else he'd have gone away long ago.

It would be wrong to take him from the work he loved, from his family, his friends. And for what? To save me from trouble I had made for myself?

Besides, there was still a chance for me to be free here in Bridges. Despite the Golden Bridges articles, and the Families' fears, and

Gardena's worries, sooner or later some new scandal would arise. People would forget about me.

I got up, went into the hall, intending to return to my study. But on the stair lay a ticket stub, edged in bright orange.

And I recalled Joseph Kerr's zeppelin tickets, edged in red. Three tickets: one for him, one for me, and one for my Ma.

I told Joe to buy a ticket for my Ma.

Which meant he knew Ma was alive.

Who had **he** told?

A shriek came from the girls' room, then a crash.

Everyone in the house rushed in. Tenni stood two steps back from the wall, staring at it, the remains of a shattered picture frame on the floor before her.

I said, "What happened?"

She pointed. "I took the picture down to dust it," at this, her hand shook, "and I s-saw the hole there —"

Indeed, there was a hole, perhaps the size of a nickel.

"- and I l-looked, and there was an **eye**!"

Sawbuck turned to his men. "Get them!"

The men rushed out, yet Sawbuck remained in the doorway.

I pressed my ear to the wall: footsteps departing. "Better hurry." I turned to Tenni. "Let's clean up this glass." It took a few minutes. Then I said to Sawbuck, "Help me move this dresser aside. And let's take down the other pictures. I want to find no more eyes."

Tenni shrank back from the dresser. "Believe me, mum," Tenni said, voice shaking, "neither do I."

She hurried out — presumably to finish making dinner — while Sawbuck and I moved the heavy dresser. We took down the pictures: there were no other holes in the wall.

"There's a listening bell set into the wall," one of Sawbuck's men said from the hole. "I can hear you breathing over there."

I felt dismayed. So this was how they knew my plans.

They'd known everything.

The Peril

I stood right next to the hole. "Wait," I said to Sawbuck. "Listen."

I heard Tenni talking to her sister in the kitchen, and the squeak of Mary turning over in bed, and the little girls giggle in the parlor. And the girls told us earlier that they could hear what was being said upstairs. "Go into my study and say something, then into my bedroom and speak again."

I could hear it all. I heard the front doorbell ring, the door open and shut. I heard Sawbuck go outside. I heard his footsteps return, all the way down the hall.

Sawbuck walked in. "This is bad, Mrs. Spadros. My men talked to the neighbors: there have been men coming in and out for two years at least."

"I'd begun to think the Red Dog Gang had some arcane ability. But this whole building ..." What had I said during this year I'd lived here? "It's as if it were built precisely to gain secrets."

Could this building have been given to me as a way to know what I was doing? What the Families were doing? Had Dame Anastasia known what this was when she left the deed to me?

When was this built? By whom? Who was here before? So many questions poured into my mind that I could hardly catch them all.

Blitz stood in the hallway, his face concerned. "We'll catch them, Mrs. Spadros. As fast as they left, they're sure to have forgotten plenty over there that we can use to identify them."

Sawbuck and his men could take care of that — once Tony found out about this, he'd surely order them to do so.

But I knew what I had to do. And I had a sudden thought: tonight I might die. "Thank you."

Blitz rested his hand high on the door-frame. "For what?"

"You have always supported me, even when you thought me an utter fool." I smiled to myself. "And you speak your truth, even if I don't accept it. That's of great value."

He chuckled. "Got me into trouble more than once at the Manor." Then he gave me a wink and a grin. "Guess that's why I came here with you."

He continued on into the kitchen.

But I stood there by the hole in the wall, listening to the conversations go on in my apartments.

What secrets had I given to our enemy?

Who had been here this year? What had we discussed? What plans had been made in these rooms?

My consultations with Mr. Pike, the talks I'd had with Jonathan Diamond and Mr. Charles Hart, the —

And then I gasped in horror.

Mrs. Diamond had been here.

"Oh, gods." I ran down the hall to turn on the light for the messenger, then rushed to write a letter:

> Our conversation was overheard by our enemies: your secret is no longer safe. Please take measures tonight to protect yourself. And speak with your sons and daughter, before they hear of this from others.
>
> They are no longer children. They would do anything to keep you from harm. They deserve to know the truth.
>
> JS

Sawbuck stood in the doorway. "What's wrong?"

I shook my head. "It's not for you to know." Hands shaking, I thrust it into his hands. "This is beyond urgent."

He peered at the envelope. "What urgent message have you for Mrs. Rachel Diamond, of all people?"

Oh, gods, I thought. Did I just reveal her secret? "Her husband or her lady's maid will read it, of course. But it's about her safety. Pay them double if you must, but it has to get there tonight. Before she leaves for the Celebration!"

Sawbuck stood gaping at me.

"Now, out! I must be ready when Amelia comes to dress me."

Sawbuck's eyebrows rose. "Well, I'm glad you're finally coming to your senses."

I snorted. "If you say so."

I shut the door in his face. Everything had changed.

The Chance

I had no intention of going to the 500th Celebration. I knew where Maria Athena was, and the Red Dog Gang now knew that I knew. If I didn't leave now, I might never have another chance.

I wrote:

Now they know we're on to them, they'll be ready for a large attack. But they won't suspect that I would arrive alone.

Make your attack as planned. I'll sneak in whilst they're distracted and find her.

I addressed it to Sawbuck and propped the note up on my bed.

Sawbuck would never agree to this unless I acted first — then he would be forced to come after me. He'd be furious, but it was the only way to get Maria Athena back to her mother.

I put on my old widow woman clothes, grabbed my cloak, and climbed out of the window. It was a bit of a squeeze to get out from behind the mesh in front of my window. And the potato plants were worse for wear afterward. But the mesh blocked me from sight of the street: no alarm raised.

I rushed past the alleyway in the twilight, lit by the ruckus of Sawbuck's men, then darted across the street to another alley. I had to get to a taxi-carriage before they found me missing.

I had the driver take me to the Spadros poorhouse. This was on 1st Boulevard, about a mile east — well, if you wish to be precise, north — of the entrance to the Gap.

The poorhouse was always open: the Dealers took turns staffing the front desk, should anyone need their aid. During the day, anyone was allowed to go inside and have a meal, or sit on the benches outside the door. But only women, infants, and girls were allowed to stay inside once darkness fell. Men lay under the benches, or camped across the wide boulevard along the Hedge. Some had small boys with them.

Once the carriage left, I walked towards what the quadrant-folk called the Rathole. The very fact they called it so said much.

From the Gap, it was another two miles to the Cathedral. And the roads were busy. It was Midsummer Night, the biggest party night of the year.

A crowd poured down Scoop Street: most walking, with the occasional man on horseback or group in a carriage. Ragtime music wafted along from player pianos. Men, women, and children stood hawking wares, or calling men to drink at their bar, eat their food, visit their brothel. Most everyone in the Pot was born in a brothel and spent their nights inside its walls, selling their bodies for safety, food, and warmth. While the Cathedral was the finest brothel in the Pot, the closer ones often got more trade.

Anything one might conceivably want was sold along Scoop Street. Party Time, weapons, clockwork toys, forbidden tech from other cities, stolen items of all kinds, an hour with a pretty child.

In the Cathedral, we were always told we could say no. And of course, my mother's benefactor the Masked Man had forbidden me to even be asked. For that reason, Tim's story had truly shocked me. The men running the Keycard Cafe should be rounded up and beaten to death for what they'd done to the boy! If I ever got the opportunity to report them, I'd make sure to do so.

But tonight, I had to blend in. Hooded, with my dark cloak around me, I could walk beside one group, behind another. I became part of them.

I stayed away from the sides of the street, allowing others to become the target of a vendor's call, a child's question.

When I was in the High-Low Split, we Low Cards would offer a good item to quadrant-folk. Then we'd take them to a back alley or abandoned building, where the High Cards would be laying in wait. Whoever did the luring split a tenth share of what the High Cards captured. It was how I made money for cigarettes and booze.

The throng moved along to where the road split. Most took the left, the most direct way to the Cathedral's entrance, although the shops were better on the right. The adventurous and those who knew this secret split off. But I followed the larger crowd, the better to hide myself in.

A road went off to the right, with bright lights and loud jazz music, and some went that way. This road met up with the right-most one, and some who'd gone that way met up with our crowd, which moved along as one.

Scoop Street ended at Shill Street. Again, most went left.

I stopped on Shill Street for a moment at a spot of wall where no one stood, staring ahead. It was over a mile off and eleven years ago to the intersection of Shill and Snow and the midwinter night which had sealed my fate.

I grabbed a little hand in my pocket. A girl, perhaps six, had made her way under my cloak. "None of that here."

I took my handbag from her. Her eyes grew wide, and she ran.

Remembering myself at that age, I chuckled, moving on down the street, then turning right to follow the road to the Cathedral.

This road was longer, and if the energy to get people to buy was intense on Scoop Street, along here it was volcanic. This was their last chance to draw people from the lure of the Cathedral. Shops were full, people sat at tables drinking, eating. The music and the shouts of the barkers were deafening.

It seemed busier than I remembered. And the crowd pushed on, almost as thickly as it had been at the Gap.

Many carriages stopped at the road which ended at the huge mass of the Cathedral. I stood gazing at the Cathedral's windows, lit from inside. People streamed past me, many drunk already.

I moved along the other side of the street beside the Cathedral, past the shops selling souvenirs. I passed the bulk of the building and had a clear view of the Cathedral's entry.

A sign said, "Closed Midsummer Night." Yet men stood on the steps arguing with several men I recognized and a few I didn't who guarded the entryway.

Ducking into my hood, I crossed the street, keeping the taller men between me and the guards so they wouldn't see me go past. Then I walked along the alley behind Benji's new home and towards what the quadrant-folk called the Old Plaza.

Past the Cathedral, the traffic declined markedly. The music and blare of the crowds decreased. Here and there were brothels, boldly stated or masquerading as cafes or bars. A few people walked the streets, shopped, sat at the tables, but not nearly as many.

Between the alleys and in the broken buildings, pitiful small piles lay around meager fires. Those who refused to join or were cast out from their brothels huddled together for warmth.

These were the people of the street, who lived on the edge of their wits in the shadows. Most were former quadrant-folk. Addicted to Party Time as my father once was when he lived here, alcoholic, or mad, without family or friends to care for them. There were few children with them: not many born in the street survived.

After a few blocks, I walked alone, keeping to the middle of the street. Here and there, oil lamps showed in the windows, a woman laughed, a baby cried. Women in tattered finery beside chipped and peeling doorways peered at me hopefully as I went past, a few even calling out. Their faces fell when they realized I was also a woman.

As I walked towards the Plaza's entrance, I remember thinking how much smaller this area seemed, now that I was grown. How much more ruined it was than I remembered. I felt astonished that I'd spent my childhood, my girlhood, in this desolate place.

Ahead, one of the many firework shows began, this one over Market Center. But it wasn't just an ordinary Midsummer show: displays for the 500th anniversary of the city's founding were going on all over the city.

But I didn't feel much happiness from it.

Was our dream — the Cathedral's dream — only a dream?

Could those golden bridges have ever been real?

The apple trees along the shattered roads of the Pot and beside the broken windows of the Cathedral were real enough: a hint of the garden city of ages past. Far too often, they were cut for warmth today, rather than allowed to bring forth fruit tomorrow.

How far we had strayed from what Benjamin Kerr planned!

He wanted a gentle garden city, where people could live in refinement and peace. The learned, the Inventors, the artisans — those were the people meant to thrive here.

What we got was the Four Families.

Most people thought the reign of the Families was a good thing. They brought an end to the constant violence. The quadrants were at peace, and if anything, life was orderly and stable. Everyone knew their place, and most had a secure future, assuming they paid their protection money. And if they didn't like it here, they could move somewhere else.

Well, the rich could, anyway.

The Families brought survival. It seemed that this was all most people cared about.

Living with Tony, I'd learned bitterly that survival was not enough. In my heart I yearned to be truly free.

Would I ever get that chance?

A boom from far off. The red firework of tales past rose and burst, as it had a hundred years past, to mark, I suppose, the doom my people brought upon themselves. I looked away.

The ruined 'scrapers of the Old Plaza loomed ahead. I approached to within a few blocks of the entrance and crouched in the alcove of a bombed-out building, contemplating my choices.

There were several ways to approach the Plaza's entrance. Only Snow Street — far to my left — could admit a carriage. The others were blocked by rubble.

But many of the buildings were destroyed, offering someone who knew the way clear passage. And I knew the way.

But where would they take Maria Athena? It all depended on whether she was prisoner or participant in their schemes. Also, how many they had to guard her.

The High-Low Split spanned the entirety of the Spadros Pot. Every living child ran in the gang until they grew old enough to take more responsible positions within their brothels. And if this Black Maria ran the High-Low Split, she may have recruited former gang members to help. Plus, they had the Ten of Spades with them. So they had guards a-plenty.

Black Maria surely knew that the Spadros Family planned to assault the Plaza's entrance. If I were her, I'd have most of my men there to defend. I'd put men with rifles in the 'scrapers to watch for attack from the side streets.

But although the side streets would be lightly guarded, the Plaza was a mile long. No one person could search a mile of 'scrapers on each side, especially if they had to watch for snipers. It would take weeks, which I didn't have.

If Maria Athena Spade were a prisoner, they'd hide her somewhere. We'd never find her until we rooted these men out. If she were dead, the same. But if she were working with them ...

Her face appeared before me: terrified, yet they had to pull her back from shooting further.

I felt sure Maria Athena Spade — a sheltered outsider spinster — wasn't Black Maria. Why would she be afraid of me if she were? Besides, the High-Low Split would never follow an outsider.

But while I didn't want to believe Maria Athena was working with Black Maria, the evidence seemed to be pointing that way. At the very least, Maria Athena was with Frank Pagliacci and wanted to help him. He'd made her believe I was her enemy. She'd shot at me once — she might want to be part of the defending force, especially if Black Maria was part of it too.

I had to get to Maria Athena before the shooting began. Somehow, I had to make her see reason, or at least keep her safe, before she ended up dead.

I crept forward, winding around rubble in the darkness, keeping myself in the shadows as fireworks flashed. The sounds echoed in the rocks around me.

A brilliant white light glared at me, seemingly placed near the far end of the entry to the Plaza.

How was this light possible? It was brighter than any light I'd ever seen. Even at this distance, its sudden appearance blinded me. Angling away, I moved to my right, deeper into shadow.

I had to stop for a few moments, because I couldn't see. What could they possibly want this light for? Surely they couldn't know I was coming, and from where.

But if they did, I was in danger. So I kept moving ahead and to my right, feeling my way towards the entrance to the Plaza.

Its entrance was wide, thirty yards or more, its carved archway now cracked in places, covered in vines. Rocks and rubble had been placed twenty yards out from the Plaza entrance to form a rough semi-circle which rose above my head.

A fortification, here?

As I crept closer, I noticed a gap in this wall of rubble, large enough to walk through. A second fortification lay ten yards behind the first, as high as my chest.

Movement came from behind it. I shrank out of view, a sharp pain in my foot making me stumble, fall. Yet no alarms raised. With my black hood and cloak, it seemed whoever hid behind these barricades hadn't spotted me.

The brilliant light went off. Yet fireworks lit the sky all around me. I shrank down in the darkness, crept through the gap to look at the outer fortification from its inner side.

The wall held small openings just below eye level which even an untrained shooter could use to good advantage. They might not be able to shoot through them — I don't know if even I could have. But they could use them to mark the passage of anyone going by.

Blinded by the light and distracted by the fireworks, Sawbuck and his men might not see these gaps. But those inside the fortification would see the men clearly.

This had to be a trap.

Horses' hooves echoed from far off, drawing closer. I crept back towards the outer wall. I needed to warn Sawbuck and his men before they reached the danger. A second beam of light appeared, this time in front of me, high on the building whose alcove I'd hidden in earlier. I dropped to the ground, still in the shadow of the outer wall, and froze.

No bullets came my way, but the fireworks still boomed overhead. The minute someone peeked over the inner wall, they would see me in the fireworks' flashes. And from here, I wouldn't be able to get to Sawbuck's men.

As if reading my mind, the light in front of me went off. I scrambled behind the outer wall, panting with fear yet feeling safer there. My foot throbbed, and the sharp pain returned when I put pressure on it. This hadn't happened before. Had I truly injured it, as the doctor feared?

I might have simply been paranoid. But it felt as if someone saw me, herded me. Was a sniper waiting for me to get within range? Would they then turn this light on, leaving me with nowhere to hide? I marked in my mind where the light's beams had originated. The piles of rubble on the way to Sawbuck which would hide me.

Then I hurried to the nearest safe area. I would not get caught in that light's glare again.

It was then the shooting started.

The Shot

New lights blazed from the Plaza buildings, directed at the eyes of anyone coming from the road. Between the fireworks, the lights, and the shooting, the scene was chaos. The noise among the rocks was deafening.

Men fell on both sides as I crept along, keeping myself below the outer wall's view-ports. When was almost to Sawbuck's men, I saw another large gap in the outer wall, large enough for men to pass through. Then the shooting on the Plaza side fell silent.

With the light in their faces, the men couldn't tell what was happening. But from where I hid in the shadows, I could see everything.

In the wild, flickering lights of the fireworks, Maria Athena Spade rose from behind the rubble, as if lifted up from below. She wore a hood and cloak like mine. A dark headband went across her forehead, matching her choker and belt. Her face was frightened, her eyes wide. But there was something missing in her eyes — like she was dead inside. Like she'd given up all hope.

I shouted, "Your mother sent us! We mean you no harm!" But my voice was lost in the booming of the fireworks above us.

Maria Athena turned her whole body away. A woman's scream of triumphant delight split the air, and I followed her gaze. Sawbuck and his men crept past, seemingly unaware of her tracking their movements. She had a clear shot up ahead for the first man to enter that gap.

The wind blew, the lights flickered, fireworks burst overhead. Hands rose, pointed towards where Sawbuck would emerge, the dark shape of a gun in them.

The lights, the gaps, everything weren't only meant to herd me to where they wanted me. They were to herd Sawbuck and his men to where they wanted them.

Sawbuck was almost to the gap, moving quickly, as if unaware the gap even existed. In seconds, he'd be in her sights.

The light from behind me flared on. I'd chosen well: I was still in shadow. But the men cowered, scrambled towards the shadow, right into the gap. Sawbuck led them.

The instant Sawbuck stepped into that shadow, he was dead. And blinded by the lights, he'd never know what hit him.

I had to capture Maria Athena Spade alive. It was our only chance to learn who these people were.

But I couldn't let Sawbuck die.

I raised my gun and fired.

A small hole appeared between Maria Athena Spade's eyes. Toppling backwards, she fell.

Sawbuck crouched in the gap ten yards to my left, lit in bluish-white, staring at me with astonishment on his face.

At least a dozen Spadros men scrambled up from behind where Maria Athena had stood and ran toward the Plaza entrance.

A terrible noise came from the Plaza entryway. Dozens of bullets tore apart the rogue Spadros men running towards the Plaza.

And then silence: whoever fired those weapons were gone.

A boy, maybe eight, rose in the distance from where the rogue Spadros men had just been slaughtered and scurried off. The sounds of crying came from where that boy had been: another, somewhat older, child hid there.

Sawbuck's men moved forward cautiously, looking for a trap. They found no men alive. One picked up a child.

I limped forward. "Maria Athena! Maria Athena!" I called to the men. "Do you see a woman?"

"Over here," one of the men called. "Looks like she's dead."

His words stopped me. How could I face her mother?

Sawbuck came up beside me, glancing back at the light, the fortification, the gaps. He pointed to where Maria Athena once stood. "We needed her alive. You could have let me die and no one would have blamed you. Yet you saved me. Why?"

I watched the light dance over Sawbuck's face as fireworks boomed above us, and I felt compassion for this man. "You're the most important person in this quadrant. Without you, he's lost."

He stood gaping at me for a long moment, as if completely astonished by my words, then nodded. Then he shouted, "Get rid of those lights." As the men shot out the lights, we walked to the scene of the slaughter, stopping just inside that second barricade.

Sawbuck's men came back. One said, "That's all of them, sir. The whole fucking lot." He relaxed, shaking his head. "Good job, Mrs. Spadros. You led us right to them. We've won."

The other men bristled. A man shouted, "Like hell we did!" He pointed at a body. "That's my cousin. Over there's my friend." He gestured to another of their number. "Look there, that's your brother. Don't you even care?" His hands balled into fists, and he took a step towards the man.

Sawbuck put his arm out to block the angry man. "We didn't win. We lost the minute they left." Regret lay heavy over his words. "It should never have come to this."

"The traitors were betrayed." I stared at the direction of the terrible sound. "The Red Dog Gang killed them, there at the end."

The men murmured angrily, looking in the same direction.

I'd never heard such a sound before. "What were those?"

"Tommy-guns," Sawbuck said. "Likely smuggled in from Chicago. We lost a shipment of them a few years back —"

"And now the Red Dog Gang has them."

Sawbuck nodded. Then he gestured to the man holding the crying child. "What's this?"

The man set the child into the light.

Little Tim stood on one foot, his other trouser leg slick with blood. "They shot me," Tim sobbed. "Why'd they shoot me?"

"He's one of them," a man said. "We should just shoot him."

"No," I said. "You can't just shoot him! I know this kid."

"We can't leave him here," Sawbuck said, "Without a doctor's care, he'll be dead in a few days. And we can't take him with us." He began to raise his gun.

Tim cowered down to the ground, hiding his face.

A dark shape rose from behind the stones. "I'll take him."

All the men jerked their guns towards the figure.

Sawbuck said, "Who are you?"

Benji walked a few steps forward, but casually, as if they were about to go out for a beer. "You don't remember me, Tensie?" Benji let out a short laugh, then shrugged. "I remember you. We used to play right here. And now look at you, a Spadros wolfhound."

Sawbuck held no recognition in his eyes.

"It's Benji," I said to Sawbuck. "He's a guard at the Cathedral. I know him. Let him take the boy." Tim lay on the ground, hiding his face, sobbing. "Tim won't bother you again, will you, Tim?"

"Nooo," Tim sobbed. "I just wanted them not to kill me. They said they would kill me if I didn't go with them."

I stepped forward. "Did you see Black Maria?"

"N-no," Tim's face was streaked with tears. "They wouldn't let me inside either."

My eyes stung, my breath caught. Had they no mercy? He was just a little boy.

"Come," Benji opened his arms. "I have a place inside for you."

Tim crawled over; Benji picked him up. "We'll see the herb women about that leg."

Tim wrapped his arms around Benji's neck. "I'm sorry I run off."

Benji murmured something as he moved the boy to his hip.

Then Tim's little voice rose. "They killed a quadrant-lady!"

I called to them, "Stop! Wait." I limped over to Tim and Benji, and the rest followed. I pointed back at Maria Athena. "You saw them shoot her?"

Tim nodded, a haunted look on his little face.

"Why? Why did they shoot her?"

"They were over there," he pointed at the entryway. "Arguing, her and this man. Everyone knew him. He s-scared me."

"What did he look like?"

Tim shrugged. "He was big. He had brown hair." He sniffled. "They argued a long time. She was real scared. She kept saying you said her Ma sent you. She started crying. She wanted to go home. One of the High Cards come out and said something in the man's ear. Then he — he shot her head!" Tim hid his face in Benji's shoulder.

Benji rested his hand on the boy's head. "Let's go home." Then he carried Tim away without even looking back.

"It would have been a blessing to finish him," Sawbuck said. "Out here, in," he gestured at the rubble, "this?"

So Sawbuck remembered nothing of our ways at all. "The herb women will care for him, Ten, never fear."

Sawbuck shook his head as the two left. "Let's see about the girl."

Maria Athena Spade lay so very still.

I crouched down, closed her wide, staring eyes. My heart clenched in grief, remorse, shame. I'd failed her. I'd failed her mother. I'd failed everyone. "We can't leave her here. I promised her mother I'd bring her home."

Morton ran up, out of breath, as if he'd run all the way from the Hedge. "Sorry to miss the party, fellows."

What the hell was Morton doing here?

Then Morton looked at the carnage before us. "Good gods."

I grabbed his lapels. "Is this her? The girl at the office with Frank Pagliacci. The girl who killed Marja." With one hand, I pointed at Maria Athena. "For gods' sakes, Master Rainbow. Tell me it's her."

Morton went closer, peered at her in the light of the fireworks booming overhead. "I'm sorry, Mrs. Spadros. This isn't her. I've never seen her before in my life."

I let go of him, feeling sick. It wasn't her. I didn't see a gun anywhere near her, much less in her hand. And there was no blood on the ground.

Sawbuck gestured towards the Plaza entrance. "It would take a thousand men to root them out of there." He shook his head. "Even if they didn't have Tommy-guns. We aren't ready for this. We need to leave before they come back."

I couldn't move. "I killed her."

Morton crouched beside Maria Athena's body, pulled her hood aside. "Not unless you've been here for hours." A large hole lay in her temple; the blood had dried around it.

Morton drew back, and a shocked laugh burst from him. "I don't believe this. She's tied to a pole!" He took out a pocket knife, cut loose the bonds around her head, her neck, her body. The pole was attached to a platform the size of a dinner plate. "There's some sort of mechanism down here — it looks like a lift!"

I peered over Morton's shoulder to get a glimpse of the gears beneath where Maria Athena's body had been as fireworks boomed overhead. How long had they been building this?

Morton seemed to have more interest in Maria Athena's wounds. He tried to move her arms. Then he glanced up at me. "She was dead before you got here."

I stared at her body, horrified.

"Grab the girl," Sawbuck said, "and let's get out of here."

Two men carried her body. I couldn't walk, and I didn't have my cane; Sawbuck carried me to the carriage. The bodies of our men were taken away. The bodies of the rogue Spadros men were left with the Red Dog Gang members to rot.

Several carriages waited for us on Snow Street. Maria Athena Spade was laid in the back luggage compartment and covered with a horse blanket.

I'd fulfilled my case. I had Maria Athena Spade. I could bring her home to her mother.

But all the way home I sat quiet, deeply shaken.

I shot an unarmed woman!

She didn't aim at me. She didn't even have a gun.

Sure, she was already dead, but I didn't know that.

These people, this Red Dog Gang, whoever led them — they were ruthless beyond imagination. To trick these men into defying the Spadros Family. Then to lure Maria Athena from her home, stage this trick with this poor girl's dead body — for what? To test me?

Then to cut down the men who had joined their cause and risked their lives for them once they had served their purpose ... "What kind of monsters do we **face**?"

I knew Sawbuck thought Joseph Kerr was involved with these people in some way, but I couldn't believe it. I'd known Joseph Kerr since I was born. There was no way he'd be involved with something like this.

Sawbuck let out a sigh. "Ones I fear are more cunning than any of us." He leaned forward, turning to me there in the darkness. "You saved my life when you could have let me die. Perhaps should have." He shook his head to silence me as I stirred to protest. "And you did it for him." He put his hand upon mine. "I regret my behavior towards you, Mrs. Spadros. I was wrong. We need you — as an ally."

I nodded, but felt unable to speak.

Morton sat there, just watching me.

"You know," Sawbuck said, "he still loves you. He's had men watching over you this entire time. Even when you," at this he let out a laugh, "floured your hair and limped around Bridges. Always. But it's not to trap you or cage you, or anything else. He'll be angry with me for telling you this — he didn't even want you to know. He doesn't want to bother you, or cause you harm. He just wants you safe and well."

Something in the way Sawbuck said this touched me like nothing else had, and my vision blurred. "I know he still loves me."

I heard the smile in Sawbuck's voice. "I envy you."

"That was never the problem."

"I know that too."

I glanced over at Morton, who never moved.

"There's nothing to forgive, Ten." Sawbuck was right to say what he did. Tony loved me, and for that, someday he would surely die, just like everyone else did. "People have died," I whispered. "To get me out of there. To keep me from going there in the first place." I shook my head. "Even if I did love him — which I don't — I wouldn't go back."

Sawbuck took his hand off mine. "He doesn't want you to. He understands now what Spadros Manor means to you. He doesn't want to hurt you. He just wants you to be happy."

But how could I ever be happy? I was a murderess in intent if not deed. I'd betrayed this woman's mother, who had placed all her hopes in me. I'd been banished from my home in the Cathedral. The Eldest — my ancestor — had named me one of the enemy. Everyone believed that the man I'd given everything up for was a — how had Ten put it? A vicious scoundrel.

I felt wounded to my very soul. How could I ever be happy again? "Then tell him to take the locks off my doors. Stop caging me. Stop trying to control where I go and what I do. It's no longer his concern. That's how he can help me be happy. Stop whatever he's doing to keep me from making my own life. I want nothing more than to be free. Really and truly free."

The Gesture

We bathed and dressed Maria Athena Spade that night, laying her on the kitchen table for her mother. Her oldest son arrived with her. "We're selling everything," Mr. Spade said. "We're taking my father and my sister home to Milan and never coming back. There's nothing here for us anymore."

All Mrs. Spade said was, "Thank you for bring a my girl home."

But how could I take her thanks? I'd taken her money and left her with nothing but grief. I saw her daughter's dead eyes, the hole in her head. "I'm sorry."

Mrs. Spade patted my hand and left. I never saw her again.

* * *

The next day, we buried Madame.

Tenni was there, and of course, Monsieur. Many of Madame's customers attended, a few embracing Tenni as if she were their sister, rather than a shop maid. Some grieved so heartily that I wondered how close they'd been.

I returned home late, feeling bleak. Blitz met me at the door. "What will you do now, Mrs. Spadros?"

What could I do? This Red Dog Gang frightened me beyond words, because they were so utterly ruthless as to chill the soul. "I have underestimated these men. But they're still men."

I needed to re-examine everything, down to the last detail. Already, I knew I'd made mistakes, assumptions, which had led me down this terrible road to disaster.

Yet this could have ended so much worse. I might be dead, or worse, captive, a tool to force the Four Families into submission.

I pictured events in my mind over and over, how they'd herded us all. They'd had me right where they wanted me!

What were they really doing?

Grasping their plan felt beyond what I was capable of, and for the first time, these people unnerved me.

But even in my terror, in my dismay and dread, I couldn't just let them have their way. Somehow, I had to fight them, even if I was just one woman. Even if I didn't know how.

If I were to beat the Red Dog Gang, I needed to be better than they were: plan better, think better. I needed to be more cunning, more ruthless than they were, if we were to survive.

Because even then, I saw what would happen if they won. Whoever led these men set afire the basest, the most desperate desires. This man's aim was to drive wedges into the Four Families, splitting each into smaller and smaller groups driven to destroy the others. He hardly had to pull a trigger!

And with their man as Mayor, this Red Dog Gang was poised to mow us all down when we'd served their purposes, just as they'd done to Roy's rebellious men.

They wish the ruin of the Pot upon the entire city.

I sighed wearily. "I fear this is just the beginning."

Blitz handed me the key. "Sawbuck said this is yours. He'll have new locks put in, so we can come and go as we please."

The doctor waited for me in my parlor. He'd been right, of course: I'd injured my foot badly. And as he'd threatened, it lay wrapped in plaster for some time.

* * *

Tony had the Inventor's summons quashed. Amelia gave me the news, a spark of proud glee in her eyes. "He told the Inventor he could either bring you to summons or he could remain in Spadros quadrant. Dear Mr. Anthony stood his ground against an Inventor!"

That made me smile. Tony deserved someone in his life who supported and loved him, even if it couldn't be me.

* * *

Eleanora Bryce refused Madame Biltcliffe's dress shop. "You should've seen the state my poor Constable was in! He doesn't want to ever see Clubb quadrant again, until the day he leaves this city."

"But what will you do?"

She snapped, "First he must recover!" Then her face fell. "I'm sorry, mum. You've done more than anyone would ever expect."

After she left, I asked Dr. Salmon to visit them. He returned later that evening. "Poorly nourished. He's been under a great deal of mental distress, but he should recover."

I'd never felt so grateful to pay someone in my life.

* * *

Tenni volunteered to manage Madame Biltcliffe's shop. "I've worked with dressmakers for three years." Then she grinned. "And I know how to sell fabric."

"Well then," Monsieur Sabacc said, "Let's give it a try."

Mr. Howell and his men helped the girls move.

"Please write if you need anything at all," I told Tenni.

"I'm forever in your debt, mum," Tenni said. "We had no place at all — now look at us! Managing a shop!"

I hugged her. "Madame Biltcliffe would be very proud of you."

Mr. Howell and I watched their carriage drive off. Tenni and her sisters would be somewhere safer. Or at least on a higher street.

I said, "Have you learned anything about the men on the other side of my duplex?"

"It was owned by a Mrs. Roberta Bird —"

Birdie. Black Maria had been behind my wall this entire time!

"— but no one is registered as such. The bill of sale dates back twenty years. But the place sat abandoned until three years ago."

Twenty years? How long had they **planned** this?

* * *

The listening tube was removed and the hole filled in, with guards set on the building behind us. The next day, a workman knocked on our door. "Here to install your Telephonic device."

From the way Blitz explained it, this was meant to be a grand surprise. "Your husband has had men laying wire from the doctor's office for a year now, so that you might call for aid without delay."

I knew Tony still loved me. But this simple gesture cut me to my very soul. I felt so overwhelmed, so anguished, that I left Blitz standing in the hallway.

How I'd hurt Tony! How I'd betrayed him, opened him to scandal, shame, and ridicule!

How did I deserve this concern, this care?

How could I ever face Tony again?

The Heirs

Two weeks later, Tony held a press conference at the statue of the first Acevedo Spadros. This time, I stood by his side. "Many rumors and lies have swirled about these past months." He spoke through a microphone, his words booming over the crowd. "We stand here today to set the matter straight once and for all.

"The dastardly slander that sent my wife to stand before a jury on Market Center not only wounded her, but this entire quadrant. It made us distrust each other. It caused cowards to rise up against their own Family, spurred on by evil men who wish nothing more than to take our land from us.

"Each of us has had times of darkness that challenge who we thought we were," he tapped his chest, "inside. My wife and I travel through such times. But we are still here. We still keep you safe. We are still strong.

"My wife wishes to live as one of you to heal the many wounds this trial has given the Spadros quadrant. As my ancestor, the first Acevedo Spadros, fought for women to be educated, so I support my wife's desire to improve this city in her own way. Do not fear to take her help, should you need it."

My eyes filled with tears. What that must have cost him!

"This quadrant shall be not only a strong, secure quadrant, but an enlightened one as well." He raised his arms as if to embrace the crowd. "You are my Family! Take pride in your place beside me. Do your good work to better your children's lives, our quadrant, and our future. Remember, Family is everything."

He took my hand, helping me to his carriage through the shouted questions, and we drove away.

Yet his public mask never slipped. He never showed how he felt. I could no longer read him. The cold, hollow Spadros Heir sat in the carriage; my gentle, sweet Tony was gone.

Our trip to my apartments was silent, and he never looked at me.

When we stopped at my home, I said, "Thank you."

He never spoke, nor did he even move, so I went inside.

It was a year before I saw him again.

* * *

A few days after Tony's speech, my cast was removed. So I went for a walk. Blitz wanted to go with me, but I wanted to be alone.

In a way, it was a comfort that Tony had men watching me. Now that the rogue Ten of Spades were dead, I doubted I'd have further trouble. But if this let him feel safe enough to let me live free, then it was worth the scrutiny.

As I walked, the names went through my mind of those who'd died because of me. Over and over they went: Air, Daniel, Herbert, Stephen, Marja, Anastasia, Major Blackwood, Madame Biltcliffe, Maria Athena.

The names cut me, they comforted me, they tormented me. And try as I might, I couldn't help feeling that Jonathan Diamond would die because of me as well.

I walked this way and that until I came across a bar. Its front had beveled glass and oak-stained wood that reminded me of Madame's dress shop.

It was even nicer inside, and the bartender was a rather good-looking fellow. "What'll you have, miss?"

I smiled, remembering the drink I'd had at the racetrack with Joseph Kerr. "Can you make a chocolate martini?"

"Never heard of it."

So I left.

Now, I never actually believed I would die if I had one drink.

But if I were going to die from one drink, as the doctor claimed, I should have some dignity about it. I'd not go to my grave clutching after a bottle of cheap swill like some pathetic sot. I'd choose a special time to have one last, very special drink, to toast the man who ruined my life.

So I walked until I found another bar.

And another.

No one knew of this drink. So I took a taxi-carriage home.

* * *

When I walked in the front door. Blitz stood in the hallway, face horrified, letter in hand.

While they slept, Cesare Diamond had seized his parents Julius and Rachel Diamond, as well as Jonathan, Jack, Gardena, and her son Roland. Then he took them by force to the Diamond Country House, where they now remained under guard.

Overnight, the bridges to Diamond had been fortified: those approaching from Spadros quadrant had been fired upon. The five older Diamond brothers now held Diamond Manor. The Clubb-Diamond alliance was suspended, and a second Diamond Purge had begun.

For all purposes, Cesare Diamond — a man who hated me simply for where I was born — was now Patriarch of the Diamond Family.

~~ This ends Chapter 5 of the Red Dog Conspiracy ~~

The Five of Diamonds

Part 6 of the Red Dog Conspiracy

Coming October 2020

Acknowledgments

I want to thank Julian White, Lenka Trnkova, and Marlys Wiest for beta reading. I'd also like to thank Erin Hartshorn for editing and proofreading.

Thanks also go to my street team, The Commission, without whom this book might not have made it into your hands.

Special thanks to my Patrons, whose monthly financial support helps make this series possible:

Melissa Williams

Julian White

Cristina

Eirlys Evans

Michaelene Alston

Jennifer Eades

Phoebe Darqueling

Rachel Heslin

Jane Kamvar

Toni Mcconnell

James Mallison, Sr.

Aramanth Dawe

Follow the Red Dog Conspiracy on Patreon

patreon.com/red_dog_conspiracy

About The Author

Patricia Loofbourrow is a writer, gardener, artist, musician, poet, wildcrafter, and married mother of three who loves power tools, dancing, genetics, and anything to do with outer space. She also has an MD. Heinlein would be proud.

You can follow her at:
- Her website JacqOfSpades.com
- Twitter @Jacq_Of_Spades
- Tumblr red-dog-conspiracy.tumblr.com
- The Red Dog Conspiracy Facebook page

Note From The Author

Thanks so much for reading *The Ten of Spades*. If you liked the book, please contact me, or leave a review where you bought this!

For news, backstory, and more, visit JacqOfSpades.com